本专著受安徽省哲社规划项目"托妮·莫里森小说中的生存美学研究"（编号AHSKY2020D129）资助

托妮·莫里森小说中的生存美学

Existence Aesthetics in Tony Morrison's Novels

应伟伟　著

吉林大学出版社

·长春·

图书在版编目（CIP）数据

托妮·莫里森小说中的生存美学/应伟伟著. -- 长春：吉林大学出版社，2022.9
ISBN 978-7-5768-0586-4

Ⅰ.①托… Ⅱ.①应… Ⅲ.①莫里森(Morrison, Toni 1931-)—小说研究 Ⅳ.①I712.074

中国版本图书馆CIP数据核字(2022)第173342号

书　　名：	托妮·莫里森小说中的生存美学
	TUONI MOLISEN XIAOSHUO ZHONG DE SHENGCUN MEIXUE
作　　者：	应伟伟　著
策划编辑：	殷丽爽
责任编辑：	殷丽爽
责任校对：	周　鑫
装帧设计：	雅硕图文
出版发行：	吉林大学出版社
社　　址：	长春市人民大街4059号
邮政编码：	130021
发行电话：	0431-89580028/29/21
网　　址：	http://www.jlup.com.cn
电子邮箱：	jldxcbs@sina.com
印　　刷：	长春市中海彩印厂
开　　本：	787mm×1092mm　1/16
印　　张：	13
字　　数：	200千字
版　　次：	2023年1月　第1版
印　　次：	2023年1月　第1次
书　　号：	ISBN 978-7-5768-0586-4
定　　价：	72.00元

版权所有　翻印必究

作者简介

应伟伟，女，安徽理工大学教师，1999年本科毕业于安徽大学英语系，2003年硕士毕业于安徽大学英语系，2012年毕业于复旦大学外文学院，获英语语言文学博士学位。2010年1月被评为副教授。2018年10月至今担任安徽理工大学外国语学院英语系主任。安徽省比较文学学会理事。主持安徽省哲学社会科学规划一般项目一项，省级教研、科研重点及一般项目四项，英语专业省级示范教研室重点项目一项。参与国家社科基金重点项目一项，一般项目一项；参加省级教研科研重点项目三项。担任省级示范课程《美国文学》的负责人。至今发表论文十余篇，参编大学英语、英语语法、专门用途英语、研究生科技英语写作教材共四部。

前　言

托妮·莫里森（Toni Morrison，1931—2019）是美国文学史上著名的小说家，于1993年获得诺贝尔文学奖，成为首位获该奖的美国黑人作家。莫里森创作了多部小说，她1966年在纽约兰登书屋担任高级编辑时主编的《黑人之书》，因记叙了美国黑人三百年历史，被称为记叙美国黑人史的百科全书。莫里森凭借她独特的女性视角，通过描述黑人跨越三个世纪的生存画卷，把黑人女性寻求自我的历程和重构黑人民族意识的进程紧密相连，形成交互共进的发展趋势，以探寻美国黑人文化的出路。

国内外对莫里森的研究已持续近四十年。传统理论视角多集中于族裔、性别、身份和文化主题的研究，近十年的理论研究视角虽有较大拓展，分别结合了马克思主义、新历史主义、空间理论、喻指理论、后殖民主义等进行研究，但仍多集中在意识美学研究范畴。部分研究虽对身体美学和死亡哲学有所涉及，但终归零散和片面，未能全面、充分和系统地对莫里森小说中的生存美学进行研究。在反本质主义和超越二元对立的后现代语境中，"身体"成了重要的话题，法国后现代哲学家福柯、法国存在主义现象学大师梅洛·庞蒂及皮埃尔·布尔迪厄等都将"身体"作为哲学研究中的重要对象。然而，对莫里森小说中以黑人女性身体美学为主要出发点的综合了意识美学的自我构建的综合研究，尤其是对其多本小说的系统解读，以期探究莫里森小说中反映出的生存美学的研究还极为匮乏。本书针对莫里森小说中的黑人女性身体表现的特征，拟从身体性出发对黑人女性的生存做出审美性思考；本研究中的身体既是作为审美主体存在的身体，又是作为审美对象存在的身体，更是以身体为主体建构的生命世界。

莫里森的首部小说《最蓝的眼睛》发表于1970年，彼时美国社会处于前所未有的大动荡之中：越南战争和反越战和平运动、反文化运动、女权运动、黑人民权运动和黑人文艺运动风起云涌，这使得美国出现空前的社会和政治大分裂。新黑人美学在这种社会背景下得以发展并达到了顶峰。作为实践第二代黑人美学运动主旨的代表作家之一的莫里森，在其文论《黑暗中的游戏：白色与文学想象》中提出了要求重新审视文学美学的主张，即全方位有机融合欧洲经典作品的美学特征和从其非洲祖先那里传承下来的表达方式和民间叙事文学的技巧，以"既此既彼"的逻辑观点强有力地反驳了"非此即彼"二元对立文论美学观。在经历了动荡年代之后，作家们开始反省地寻找自我本质，进一步探索黑人文化并对世界持更广博的看法，黑人作家拓宽自己的创作主题，从早先在作品中反映的种族矛盾与种族斗争中延伸出来，同白人作家一道，共同在作品中探索当代西方文化中面临的重要问题：人与人的关系及对自我本质的重新认识。在这个意义上，除了莫里森、爱丽丝·沃克等作家的作品同样开始摆脱表层的社会抗议型方式，成功地将黑人文化传统和当代美国社会有机地结合起来，把种族道义责任提升到弘扬生命意义的层面上，给黑人美学思想注入了新的内涵。

莫里森的后五本小说《秀拉》（1974）、《所罗门之歌》（1977）、《柏油娃》（1981）、《爱娃》（1987）、《爵士乐》（1992）均出版于20世纪与21世纪之交。随后，莫里森陆续发表了《天堂》（1997）、《爱》（2003）、《慈悲》（2008）等作品，作品中的绝大多数的黑人角色都在不同程度上因美国白人对其长期的精神压迫及主体异化而自我否定，忘记了自己的文化身份、迷失了自我，成为奴隶制和种族主义的无声的牺牲品。在最后的两部小说《家》（2012）、《上帝拯救孩子》（2015）中，莫里森更是重新认识了黑人与白人之间的关系及自我本质，并展现出与白人作家一致的步调，即在其作品中探索当代西方文化乃至人

前言

类文明未来命运的重要问题。

纵观莫里森的小说，其中的生存美学从超主客二元对立关系出发，强调本质并不存在，存在的只是相互联系、相互补充的现象，以及在人的生存世界中形成的体现对自由的追求超越性。它不再属于认识论范畴的美学问题，而是属于生存实践论的美学问题，着重关注现实中的人并探讨改善现实中的人的生活品质的种种可能。如在早期小说《秀拉》里，莫里森便以充满反叛精神的秀拉的个案，表明了自己的生存论美学观点：个体的审美生存既是确立自我的形式，也是对抗"规范化"的手段，引导我们摆脱受传统主体性约束的困境，进行自我改造和自我修养的生活实践。生存美学以生活实践为出发点，较之自然属性和生命本性，它更多地体现出人的社会属性和超感性生命的审美性，寄寓着生活在现实世界里的人类对自由、平等、和谐的生存愿景的渴望。在莫里森小说中体现的生存美学中，身体成了人的感性生存的重要途径，是人与世界之间建立的最初关联，对黑人女性的自我构建有着不可或缺的作用。

本书的第一章对理论研究的视角进行了相关阐释，从西方哲学的本体论、认识论和价值论入手，溯源"自我"和"身体"的密切关联。指出正是传统哲学在存在者状态上研究存在导致了对人的存在的遗忘，而海德格尔的"此在"，因其是"在世界之中存在"的基本建构，表明了人在世界中存在的真实境域。梅洛·庞蒂的《知觉现象学》则给予了肉身存在以适当的存在论说明：身体被用来感知世界，世界的意义是通过身体的存在而得以体现的；身体是表达现象的场所，是意义表达的现实性本身。对于黑人女性而言，身体既是她们拥有世界的一般方式，对于被感知的世界而言，身体又是她们理解世界的一般工具。是身体使黑人女性能够"感知"这个世界，"理解"这个世界，"作用"于这个世界。

在第二章和第三章，本书将分别从黑人女性身体的族裔维度、空间维度对莫里森早、中创作期的作品中身体与自我的构建关系进行研究。本书的第二章借鉴了存在主义女性主义者波伏娃的《第二性》及福柯对女性身体的重要观点，论述从佩科拉的悲剧，到《秀拉》里的秀拉通过身体抗争蔑视男性，再到《所罗门之歌》中帕立特的身体救赎，黑人女性的自我完成了从"自贬"到"自省"的过程。然而，从实体层面出发困囿于女性个体的静态自我的构建，是对"黑人女性"的物化。女性对自我的全面构建需回到其所置身的生活世界中。在第三章里，针对黑人女性身体的空间维度，除了梅洛·庞蒂外，本书还借助列菲弗尔的《空间的生产》对黑人女性的生活世界进行研究，突出其身体的动态空间性意义，从《柏油娃》中吉丹"越界"的身体到《宠儿》中的"交纵"的身体，再到《爵士乐》中"冲突"的身体，身体在其与世界的关系中处于一种能动性的地位，分别经历了"物质空间""精神空间""社会空间"的自我构建过程，动态地完成了"现象"自我的构建。

莫里森后期创作的三部小说《天堂》（1997）、《爱》（2003）、《慈悲》（2008）突显了黑人女性身体的话语维度，以及黑人女性群体身体的对话和交往意义。在《天堂》中，黑人女性身体经历了从"排斥"到"融合"的过程；在《爱》中，黑人女性身体经历了从"异化"到"和谐"的过程；在《慈悲》中，黑人女性身体从"自由"回到"再次被奴役"的状态，莫里森对人类整体的命运发展投入了深刻的悲悯和关注。梅洛·庞蒂在《知觉现象学》里的"作为表达和言语的身体"一章里指出：身体是思想的无声表达，是言语意义的有益补充。武汉大学哲学系教授彭富春同样指出身体的哲学维度主要在于"任何一个身体都是被话语所建构的活生生的身体"[1]；身体的话语维度既是身体存在的最高形式又是身体存在的真实状态。正是在这个意义上，莫里森笔下的黑人女性在身体的话语性特点中建立了体现主体间性的"交互自我"，完成了以差异为基本内容，以身体的内在超越性为特点，以自由、平等为目标的自我构建。

笔者在本书的第二、三、四章的最后一节中指出莫里森的生存美学除了关注身体和自我的建构关系外，还聚焦了小说中的死亡哲学。其早、中、后期三个阶段的小说均突出了若干黑人女性的死亡：第一阶段中以帕立特为代表的女性死亡，第二阶段中宠儿的最终死亡，以及第三阶段中康索拉塔的死亡。她们的死亡不仅蕴含着莫里森对黑人女性悲剧的意识，更有着深刻的生存美学的意义。莫里森小说中以"自然""自在""自

---

[1] 彭富春. 身体与身体美学[J]. 哲学研究, 2004（4）: 59-66.

为""自由"为递进属性的死亡哲学体现了对黑人女性身体的审美超越性,既体现出梅洛·庞蒂的身体审美超越性,又反映出对海德格尔"向死而生"的继承发展,体现出"死后有生""死后新生"等与生命的亲缘共在的辩证关联。

本书的第五章指出莫里森小说中的黑人女性主体的存在和发展不是一个单一的线性过程,而是呈现螺旋运动状态的永恒发展过程。关联着以身体为基点的主体的自我认同。身体不仅构成了主体存在的本体论前提,而且是主体直接的外部符号和表达形式;在与外界的交往过程中,主体总是以身体为其存在的最初表征。黑人女性的身体所体现出的能动作用乃至死亡,都体现出黑人女性自始至终追求的目标,即通过人类的审美自由境界而达到政治上的自由,实现"人性完整"和"人的自由全面发展",进而实现人类自由、美好、幸福的生存状态。

总之,莫里森的生存美学立足于个体生命意义的重建,它采用的不是关注黑人女性"是什么"的本质论思维,而是关注"生存得怎样"及"怎样生存"的存在论思维。它倡导在主体间性理论基础上的生成性的多元共生的辩证思维模式。此外,还通过对黑人女性死亡的审视,体现了身体的内超越性及黑人女性不满足于有限、不完美的生存境况而追求无限、完美的生命存在状态,渴求超越自我的强烈的生命意向。从这个意义上说,莫里森的生存美学是以小说的形式表达人对自我生命本性意义的自觉理解;人不仅是为生存而生存,更是为一种人生价值和意义而生存。生存美学是从存在走向理想,也是从现实走向未来的要求。莫里森的最后两部作品《家》(2012)、《孩子的愤怒》(2015)更是体现了其更宽广的生存美学境界,它超越个体、民族、国家及意识形态的历史现实的局限,从封闭的自我生存美感走向开放的普世生存价值张扬,从基础的微观生存状态批判到高维视角的终极生存理念思考。

Toni Morrison's Works

Novels

The Bluest Eye (1970, abbreviated to *Bluest*)

Sula (1974)

Song of Solomon (1977, abbreviated to *Solomon*)

Tar Baby (1981, abbreviated to *Tar*)

Beloved (1987)

Jazz (1992)

Paradise (1997)

Love (2003)

A Mercy (2008, abbreviated to *Mercy*)

Home (2012)

God Help the Child (2015)

Children's Literature (with Slade Morrison)

The Big Box (1999)

The Book of Mean People (2002)

Short Fiction

Recitatif (1983)

Plays

Dreaming Emmett (performed in 1986)

Desdemona (first performed in 2011)

Libretti

Margaret Gamer (first performed in 2005)

Non-fiction

The Black Book (1974)

Playing in the Dark: Whiteness and the Literary Imagination (1992)

Race-ing Justice, Engendering Power: Essays on Anita Hill, Clarence Thomas, and the Construction of Social Reality (editor) (1992)

Birth of a Nationhood: Gaze, Script, and Spectacle in the O.J. Simpson Case (co-editor) (1997)

Remember: The Journey to School Integration (2004)

What Moves at the Margin: Selected Nonfiction (edited by Carolyn C. Denard) (2008)

Burn This Book: Essay Anthology (editor) (2009)

Contents

Introduction 1

Chapter One Self: a Theoretical Point of Departure of Body Studies 18

    1.1 Philosophical trace of self and its linkage with body 19

    1.2 Perspectives of body studies: ontology, epistemology, axiology 27

    1.3 Dimensions of Morrison's somathetics: racial, spatial, discursive 39

Chapter Two The Ethnic Body in Bluest, Sula and Solomon 52

    2.1 Pecola: "lure of blue eyes" and the victimized self in the superior

        white culture 53

    2.2 Sula: "unbridled sexuality" and the rebellious self against the

        patriarchal society 62

    2.3 Pilate: "missing naval" and the constructive self

        of the black women 71

2.4 Transcending "gendered" body in individualized black women 77

Chapter Three   The Spatial Body in Tar, Beloved and Jazz 84

3.1 Jadine: "transgressed" body and self in "physical space" 85

3.2 Beloved: "traversing" body and self in "spiritual space" 95

3.3 Violet: "conflictory" body and self in "social space" 104

3.4 Transcending "bound" body in the individuality of black women 113

Chapter Four   The Discursive Body in Paradise, Love and Mercy 120

4.1 Paradise: collective self in the bodies from exclusion to assimilation 121

4.2 Love: collective self in the bodies from alienation to harmony 135

4.3 Mercy: collective self in the bodies from freedom to
   "re-enslavement" 144

4.4 Transcending "individual" body in the community of black women ... 155

Chapter Five   The Construction of Self in Black Women's Body 161

5.1 Static construction of "ontic" self vs. "finished" self 162

5.2 Dynamic construction of "phenomenal" self vs. "finite" self............ 166

5.3 Spiral construction of "reciprocal" self vs. "infinite" self 171

Conclusion 178

Works Cited 185

References 186

Introduction

As the only African American woman laureate for Nobel Prize in Literature so far, Toni Morrison (1931—2019), is a pivotal figure in the African American literary canon and cultural history. She used her novels and non-novels to grapple with vital social and aesthetic challenges by exploring diverse aspects of African American experience. In 1993, when Morrison was awarded the Nobel Prize for Literature, she was described as one, "who, in novels characterized by visionary force and poetic import, gives life to an essential aspect of American reality."

Despite the fact that the studies on Morrison have constituted a fruitful academic field throughout the years, the present paper endeavors to anatomize the bond between black women's bodies and the construction of themselves in the nine of Morrison's novels, which reflects the predicaments and breakthrough the black women are encountering in their life in America, have an inalienable kinship with their inborn physical qualities of being black and women.

The black, the woman, and the body

Therefore, before embarking on such exploration, it is a requisite to redefine black in this paper. When receiving the Nobel Prize in Literature for her work, Morrison insisted upon being called "a black woman novelist" rather than "a great American novelist" or "a wonderful woman novelist". She explained,

> So I've just insisted–insisted–upon being called a black woman novelist. And I decided what that meant–in terms of this world that has become broader and deeper through the process of reclamation, because I have claimed it. I have claimed what I know. As a black and a woman, I have had access to a range of emotions and perceptions that were unavailable to people who were neither. (Taylor-Guthrie 243)

Theoretically, black covers connotations of both race and ethnicity, in which the former is a static, narrow, and biologically determined category that serves as the primary ideological context for racism in America and the latter is a much more dynamic and fluctuating category centrally based on cultural affiliation (King 11-32). According to Audrey Smedley' definition, ethnicity is composed of all those traditions, customs, activities, beliefs, and practices that pertain to a particular group of humans who see themselves and are seen by others as having distinct cultural features, a separate history, and a specific socio-cultural identity. Moreover, Smedley made an explicit distinction between the two: "Race signifies rigidity and permanence of position/status within a ranking order that is based on what is believed to be the unalterable reality of innate biological differences. Ethnicity is conditional, temporal, even volitional, and not amenable to biology or biological processes." (Smedley 31-32)

Paul Gilroy described blackness as a metaphysical condition that creates, as much as it is created by, the social surroundings of modern existence, rather than any fixed and static identity (Gilroy 160). To Gilroy, by describing "... creates, as much as it is created by ...", he focused on the process of identification that blackness is intangible and fluid. With the use of black, the construction of African American women's subject, or in other words, the reclamation of their ethnic identity becomes a dynamic and infinite process of creation and re-creation that is relevant throughout Morrison's writing career. So, the use of black in this paper is intended to bypass, or transcend the inhibiting term of "race" in the development of African American women.

Returning to Morrison's novels, a multitude of black female characters are depicted in them with diversified connotations in shifting time and space. With regard to the bodily features of black femaleembodied in the novels, Morrison's novelistic creation can be arguably divided into three stages: the first stage (1970—1980) covering *The Bluest Eye* (1970, abbreviated to *Bluest*), *Sula* (1973), and *Song of Solomon* (1980, abbreviated to *Solomon*), during which Morrison, still a novice in literary arena, was much concerned about the racial features of black women from the perspective of black feminism; the second stage (1985—1993) inclusive of *Tar Baby* (1981), *Jazz* (1987), *Beloved* (1992), during which Morrison, despite her still profound touch of racialism in *Beloved*, had risen above the static limitations of black women's physical features and expressed deep meanings of their female bodies placed in changed physical and social spaces along with the proceeding time in American history. When she entered her third stage of novelistic creation, Morrison tactically extended the spatial meanings conveyed by black women's bodies to the inter-communications among female bodies or between opposite sexes, exhibiting her profound concern for the black community and the humankind as a whole. Different from the previous two stages, there was no protagonists in the strict sense in he third stage, but a collective portrait of black men and women. In this stage, she continued her focus on the spatial dimension of bodies in the second stage and developed it into the discursive dimension of bodies that spanned distant times and used space as the medium. The development of the discursive meaning of black women's bodies was conducted in flashbacks.

In *Paradise* written in 1996, it is in the fierce conflict and dialogue between male and female bodies that the reconciliation between the two sexes is ultimately reached. *Love* relates back to the alienated love against the setting of Second World War (the Civil Rights Movement included) and narrates how another group of black women venture to love, to rid their life of plight and free their love from alienation, highlighting the internal unity and affection within the black community. In *A Mercy* published at the end of 2008 (abbreviated to *Mercy*), Morrison successfully extended her concern for the black culture to the culture of the entire mankind, tracing back to as early as 1680–the year of the evil slavery when the white, just like the black, were enslaved in the northern American colony.

Although her novels typically concentrate on black women, Morrison did not identify herself as a feminist. She argued, "It's off-putting to some readers, who may feel that I'm involved in writing some kind of feminist tract. I don't subscribe to patriarchy, and I don't think it should be substituted with matriarchy. I think it's a question of equitable access, and opening doors to all sorts of things."[1] Judging from her words, it is sufficiently clear that Morrison did not view herself as a feminist writer, nor did she expect to confine her novels to feminist interpretations, but rather she aspired to an open, integrated and developing attitude towards the understandings of the black women in her novels.

---

[1] Jaffrey, Zia (February 2, 1998). "The Salon Interview with Toni Morrison". Morrison's answer on " Why distance oneself from feminism": In order to be as free as I possibly can, in my own imagination, I can't take positions that are closed. Everything I've ever done, in the writing world, has been to expand articulation, rather than to close it, to open doors, sometimes, not even closing the book–leaving the endings open for reinterpretation, revisitation, a little ambiguity. I detest and loathe (those categories). I think it's off-putting to some readers, who may feel that I'm involved in writing some kind of feminist tract. I don't subscribe to patriarchy, and I don't think it should be substituted with matriarchy. I think it's a question of equitable access, and opening doors to all sorts of things.

Besides Morrison's above confirmation, several other causes also account for why a female, before being viewed as a woman, must be beforehand seen as a "man" or "human". With reference to the core of existentialism, or "existence preceding essence", the physical bodies of the American black women in which their selves reside are prerequisite to the identification of their essence. Satre's statement was welcomed by Beauvoir, who, as an existential feminist, astoundingly stated "one is not born, but rather becomes a woman". This also resonated with Heraclitus, an ancient Greek philosopher, who proclaimed that "nothing ever is, everything is becoming" and that "nothing steadfastly is". In terms of black women, it is their bodies in existence rather than their existent bodies that decide their social essence; it is their right of being "humans" that serves the primary basis of their existence as "women". The deprivation of the basic level of "humans" in black women traps them in twofold fetters of the "female" gender and "black skin".

Moreover, even the feminist criticism does not exclude black women's nature as humans. As feminist criticism is based on the three waves of feminist movements, its core is women's social existence and self-perfection. If such abstract existence is specified in literature, feminism will seek the overlapping part between women and men as well as the part belonging to women alone, since women exist in a society that is centripetally complemented rather than centrifugally opposed by men. This is in line with what Beauvoir said, "The selection of one's own liberty is the selection of the others' liberty" (Beauvoir 1997: 73), which, by pointing out the deep symbiotic relationship between women and men, can well be comprehended as the fact that "the concern (most probably from the society) for women is also the concern for men". With this, feminism is featured by its dualism of symbiosis and independence in terms of women's dialectical relationship with women.

As early as the liberal feminism in the Enlightenment, Elizabeth Stanton held that "women are men's equals", "As independent individuals, women are first of all humans before becoming daughters, sisters, wives and mothers at different stages."(Donovan 27) The National Organization for Women's 1966 Statement of Purpose goes: "Now is dedicated to the proposition that women, first and foremost, are human beings, who, like all other people in our society, must have the chance to develop their fullest human potential. We believe that women can achieve such equality only by accepting to the full the challenges and responsibilities they share with all other people in our society, as part of the decision-making mainstream of American political, economic and social life."[1]

In the philosophical study of women, the introduction to The Cambridge Companion to Feminism in Philosophy[2] points out "It has come to be a central feminist philosophical project to respect difference by treating the subject (or self) so that she is represented as socially situated in many dimensions of power and identity besides gender."(Fricker and Hornsby 6) Noticeably, Toril Moi, during her interview at Nanjing University in 2009, pointed out that to meditate on feminism from the perspective of man is a good solution to the dilemma proposed by Beauvoir. She was in favor of incorporating feminism into the general framework of the general context and seeking an organic blend of women's particularity and commonality. "To seek (women's) commonality will lose the (ir) particularity, but if trapped in (their) particularity, no one will think your concern is a common one." (He Chengzhou 155)

Worse still, despite the varied perspectives of new feminists, they are all aware that in a patriarchal society dominated by men's wills and interests, women have almost lost all their selves as well as their "communal" identities.

Since the patriarchal society, women have never fully realized

---

[1] http://www.now.org/about/history/statement-of-purpose/
[2] Edited by Miranda Fricker and Jennifer Hornsby, published by Cambridge University Press in 2000. The thirteen chapters in the volume are written by philosophers at the forefront of feminist scholarships, and are designed to provide an accessible and stimulating guide through a philosophical literature that has seen massive expansion in recent years.

their selves with a "communal" identity. In the past several thousand years, they scattered in every one of "his" family, with their personalities specifically disappearing in their affiliation to the "single" man. The individual patriarchal family's encroachment on female community- dissolved the communal quality of women as a category of community, and their communal identity and interest dissipated in the individual family... (translated by Li Xiaojiang 53-54)

This view comes close to Judith Butler's arguments about the culturally-constructed status of the body in her *Gender Trouble: Feminism and The Subversion of Identity* (1990), where she criticized all feminist efforts have been trying to liberate the female body from the determinations of patriarchal power and by referring to Foucault, further argued that the body assumes meaning within discourse only in the context of power relations. To her, body "is not a being, but a variable boundary, a surface whose permeability is politically regulated, a signifying practice within a cultural field of gender hierarchy and compulsory heterosexuality." (Butler, 1990: 139) Moreover, to Butler, the culturally-constructed body cannot be liberated to its "natural" past, or to its original pleasures, but only to an open future of cultural possibilities. (Ibid 93)

In the contemporary society, "As the favorite writing subject matter of modern culture, body is not only a commodity, but also the object restricted by such modern techniques as weight reduction, keeping fit, face-lifting, etc. With the gradual weakness of grand narratives (or meta-narratives), the worship of body has imbued the margin with direction and meaning unachieved by grand narratives. Meanwhile, women's bodies, which accommodate power, sexual communication and identity issues, have become an important domain of feminists' struggle for their subjectivity."(Song Jianfu 149-150) In specific, "A black woman's body, as a cultural construction controlled and molded by restrictive society and political power, has become a surface on which the predominant power relationship writes and projects its meaning. That's why bodily text bears distinct structural features of social hierarchy. Nonetheless, a black woman's body is not only a place where the mainstream discourse realizes its control, but also a base where she resists power oppression and fulfills her subjective experience." (Song Jianfu 149-150)

So, to explore women's construction of their selves from the perspective of their bodies is in accordance with the third-wave feminism. Such feminism absorbs the basic concepts of post-modernism that deconstructs the conventional culture and doubts the fixedness and stability of all existent disciplines and regulations, negates the popular and grand theories established since the Enlightenment and the subject/object dualism as the basis of the Enlightenment epistemology, and provides diversified methods of complexity to anatomize the formation of subject. Quite a part of feminists no longer make macro analyses of gender, race and class, and with their doubts about the hue of essentialism of such concept of "women" and "patriarchy", negate the conventional sexual dichotomy. Against this background, feminism tends to develop more complex theoretic framework to analyze the complex histories and realities undergone by women.

Accordingly, after the 1980s, the academic research on feminism has embodied increasingly complex living status of women, and women in the third world and the marginalized colored women in the first world have come up with more and more unique thoughts on feminism. In 1981, Cherrie Moraga and Glaria Anzaldua, two well-known American feminists pointed out in their co-edited book *My Back Is a Bridge*, the American women of minority nationalities need to fight against such phenomena as racialism, prejudice, privilege, and violence to women, "to subvert the rule of colonialism inside and outside America."(edited by Bao Xiaolan 39) In 1984, Bell Hooks, a contemporary American black feminist made it clear in *Feminist Theory: From the Margin to the Center* that, due to the hierarchic limitations and cultural misunderstandings, the existent theories of women's liberation had failed to construe the complexity and multiplicity of women's experience, and therefore were unable to represent the black laboring

Introduction

women who were most seriously oppressed (translated by Kang Zhengguo 110). The third-world feminist Chandra T. Mchanty also keenly showed, "Except for the oppression of women, there still exist racialism, colonialism and imperialism" (Bao Xiaolan 29).

As a solution, feminists have since the 1990s reached such a consensus that social gender is not born in the single, common, non-historical "root", so the exploration of it shall be placed in the specific class, race, nationality, country, culture and history. They assumed that the changed meanings of social gender wee produced in the intersection and interplay among diverse factors, and that as the simple stereotyped mode of depicting women merely as victims was undesirable, their dynamic role in history and reality should be found. In a word, the way of respecting difference through subject (or self) so that she will be exhibited as a social existence with multi-dimensions of power and identity in addition to gender has become the core scheme of feminist philosophy. Morrison approved in an interview with Rosemarie K. Lester in 1983 her privileged status as a black woman writer, "I am valuable as a writer because I am a woman, because women, it seems to me, have some special knowledge about certain things".(Lester 54)

> Toni Morrison, however, offers no simple solution to a black woman's search for identity. Rather, she reveals the complexities that attend such a search and uncovers basic moral ambiguities in cultural forms and ideas that stand between women and their attempts to sacralize their identity. Moreover, she shows that sacrality, like identity, is not a permanent quality but one that grows and changes throughout time and experience. (Connor 178)

Morrison study: a literature review

Generally speaking, Morrison's earlier novels in the 1970s invited feminist approaches to deal with the subject of female self-discovery in her novels like Jacqueline de Weeker's "The Inverted World of Toni Morrison's The Bluest Eye and Sula" (1979), Davis's "Self, Society and Myth in Toni Morrison's Fiction,"(edt. by Linden Peach in 1998), Jane S. Bakerman's Failure of Love, "Female Initiation in the Novels of Toni Morrison" (1981), Babara Christian's "The Contemporary Fables of Toni Morrison".[1]

In the 1990s, narratology, feminism and anthropological/cultural criticism have integrated in the discussions of Morrison's fiction in relation to narrative strategies and female discourse. There are several critical works concerning self-construction: Jennifer Fitzgerald's, "Selfhood and Community: Psychoanalysis and Discourse in Beloved" (1998), Ashraf H. A. Rushdy's "Rememory: Primal Scenes and Constructions in Toni Morrison's Novels" (1991).[2]

Just as Linden Peach summarized in his revised edition of *Toni Morrison* in 2000, the latest development in Morrison criticism was the tendency to stress the interconnection among history, memory and trauma in Morrison's work (Peach 172). Furthermore, "Morrison's work explores the shifting notions of self in

---

[1] For convenience's sake, the above quoted papers are as follows: Jacqueline de Weeker's "The Inverted World of Toni Morrison's The Bluest Eye and Sula", CLA Journal 22(1979): 402-414; Davis's "Self, Society and Myth in Toni Morrison's Fiction", in Toni Morrison, Linden Peach, ed. (New York: St. Martin's Press, 1998) p 27-42; Jane S. Bakerman's "Failure of Love, Female Initiation in the Novels of Toni Morrison," (1981) American Literature 52 (1981): 541-563; Babara Christian's "The Contemporary Fables of Toni Morrison", in Black Women Novelists: The Development of a Tradition, 1892—1976, Barbara Christian ed., p 117-179.

[2] For convenience's sake, the above quoted papers are as follows: Susan Lanser, "Fictions of Authority: Women Writers and Narrative Voice" (Ithaca and London: Cornell University Press, 1992); Jennifer Fitzgerald, "Selfhood and Community: Psychoanalysis and Discourse in Beloved" (1998), in Toni Morrison, Linden Peach, ed. (New York: St. Martin's Press, 1998) pp. 110-127; Ashraf H. A. "Rushdy's'Rememory': Primal Scenes and Constructions in Toni Morrison's Novels", Contemporary literature, 32:2 (1991), p194-210.

Introduction

direct relation to the social and physical environment" (King 12). Criticism puts premium on the memory and reconstruction of black history, and the connection and symbiosis between the black and white and their cultures. Yet, all the above criticism is inseparable from the analysis of the black women who are set in the center of the texts; the construction of subject of the black women is a life-long concern to Morrison.

So far, there has been an undesirable situation concerning an overall evaluation of self-construction in all Morrison's novelsd, and there has been even fewer papers on Morrison's more recent works which include Love (2003) and Mercy (2008) in China. For the former there is Zeng Mei's "'Love' Trudging in Mud", and for the latter, there is Wang Shouren and Wu Xinyun's paper published in the journal Contemporary Foreign Literature. With scanty comments on these latest two novels, there is even an absence of comments on the discursive dimension of bodies exhibited in them.

However, the above studies on Morrison's novels, attaching considerable attention to the two layers of "women" and "blackness", lack requisite concern about the basic features of "humans". As the definition of "self " remains equivocated, its construction is hardly appropriately clarified in depth, nor is it fully expounded in all Morrison's nine novels. Worse still, there has been rare elaboration on the bodies in Morrison's novels. Some notable discussions include Mae G. Henderson's "Toni Morrison's *Beloved*: Re-Membering the Body as Historical Text" (1990); Rafael Perez-Torres's "Between Presence and Absence: *Beloved*, Postmodernism, and Blackness" (1999); and Linda Krumholz's "The Ghosts of Slavery: Historical Recovery in Toni Morrison's *Beloved* " (1999). At home, the deformed body symbolizing cultural deficiency is concerned about by a few scholars like Zhang Ruwe in his book entitled *Study on Toni Morrison*[1], as well as Wang Yukuo in his *Study on Morrison* with fragmentary discussions on

---

[1] For these papers, please refer to Zhang Ru-wen's book *Study on Toni Morrison*, Beijing: Foreign Language Teaching and Research Press, 2006.

Bluest and *Sula* respectively.

Undeniably, as components of a dynamic process, the birth and existence of self correlate with the self-identity of subject that has body as its prerequisite. Body not only constitutes the ontological precondition of the existence of self, but also serves as the direct, external symbol and mode of its expression. In interpersonal communications, body is also the primordial representation of self's existence.

Furthermore, regarding Western philosophy, despite reason representing the general nature of humankind from one single aspect, perception correlates more with the individual existence of humankind. As subject in real life, humankind has their general, rational nature as well as their perceptual existence of life. Admittedly, reason is the prime motivation in transforming humankind from the object of "being-in-itself" to the subject of "being-for-itself", yet the existence of his/her bodily perception is also inalienable in directing him/her towards such a transformation.

To connect black women's bodies to their perception and to their construction of selves, the theory for body study in Morrison's three stages of novels, in addition to some feminist theories, mainly derives from Merleau-Ponty's *Phenomenology of Perception*, which is "a prominent example" in "the engagement of feminist philosophers with the phenomenological tradition, and particularly with the work of Merleau-Ponty"(Fricker and Hornsy 30). Papers on such engagement include: Sharon Sullivan, "Domination and Dialogue in Merleau-Ponty's *Phenomenology of Perception*"; Judith Butler, 'Sexual Ideology and Phenomenological Description: A Feminist Critique of Merleau-Ponty's *Phenomenology of Perception*, in Jeffner Allen and Iris Marion Young, "*The Thinking Muse: Feminism and Modern French Philosophy*; Iris Marion Young, "Throwing Like a Girl: A Phenomenology of Feminine Body Comportment, Motility, and Spatiality", in *Throwing Like A Girl and Other Essays in Feminist Philosophy and Social Theory*.

Introduction

In *Phenomenology of Perception*, Merleau-Ponty's exposition on the spatial dimension of body appears in the two sections of The Spatiality of One's own Body and Motility and The Synthesis of One's own Body in Part One–The Body; likewise, his exposition on the discursive of body appears in the section of The Body as Expression, and Speech in Part One–The Body. He even puts forward a section in this part concerning the body in its sexual being, yet from a different angle of what is to be elaborated in this paper. However, taken as a whole, his thoughts successfully restore the lost link between body and mind, which has long been eliminated in binary body/mind opposition. His efforts in the book reintegrates body, as a lived-through experience into humankind's existence among his/her relationships with the world. Noticeably, *Feminist Interpretations of Maurice Merleau-Ponty* (edited by Olkowski and Weiss) denotes how closely feminism is tied to the interpretations of "body-subject" proposed in Merleau-Ponty's *Phenomenology of Perception*, especially in the papers such as "Merleau-Ponty and the Problem of Difference in Feminism" by Sonia Kruks (p25-48), "Sexual Difference as a Question of Ethics: Alterities of the Flesh in Irigary and Merleau-Ponty" by Judith Butler (p107-126), "Female Liberty: Can the Lived Body Be Emancipated?" by Johanna Oksala (p209-228).

Moreover, in this book still, papers like "From the Body Proper to Flesh: Merleau-Ponty on Intersubjectivity" by Beata Stawarska (p91-106), "Vision, Violence, and the Other: A Merleau-Pontean Ethics" by Jorella Andrews (p167-182) and "Language in the Flesh: The Politics of Discourse in Merleau-Ponty, Levinas, and Irigary" by Ann V. Murphy (p257-272), "Female Freedom: Can the Lived Body Be Emancipated" by Johanna Oksala (p209-228)[1] well complement Habermas's theory of inter subjectivity and Merleau-Ponty's exposition on the discursive dimension of the body as expression and speech in the section of body in *Phenomenology of Perception* in facilitating the research on the discursive

---

[1] All the four papers are selected from *Feminist Interpretations of Maurice Merleau-Ponty* edited by Dorothea Olkowski and Gail Weiss, The Pennsylvania State University Press, 2006.

dimension of body studies in Morrison's third stage of novelistic creation.

It is noteworthy that the maneuver to study black women's selves from the perspective of their bodies helps to bring their consciousness back to the living world with the notion of "intentional arc" proposed by Merleau-Ponty and counteract the fault of existentialism that lies in the void of the external reality and historical conditions. In concrete, the discursive dimension of body, via forging dialogues with the outside world, among women and between sexes, combines the twin aspects of the internality and externality of human life and builds up an existential ontology of life-subject in the real sense.

Guided by the above theories, Morrison's nine novels are to be examined in three dimensions of race, space and discourse. In the first dimension, with "finished" self obtained in individualized black woman, the gendered body outruns itself through its own racial features. In the second dimension of space, the "bound" body is transcended in the "finite" self in the individuality of black women. The last dimension of discourse, a spiral one transcending the foregoing bonds of static race and dynamic space, accomplishes "infinite" self in the community of black women, realizing the transcendence of individual body. Though in the ninth novel *Mercy*, the issue of slavery is rementioned, it is expounded at a much higher level. Taken as a whole, the self in Morrison's novels witnesses the ensuing evolution: static construction of "ontic" self in *Bluest*, *Sula* and *Solomon*, dynamic construction of "phenomenal" self in *Tar*, *Beloved* and *Jazz*, spiral construction of "reciprocal" self in *Paradise*, *Love* and *Mercy*.

Undeniably, the foregoing process of subject's existence also displays the diachroneity of subject, which, viewed as an organic integrity, constitutes the self of the community of black women. As subject is not a lonely "I", it symbioses with others and exhibits his/her external aspects; if the process of an individual displays the relationship between the existents and time, then his/her coexistence shows the relationship between existence and space. Such intangible yet perceptible "existence" assumes both the dimension of time (that unveils as a historical process), and the dimension of space (that symbioses with others), which, by forming the historical constitution of black women's subject in space and time and emphasizing their transcendental intersubjectivity in language and community, complements the "body-subject" proposed by Merleau-Ponty.

The present dissertation

To prepare for the integrated analysis of the construction of black women's selves, this paper, after departing from the fundamental layer of humans, takes existentialism for the theoretical foundation, which serves as a philosophical position seeking in the analysis of black women's body structures as a universal and steady foundation for their subjectivity.

Specifically, in Chapter One, the theoretic part of the paper, what are integrated are the ontology, phenomenology as well as the existentialism-based axiology. Firstly, three stages of ontology are outlined in the part: substantial subject, cognitive subject, and life subject. Secondly, the part of phenomenology mainly absorbs Merleau-Ponty's *Phenomenology of Perception*, which makes theoretical preparations for the two dimensions of space and discourse of body studies in Morrison's novels. At the end of this chapter, based on the rough definition of axiology, the connotation of axiological subject is briefed as follows: with difference as the basic content, with transcendence as its feature and liberty as its goal, black women's bodies have a lot to do with their construction of axiological subject.

From Chapter Two onwards, the paper, following the three coordinated dimensions of race, space and discourse, expounds in succession black women's bodies in all Morrison's nine novels. It needs to be noticed that not coincidentally, the first dimension of body study covers the first stage of Morrison's novelistic creation. Racial dimension of body expounds how black women's construction of subject goes through the process from self-deprecation to self-reflection (reflected from the tragedy of Pecola's misconception of body in *Bluest* to Sula's contemptuous fight against men with her body in *Sula* till naval-lacking Pilate's salvation of the degenerated male world represented by Milkman). In this stage, black women's ignorance of themselves is foregrounded from Morrison's very first girl image of Pecola that impedes their facing up to their identity as women in the connotations of "humans". Despite the efforts made by Sula and Pilate, such construction of women's subject is a static one as is repressed by the level of entity, or the racial features of the physical body, and takes black women for objects. In this sense, the overall construction of black women has to return to the living world in which the black women's bodies exist.

The second dimension of space implicates an existence that is dynamic since bodies, while moving from place to place, allow for the appearance of phenomenal subject. This is an overturn of the absolute primacy of physical bodies of black women, as well as a breakthrough of the acquisition of self with regard to the organic synthesis of subject and object. In the specific texts, from Jadine's "transgressed" body in *Tar Baby* to Beloved's "traversing" body in *Beloved*, and to the "conflict" body of Violet and Dorcas in *Jazz*, black women's bodies are set in an active position in their relationship with the world and experience the construction of subject in the three consecutive spaces of material, spirit and society.

As both dimensions of body study belong to the category of the construction of individual black women, the paper needs to resort to the third stage of Morrison's novels to make black women's construction of self complete. Body, as a tacit expression of thoughts and a beneficial complement to langue, highlights the dialogic and communicative meanings of the communal bodies of black women. In the living world, the moving bodies simply "talk", and conduct communication between sexes, between classes, and between races. As has been exhibited in Morrison's last three novels, from "excluded" body to "assimilated" body in *Paradise*, from "alienated" body to "harmonized" body in *Love*, and from "freed" body to body that is symbolically "enslaved" anew in human history in

Mercy, the construction of reciprocal self is achieved through the retrieved human history and hence there is an accomplished axiological subject for black women. This on the one hand accomplishes the construction of subject in Morrison's novels; on the other, shows more profound compassion and care for the destiny of the entire humankind at an even higher level.

Chapter One

Self: a Theoretical Point of Departure of Body Studies

    Until the two World Wars, self in modern Western philosophy had for the most of the time almost been veiled in the shadow of reason and as a result, man's "corporeal existence" had almost long been neglected. Heidegger, by his coinage of the word *Dasein*, overturned the epistemological study on man as an existent in the traditional philosophy, and highlighted man's "existence in the world". As his successor, Merleau-Ponty provided an appropriate existential expatiation of humankind's corporeal existence in his *Phenomenology of Perception*: body is a tool used to perceive the world, and the meaning of the world is expressed in the existence of body. To black women, body is the general way of owning the world, and the existence of their bodies has aroused their perception of their existence in the world. It is the existence of body that renders the black women to "perceive" the world, "comprehend" the world, and "work" upon the world.

Chapter One   Self: a Theoretical Point of Departure of Body Studies

1.1 Philosophical trace of self and its linkage with body

1.1.1 Philosophical trace of self

To conduct a philosophical trace of self needs to retrieve the maxim "know thyself" inscribed in ancient Greek temple, which was defined by Socrates as the supreme task of our philosophy and inherited by all the successors regardless of the great differences on their ways to approach the sublime mission. Similarly, "know thyself" is also one of the fundamental themes of Confucianism, Buddhism, and Taoism, setting direction for the spiritual life of Eastern people[1].

Then what is self ? Indubitably, self is the "I" experienced by an individual and has gone through a long history of wide coverage and complexity (Cassirer 7). Among the earliest ancient philosophers, Socrates proved to be the first one to propose the question as to what man really is. His predecessors, together with his other contemporaries were primarily concerned with the genesis and physical constitution of the physical universe, which bracketed them as natural

---

[1] It is in the sense that of all the three mainstream religions of Confucianism, Taoism and Buddhism in China, the notion of knowing oneself is involved in the kernel concept of each. See Taoism and Buddhism as follows: Taoism is a philosophical and religious tradition that emphasizes living in harmony with Tao, which is ineffable and means "way""path" or "principle". In Taoism, however, Tao denotes something that is the source and the driving force behind everything that exists. The keystone work of literature in Taoism is *Tao Te Ching*, a concise and ambiguous book containing teachings attributed to Laozi. Taoist propriety and ethics in general tend to emphasize wu-wei (action through non-action), "naturalness", simplicity, spontaneity, and the three treasures: compassion, moderation, and humility. Buddhism is a religion indigenous to the Indian Continent that encompasses a variety of traditions, beliefs, and practices based on teachings attributed to Buddha who is recognized by Buddhists as an awakened or enlightened teacher who shared his insights to help sentient beings end suffering through eliminating ignorance, craving, and hatred, by way of understanding and seeing dependent origination and non-self, and thus attain the highest happiness.

philosophers. In ancient Greek philosophers, Heraclitus believed that it was impossible to probe the secret of nature without pre-studying man. This original idea reached maturity in Socrates who initiated the world of man other than the world of nature, which testified that his philosophy was an anthropological one.

To Socrates, man was a being who was constantly exploring his/her own existence and living condition; man was a being who tried to ensure a rational answer to a rational question. It was this basic ability to make answers either to him/herself or to others that qualified an individual as a responsible existence with a moral subject.

Following Socrates, Plato and Aristotle made similar explorations into the self. Specifically, Plato's philosophy emphasized humankind's generality rather than individuality, believing that their reasons were reliable whereas their bodies and senses were not; in Plato's eyes, humankind's consciousness of self was a concept abstracted from the individual. With slight difference, Aristotle, proposing that humankind was a rational, political, and social animal, held that man was a small universe and the ultimate goal of nature, and attributed his difference from other creatures to their rationality. To Aristotle, the maximal perfection was the self-realization of humankind.

After Aristotle, with Epicurean school departing from sensationalism and Stoic school departing from the latter rationalism, both schools tried to render humankind to transcend the real, secular world with emphasis on a consciousness of their subjective inner life. In particular, while the Stoic school embraced an internal impulse of unity requirement between consciousness of self and the object, the Skeptics, despite doubting the existence of objective things, suspected humankind's cognitive capacity and finally entered agnosticism.

Nevertheless, the predominance of reason in the primordial conception of self held by Socrates to Stoics was interrupted by the Middle Ages when Christian theology featuring God overwhelmingly dominated the secular life. Its greatest representative, Augustine, argued that all the philosophies anterior to the birth

Chapter One Self: a Theoretical Point of Departure of Body Studies

of Jesus Christ has a fundamental error of worshipping reason as the supreme essence of humans. According to Augustine, reason was precisely the biggest problem and ambiguity in the world that had led to the fall of man and only by relying on the supernatural power of God could humankind start a new life.

Modern philosophy began with the Renaissance, which was characterized by two discoveries: the discovery of nature and the discovery of man. Opposed to the medieval Christian theology that despised humankind and nature, Renaissance freed humankind and nature from the shackles of theology and divine rights. Besides, the Renaissance, by antagonizing subject with object, promoted the study of natural science and offered a new direction of the study on humankind. In this way, the Renaissance marked the start of man's consciousness of self into which human knowledge was later to develop.

After the Renaissance, the modern philosophy fell into two mainstreams: rationalism and empiricism. While empiricists emphasized humans' natural attributes of feeling and perception through which to connect object and subject, rationalists tempted to relate subject to object by ideas and concepts, assuming that man's rational power actually controlled nature and supplied man with new discoveries and powers. René Descartes's cogito, i.e. "I think, therefore I am", was the mantra of the rational self. By cogito, he declared, "I think, so I am not plants, not animals; I think, so I exist, I exist as a human being" and "I am here not only thinking of the activity itself, but also thinking of thinking activities".

Despite the historic strive in the rational cognition of man, both rationalists and empiricists, as they examined man from the perspectives of mathematics and mechanics, shared the common fault: humankind is mistaken for a machine regulated and determined by God, which further subjected humankind to the causality of nature and therefore denied their innate subjectivity.

In this case, the task of further developing humankind's initiative failed to be accomplished by rationalism or empiricism, so it had historically fallen on Kant, Fichte and Hegel who were the representatives of the German classical philosophers. In the Western world at the turn of the 19th century, Hegel, with his extraordinary speculative power, integrated almost all the primary thoughts since the ancient times into a huge system of rationalism. Yet, abstract reason, due to its separation from emotional life, could only mask rather than eliminate the profound contradictions and conflicts in the world of man. That was part of the reasons when rationalism dominated the domain of philosophy, Europe's capitalist society was still apparently in its period of prosperity and development.

Such superficial prosperity made the West akin to the soundest society in human history. However, the outbreak of the two World Wars in the 20th century stunned the Westerners with unprecedented scale and brutality. Their mental shock woke the world up to the fact: neither could abstract reason ensure a sound human nature, nor could it provide reliable spiritual beliefs, and instead it caught people in blatant sin. Along with two rampant World Wars sided by abundant disciplines of anthropology, reason was overturned and severely challenged. As Marx Sheler has reflected,

> In any other era of human knowledge, man has never been filled with as much self-doubt as we do today. We have a scientific anthropology, a philosophical anthropology and a theological anthropology, which share no communication at all. Therefore, we no longer have any lucid and coherent conception of man. The growing complexity of the engagement in a plurality of special sciences is not so much to clarify our concepts about people as it is to make this concept even more chaotic. (Sheler 13,)[1]

In this situation, how the subjectivity of humankind's self could be possible

---

[1] Marx Scheler, *The Position of Man in the Universe*, Darmstadt, 1928. German philosopher Marx Scheler established philosophical anthropology in the 1920s, the innovation of which lies in its research method of humans and overcomes the one-sided understanding of humans in the traditional philosophy. With the method of combining experience of science and metaphysics, philosophical anthropology compares humans to animals, proposing the idea that humans are open to the world, which exerts a great impact on the advancement of the entire modern Western philosophy.

Chapter One Self: a Theoretical Point of Departure of Body Studies

and constructed became a top priority. Philosophers like Heidegger, Jaspers and Sartre ushered in the existential movement and directed the "forgotten" existence to the primordial association between man and the world, in which man was not a given entity or nature (i.e. not as "the existence of biological body" or "rational beings", but as Dasein (there being). Heidegger's coinage of the word Dasein formed a rebellion against the world of reason in that what was predominated was "how a man lives in the world" rather than "what makes up a man".

As a solution, Dasein connects humankind's physical body with the world and highlights the long-neglected role of body, which, though supposed to supplement the insufficiency of the rational understanding of self, had from Plato through Descartes to the beginning of the modern times, been ignored until it was awakened by the modern philosopher Nietzsche.

1.1.2 Body's philosophical linkage to self

The opposition between man's consciousness and body dated as far back as the ancient Egypt, which first appeared in Plato's philosophy and was later approved in Descartes. In Plato's belief, with body being an obstacle in the way of acquiring knowledge, wisdom and truth, one's ghost will be deceived if she/he explores everything with flesh(Cassirer 7), and there exists a domain of thinking completely practiced by a soul. Such a soul obstinately rejects body as well as all five senses of sight, hearing, touch, taste and smell. In the Christian theology in the Middle Ages, Austine unveiled asceticism by opposing the city of God to the secular city. Love in the secular city derived from the momentary joy brought by body became an evil abyss. To get God's love, one must practice asceticism and abandon the secular world. So, "the long history of churches and monastery becomes the history of tacit bodies in which basic body-suppressing methods like restraint, ascetic practices, meditation, prayer, celibacy, fast, poverty prevail so as to extinguish the boiling energy of body" (Wang Min'an 7).

In the late Middle Ages when the holy transcendental world of God waned, the landscape of the secular world entered man's view. After the brief transition from the Renaissance to the Reformation, philosophy and science gradually repelled theology, state repulsed churches, and reason combatted belief in the 17th century. Despite the transient praise of body in the Renaissance, body, despite ridding itself of the confinement of theology, was still far from being liberated. At that time, knowledge, by replacing theology, had become the center of the secular world, which could destroy God and disclose the mystery of nature. Descartes even made a division between soul and body with the belief that the perceptual abilities of body are insignificant and only the ability of heart can discover the secret of knowledge and truth. Knowledge is acquired through repeated rational calculation and body is only viewed as a perceptual fact. In a word, body has nothing to do with the Enlightenment, and what went through the Enlightenment philosophy is the implementation of reason proclaimed by Kant. Hegel's secret lied with his spiritual phenomenology, where he concentrated on the abstruse and systematic development of consciousness towards absolute spirit. To Hegel, man is distilled into consciousness and spirit and humankind's history is distilled into history of consciousness and spirit. During this period, body is for another time embogged in the endless darkness in man's history.

With Nietzsche's endorsement of body, its decisive status was established and the "bodily turn" appeared. Overturning the metaphysical definition of man's reason with his slogan that "everything starts with body", body became the yardstick to Nietzsche, against which the development of all organic lives restored their "flesh" and energy. "Body" was in fact a more amazing thought than the decayed "soul" (Nietzsche 37-38). In *Genealogy of Morality*, Nietzsche analyzed "meditative life" and "consciousness", pointing out that the profound transformation of history has pushed the semi-beast-like men into thinking, reasoning and calculation, and that they shall be superseded by bodies which have long been degraded and can restore the instinct long been suppressed by

Chapter One Self: a Theoretical Point of Departure of Body Studies

consciousness.

However, to Heidegger, "Animality belongs to body, in other words, body is overwhelmed with impulses; the term of body refers to the totality in the predominant structure of impulses, drives and passions which are suffused with life will. As an animal survival is purely concerned with body, the animality itself is the will of power." (Heidegger 218). With this, body returns to the level of animality and amounts to will power. To Nietzsche, since will power constitutes the basic quality of all existences, animality turns out to be the basic requirement of humankind's existence. In this sense, body, together with its animality, overthrew the predominance of reason in metaphysics: man is the primary existence of body and animality, with reason merely as an adjunct. In Deleuze's theory, body is interwoven with force. Instead of the form, the place, the medium, or the battlefield, body is the force itself, or the conflict between forces, or even the relationship between competitive forces. "What defines body is nothing but the relationship between the controlling force and the controlled force; each relationship between forces forms a body, be it chemical, biological, social or political one. With any two of the unbalanced forces, provided a relationship is formed between them, body is thus constituted." (Deleuze 59)

In the 1970s, Foucault, one of Nietzsche's disciples in France, originated his own social theory of genealogy from body studies. Following Nietzsche, Foucault recognized the role of body rather than of consciousness that was put at the critical moment of history, "Body is the surface on which incidents are inscribed (language records incidents while thoughts dissipate incidents), the place where self is taken apart (self possesses an illusion of material totality), and is a vessel which is in eternal disintegration." (Foucault 148) Such investigatory pheneaology must be immersed in the complex merger of body and history, in which body bears the marks of history and in turn dismantled and molded by history. Therefore, with body and power relationship as the kernel of Foucault's social theories, history becomes predominated by such a closely-connected yet disputatious combination. To Foucault, "power" is not a prescribed, rational and non-subject-oriented productive process, but rather it constructs and adapts humankind's subjectivity to certain mainstream social norms at all times. It is productive rather than oppressive. In his *Discipline and Punishment*, Foucault held that unsynonymous with physical force or penalty, "power" was a social force to discipline and transformed man through social norms and political measures. Such new mode of power was later called "life—power" by him, which centers on body and integrates it into the knowledge and power and becomes the subject of all norms.

The ensuing are the differences between Foucault's body and Nietzsche's body. Setting aside the fact that presides over history, politics and philosophy, Foucaults' body mainly gets embodied in the passive transformation of power, and is a newly-born force after body being attacked by power. Yet, Nietzsche's body, as representing will power, is never static; it is the relationship of discrepancy, and the relationship between contesting forces. In this case, body becomes a basic subject, which is paradoxically dynamic, generative, and accidental.

Such "productive" quality of body was even echoed in Marx, the founder of historical materialism. To Marx, man is a corporeal, natural, living and active existence that is tantamount to a passive, restrained, and restricted existence like animals and plants. He accepted Feuerbach's (1804—1872) interpretation of the term leidend (German word of passive) that it is the form and method of the effect the surroundings and the outside world is making on man, and that only existences that are passive and in need are necessary existences while the existences that have no needs are superfluous and unworthy. Moreover, Marx made a significant expansion of the term that "social practice is actually man's inclusion of conscious and purposeful activities so as to grasp and transform the outside world" (Marx 105). To Marx, Leidend represents man's reliance on nature and nature's restraint on man, which is the objective basis of active generation.

To sum up, the inalienable bond between body and self is illustrated in the above. Similarly, the vicissitudes self has undergone are also experienced by body. However, it is insufficient to delineate the philosophical trace of either. In a sense, as self is strung together by reason, so body is threaded together by perception. Both have different starting points, yet intersect with each other at their attention to subjectivity. This suggests that only a rational study on subjectivity is not enough and has to be complemented by the perceptual study of bodies. The following will deal with three perspectives of body studies.

1.2 Perspectives of body studies: ontology, epistemology, axiology

1.2.1 Ontology of body studies

As has been elaborated above, from Socrates to Stoics, despite their discussion of humankind's epistemology of the objective world, their top concern was the problem of ontology, except that they failed to make a clear-cut distinction between subject and object. Even so, they still acknowledged the existence of self, which seeded the concept of subject.

Based on the inseparable link between humankind's self and body, there are two stages of ontology in the history of the Western philosophy. As has been slightly touched, ontology concerns the study of the essence of existence. Originally, when the word was coined, ontology was mistaken for the study of the existent, in other words, the study of entities, or substantial beings rather than the study of "existence" introduced in the modern times. The ontology of existents was the first stage of "substantial" ontology and such a focus is precarious, for it is at the risk of inducing the segregation of physical body from the fact of existence per se, which would lead to an isolated and static study of the body. As a beneficial supplement, the second stage of ontology effectively integrated the body in its existence and connected it in its existence with the physical and social world.

It needs to be pointed out that such existential ontology is also known in contemporary philosophy as "basic ontology" as held by Heidegger through his coinage of Dasein (there being). His terminology tactfully denotes how to access the core concept of existent. His division between Sein and Seiendes (existent) is the universally-known ontological division. For the former, Heidegger collocates with the modifier of ontic; for the latter, he is with the modifier of ontological. To distinguish "ontological" from "ontic", Heidegger construed the connotation of "ontological" as is involved in "existence", "The understanding of existence is in itself a distinct feature of Dasein as an existent; what differs Dasein from other existents lies in its existence at the level of existentialism."(Heidegger 12) In other words, "only when we are living in the world and constructing ourselves can we gradually understand the existence of the self of us" (Johnson 18-19).

Therefore, according to the second stage of "existential" ontology, the existence of humankind, like the existence of things, is composed of two parts: the existence of "being-in-itself" and the existence of "being-for-itself" at two ascending levels. The former is chaotic, opaque, making no sense to the existence of humankind, for it neither adds anything to nor subtracts anything from humankind. In other words, it is "what it is" or "what originally happens to be". In contrast, the existence of "being-for-itself" implicates "what it is not", for the fact that it is dynamic, transcendent, always pointing to the future creation, which is the characteristics of man.

When the first level of existence of "being-in-itself" is applied to the concrete study of man, all his/her physical features will be ill-received and lead to his/her sufferings. It is certain that the physical body does matter in one's life, especially in his/her reception by other people who consciously and unconsciously hold divergent social norms of beauty and value. Yet, such identity judgment on one's physical appearance is far less sufficient, but sadly, as a result of such a

Chapter One Self: a Theoretical Point of Departure of Body Studies

criterion, racial discrimination, segregation and even slaughter are rampant in the history of humankind.

To rid the "malignant" existence of "being-in-itself", one needs to step into the second level of existence, the existence of "being-for-itself", which involves the momentary identification of intentionality of consciousness with the object. Such identification is not a process of reflection but a recreation, or a process of endowment of meanings. The identification tears open the gapless existence of "being-in-itself", and from the fissures, some parts of the existence of "being-in-itself" are given regularity, order and possibility of being understood by others. So, in a way, the process of intentionality is the process of creation of the consciousness, and the process of endowing the existence of "being-in-itself" with value and meanings. All this suggests that creation is the true essence of man. As man continues his process of creation, the world of "being-in-itself" existence is marked by humankind's characteristics on a larger scale and to a deeper degree. Meanwhile, intentionality always means a pursuit directed toward something absent, which explains why humankind always positions the present towards the future. In the process of creating object and her/his self, she/he is always transcending the present, and such transcendence, together with self-creation gradually forms humankind's subject.

In the endless process of humankind's subject formation, more parts of "being-in-itself" are transformed into the existence of "being-for-itself", and the essence of man is gradually unfolded. This is why humankind's existence precedes essence, as was held by Satre. However, it is noteworthy that such intentionality cannot be divorced from humankind and their activities. Moreover, intentionality endows subjects with passion, impulse, endless expansion, and heterogenizes the history of life as a process of constant creation.

As existence is a quality preceding essence, such understanding of life-subject paves the way for the turn of epistemology to existentialism. The gradual shifts from cognition to existence, from the intentionality of consciousness to man, from substantial subject to man's activities are what distinguish existential subject from epistemological subject. It is from these shifts that a deeper understanding of subject in the aspects of individual liberty, creation of transcendence, and historical process is born. All this prepares the study of the process of intentionality, which is the core in the phenomenology of body studies.

So, to some extent, it may well be concluded that the new connotations of contemporary philosophy, entirely different from the conventional philosophy, merely take ontology for the theoretical presupposition or logic basis of man's cognition, for a supposition and belief that serve man's own needs and goals. Ontology doesn't decide its own significance; on the contrary, the value of ontology is embodied in whether or not man's explanation of the world is plausible. Ontology has no significance except in man's understanding and application of it. (Xie Weiying 108)

1.2.2 Epistemology of body studies

As has been afore-mentioned, ontology and epistemology are the two sides of the basic issue of "thinking and existence", in which the latter presupposes the former, which is echoed by Engels that the philosophy about the basic issues in modern philosophy is concerned with the relationships between thinking and existence. (Marx and Engels 219) The establishment of such a fundamental issue marks the philosophical revolution called "epistemological turn" that has emerged in modern philosophy. Its criticism lies in the improperness to assert the world without the concern for "the relationships between thinking and existence"; what it requires is the inexorable emergence of cognitive theory before the theory of the world is constructed. This denotes the principle of the epistemological turn that the ontology without epistemology is futile (Sun Zhengyu 144-145).

In the modern era, philosophers have become aware that it makes no sense to aver what "existence" actually is without investigating humankind's

Chapter One Self: a Theoretical Point of Departure of Body Studies

capability of perception. Such an "epistemological turn" is contrary to the ancient "ontological" philosophy, as the latter attempted to ignore the contribution of thinking to existence, to seek a certain experiential or transcendental "existence" and to take it for the "genesis" of the world. It is in this sense that phenomenology has solved the contradiction between thinking and existence by surmounting the essential disparities between phenomenon and essence via describing the basic structure of consciousness, and by exploring the contradictions between subjectivity and objectivity, between subject and object, as well as by exploring the perception of subject.

However, it is a requisite to differentiate between epistemology here and the epistemological attitude towards ontology in the Western tradition. Whereas the former emphasizes the basic regulation and formation process of subject's cognition of the world, the latter, just as mentioned above, separates the subject from the object and shelters humankind's perceptual life with logic reason. In this case, "basic ontology" or existential ontology turns to be an outright revolt against the ontology in the Western tradition, diverting the basic direction of ontology from epistemology to existentialism. So, existentialism is the description of the living situation of man who has long been neglected in the rational regulations and takes man's existence for its content of study, man's liberty for its goal of pursuit, and man's value and meaning as its future orientation.

In this sense, body, as the crucial means of humankind's perceptual existence, serves as their primordial link to the world and associates their rational knowledge about it. The epistemology of body helps supplement the study of body in existence. Despite the physical features, bodies as existents are actually under the interwoven influences of gender, race, class, society, culture and history.

Edmund Husserl's phenomenology in 1900 can well serve as the method of epistemology towards body. He set out to analyze human consciousness–that is, to describe the concrete "Lebenswelt" (lived-through world) as is experienced independently of prior suppositions, disregarding whether these suppositions come from philosophy or from the common sense. He proposed that consciousness is a unified intentional act. By "intentional", he did not mean that it is deliberately determined, but that it is always directed to an "object"; in other words, to be conscious is always to be conscious of something. Husserl's claim is that in this unitary act of consciousness, the thinking subject and the object it "intends" or is aware of, are inter-involved and reciprocally implicative.

As a proponent who further advances phenomenology, Martin Heidegger stressed that what the concern of phenomenology is how things are accessed, which helps to expose what has been hidden or covered. He interpreted phenomenology as a way to acquire understandings without opposing subject to object. "Dasein does not seek to define its own quality, but to acquire the possibility of its existence." (Sun Zhengyu 21) In other words, phenomenology unveils the structure of existence of Dasein rather than the quality or category of it.

If Heidegger's Dasein (being there) functions as the link between phenomenology and humankind's existence, implicating the unified structure of body and soul, then Maurice Merleau-Ponty, another inheritor of Husserl, is the one who initiated the relationship between phenomenology and body. Merleau-Ponty once stated that "man is a rational animal, (yet) his/her reason and mental phenomena don't leave in him/her a self-enclosed domain of instinct" (Merleau-Ponty, 1963: 181). Both Heidegger and Merleau-Ponty benefited from Husserl in terminating their ontological judgment and by replacing it with an outright, essential process of transformation, and returned to the research on existence in existence.

To validate "existence in existence", Merleau-Ponty put forward the concept of body-subject. To him, body-subject is the presupposition of all man's experience and humankind's cognition of their subject. As for the positive bond between body and the outside world, he resorted to the concept of the "intentional arc" to project us onto the surroundings, to place man in the world and exhibit his/her past, present and future and the different situations of humans, non-humans,

Chapter One Self: a Theoretical Point of Departure of Body Studies

material, ideology, moral, etc. In a word, the "intentional arc" sets man in all these relationships and supports their conscious lives of epistemology, desire and perception. It is man's body that enables him/her to change his/her perspective of perception and to further change and transform the meanings.

Merleau-Ponty's phenomenology is to restore our robust contact with the "things themselves" and "our world of actual experience" as they "are first given to us" (Merleau-Ponty, 1962: IX). This means renewing our connection with perceptions and experience that precede knowledge and reflection, "to return to that world which precedes knowledge, of which knowledge always speaks" (Merleau-Ponty, 1962: IX). Phenomenology is therefore "a philosophy for which the world is always 'already there' before reflection begins–as an inalienable presence; and all its efforts are concentrated upon re-achieving a direct and primitive contact with the world, and endowing that contact with a philosophical status."(Merleau-Ponty, 1962: VII)

In other words, without body-subject, there would never be our existence, nor would there be the experience, life, knowledge and meaning of the mankind. This is mainly because within the bounds in which the world makes sense to us, the structure of phenomenon is not an isolated entity from us, but associated with the existence of our body-subject, the existence that produces meanings. As body is dynamic living and directing itself in the world, so body offers meanings to the world our mankind is experiencing. Merleau-Ponty commented as follows,

> I experience my own body as the power of adopting certain forms of behavior and a certain world, and I am given to myself merely as a certain hold upon the world: now, it is precisely my body which perceives the body of another person, and discovers in that other body a miraculous prolongation of my own intentions, a familiar way of dealing with the world. Henceforth, as the parts of my body together comprise a system, so my body and the other person's are one whole, two sides of one and the same

phenomenon, and the anonymous existence of which my body is the ever-renewed trace henceforth inhabits both bodies simultaneously. (Merleau-Ponty, 1962: 353-354)

In addition to body's primordial link to the natural world by Merleau-Ponty, Karl Marx also could not deny the role of his/her body in man's interactions with the secular world. For Marx, he expounded the existential basis of his philosophy in his *Manuscripts of Economy and Philosophy of 1844*. Moreover, he pointed out that humankind's perceptive activities are more primitive than their activities of theoretical reflection: their feelings, passion define not only anthropology but also true ontology, or existentialism (Marx 140). Similar to Merleau-Ponty, Marx also highlighted man's perceptual activities as the starting point in his/her social practice in which she/he steps out of herself/himself and builds relationships with other existences (be them the objects in nature or other people). The possibility of such perceptual activities lies in the fact that man possesses a corporeal body. Therefore, humankind's corporeal bodies not only need to enjoy human-centered living, but also deserve their own historical exposition. Marx's supplement of individuals' social practice is verified in Merleau-Ponty, who agrees by stating,

Probably the chief gain from phenomenology is to have united extreme subjectivism and extreme objectivism in its notion of the world or of rationality. (Merleau-Ponty, 1962: 19)

To sum up, Merleau-Ponty's *Phenomenology of Perception* is a proper existential epistemology of body in that it not only combines subject and object in the subject's cognition of the world, which conforms to the existential view of ontology, but also integrates corporeal body in such cognition process. Moreover, it truthfully stresses body's inseparable kinship with the natural and social world through its two dimensions of space and discourse as to be elaborated in next section in this chapter, which constitutes theoretical basis for the two dimensions of body study in Morrison's later six novels: the dimension of space and the dimension of discourse.

1.2.3 Axiology of body studies

Axiology is a concept about the meanings or value of all the things in the objective world to the existence of the mankind; it is not epistemology whose aim is to know the inner quality and rules of the objective things and form a knowledge system about experience of humankind's life or existence. Viewed from the perspective of existentialism and based on social practice, the specific relationship between whether or not and to what extent the object the object can meet the needs of the subject is regarded as value. Without social practice, neither object nor subject can produce value: value is determined by the interactions between both sides. As it is, axiology is to a large extent rooted in the domain of existentialism, which emphasizes the interdependency of man and nature as well as the interpersonal relationships and coexistence of the humankind.

Accordingly, the concept of man from the perspective of substantial ontology is utterly different from that of axiology. Whereas the former departs from "what man is actually composed of" and views him/her as a given, static being trapped in reductionism and investigates a fixed and unchangeable quality for man's essence, the latter, or the understanding of man from the angle of axiology becomes an issue of "what she/he should be like". This shift takes man for a process of transformation, a process of practical activities, a process of opening up to the future. In other words, only from the perspective of axiology can man be comprehended as an existence in activities, which to a large extent constitute the humankind. Under this circumstance, man's substantial existence or "ontic" existence is merely a carrier of his/her real existence and shall not be overestimated. Therefore, an axiological perspective of subject stresses the active existence of subject in the domain of his/her axiological relationships with other subjects in practical activities, in which the pluralism of axiology can unify differences of subjects.

In fact, the construction of axiological subject is the theoretical solution to body studies, as combines axiological reason with body's perception. Providing, however, that ontology is the theoretical starting point of body studies and epistemology the tool of application, the subject based on axiology will inevitably be the goal and way out. At the stage of substantial subject or "ontic" subject, despite constraints of the subject by the material regulations of body, its axiological connotations are neglected. Though the substantial concept has the connotation of presence as a physical existent, subject still belongs to the category of axiology that makes judgment of its meanings. Besides, the conception of humankind as subject is not restricted to understanding him/her as a physical unity of body and mind, but promotes their active statuses in the world and relationships with other existents. Therefore, humankind's subjectivity is what differentiates themselves from their substantial existence. It is characterized by such qualities of initiative, self-independence, transcendence, and liberty. To this, Heidegger once concluded that it is man's subjectivity that makes his/her subject.

As it is, the philosophy of subject suggests that man, as an initiative existence is the center of the world and the doer of perceptual activities (with "subject of practice") and cognitive activity (with "subject of cognition"). So, man as subject should exert a predominant effect on objects. Guided by this, the explanation of man's relationships with the world should stem from and aim at man through his/her existence or activities of perception, reason, practice, will, or feelings, etc. Such an axiological subject functions in man's axiological existence, since his/her substantial existence cuts off his/her relationships with the world and rejects his/her social relationships as alienating, exclusive, and restrictive of his own liberty. Only by regarding man as an axiological subject can man construct his/her relationships with the outside world and become subject.

Chapter One Self: a Theoretical Point of Departure of Body Studies

As has been partly mentioned, man's relationship with the outside world is embodied in his/her social relationships, which is, despite Heidegger's Dasein and Merleau-Ponty's *Phenomenology of Perception* or phenomenology of body, further supplemented by Habermas's intersubjectivity in the contemporary Western philosophy. Habermas developed the theory of intersubjectivity with the purpose of reconstructing humankind's subject in their relationships of discourse and contact. It, on the one hand, overcomes the disadvantage of lonely individuals' self-centeredness and demands the understanding of subject in his/her interplay with the world, and on the other hand, accords with the reality of the contemporary Western capitalist society, in which, the excessive expansion of instrumental rationality and utilitarianism has led to new problems of survival like indifference of interpersonal relationships as well as fierce conflicts, etc. This renders the understanding of man's subject in his/her relationships with the world significant to eliminate his/her extreme selfish utilitarianism of individuality.

Moreover, Habermas's intersubjectivity helps to counteract the demerit in Heidegger's Dasein that only touches upon the visible relationship of the substantial existence rather than the internalized axiological relationships that are unique to man. There are demerits with Habermas's intersubjectivity as well. By weakening his/her centered place and own initiative, intersubjectivity is apt to shape man by his/her social relationships and make him/her an object. Nevertheless, as social relationships are created by man in his/her practice, it is inadvisable to cut off his/her relationships with the society. On this occasion, the only solution lies in their internalization of such relationships, which negates neither their relational quality nor their quality of self-autonomy. In this way, man can exist both as a substantial being and an organic part in the society with all his/her social relationships serving the conditions for his/her own development.

Marx Scheler was the forefather of philosophical anthropology in the 1920s, which overcame the one-faceted understanding of humans in the traditional philosophy. He compared humans to animals, proposing the idea that humans are open to the world, which exerts a great impact on the advancement of the entire modern Western philosophy. Moreover, his ideas on humans and their essence that promote subjectivity and value are particularly appreciable nowadays. To Scheler, man's pursuit of perfection is an eternal dynamic process; human is an "X" that constantly pursues to achieve "what it should be like".

According to Mirander Fricker, the chief editor of *The Cambridge Companion to Feminism in Philosophy*, in her "Feminism in Epistemology: Pluralism without Postmodernism", epistemology also facilitates axiology featuring difference-based pluralism, and "epistemology should be made accountable to difference by incorporating an epistemic pluralism into it, not an ontological or a metaphysical or an epistemological one." (Fricker and Honsby 161)

Furthermore, axiology is in tune with the post-modern third-wave feminism in the 1980s and 1990s that opposes essentialism in gender theories. Rather, axiology favors social constructivism. As it is, the third-wave feminism, by subverting the grand theoretical systems that have a unified standard, rejects the conventional concepts of class and dominance and advocates a plurality of difference, peculiarity, specificity, multiplicity, contradictoriness, and identity recognition. Between axiology and feminism, the overlapping part is their concerted concern for women's self-identification and self-construction in their multiple identities.

Taken as a whole, it is beneficial to integrate the axiological perspective into the study on body's contribution to the construction of humankind's subject. To do so, the study shall return to various analyses of the living states based on diverse phenomena of bodies demonstrated in specific social and cultural environments.

Chapter One Self: a Theoretical Point of Departure of Body Studies

1.3 Dimensions of Morrison's somathetics: racial, spatial, discursive

1.3.1 Racial dimension of somathetics in Morrison's novels

The issue of race is the major concern in Morrison's early stage of literary creation in which the majority of Morrison's black women fall victims to the western parameter of beauty. As it is, the concept of "race" in the United States is based on physical characteristics and skin tone, which plays an essential part in shaping American society even before the nation declared its independence. The perception of black people has been closely tied to their social strata in the United States. Black people usually have the following physical characteristics: radiant dark skin tone, big full lips, round perky butt, almond eyes. Among them, the darkskin tone is the most distinct racial stereotype and cause of racial prejudice against them, and it is impossible to be both prettiest and black.

To a black young woman, her hair, body, and color are the society's trinity in determining female beauty and identity; the cultural and value-laden gang of three that have formed and for the most part are forming the boundaries and determining the extent of women's visibility, influence, and importance. They learn as girls that in ways both subtle and obvious, personal and political, their value as females is largely determined by how they look. As they enter womanhood, the pervasive power of this trinity is demonstrated relentlessly in how they are treated by the men they meet, the men they work for, the men who wield power, and how they treat each other and themselves. To black women, the domination of physical aspects of beauty in women's definition and value render them invisible, partially erased, or obsessed, sometimes for a lifetime. For that, black women find themselves involved in a lifelong effort to self-define in a culture that provides them no positive reflection.

In practice, what Morrison's black women have suffered still proceed today. When Morrison's earliest two novels got published, the second wave of feminism reached its peak. Driven by the Civil Rights Movement, the feminist movement vehemently deplored the man-centered society, holding that gender oppression, derived from social and family structures in patriarchy, is the core and genesis of all other forms of social oppressions. Against this background, the primary aim of women's liberation was to shatter the male-dominant patriarchy. Nevertheless, such concept of glorification of women through debasing men denies the differences of class, race and nationality among women. This signifies the construction of a new gender oppression while overturning the old one, for which Simone de Beauvoir's *The Second Sex* (1952) is the manifesto of the second-wave feminism.

In addition to patriarchy, the "Otherness" is another arch criminal of racial discrimination. Black women should reject the omnipresent "gaze" of men and their role of being the Other. The biggest affinity between Satre's *Being and Nothingness* and Beauvoir's *The Second Sex* is the concept of the Other. Satre's concept of the Other partly originates in Heidegger's theory of the untrue state of all living things, and regards the Other as representing the concretion of public concept, which casts the powerful "gaze" towards women and allows no existence of woman as a true, independent and individual being. So, the gaze or concept of the Other is internalized to facilitate the formation of "being-in-itself".

As for Beauvoir, she followed Hegel in his belief that Otherness is the basic concept of mankind's thoughts, though in fact she was enlightened by Levi Strauss[1], who proposed that the evolution of culture is marked by the

---

[1] Levi-Strauss's seminal work on the primitive society–*The Elementary Structures of Kinship* was the most important anthropological works on kinship that was published in the same year with Simone de Beauvoir's *The Second Sex*. The former's work was reviewed favorably by the latter, who viewed it as an important statement of the position of women in non-western cultures.

Chapter One Self: a Theoretical Point of Departure of Body Studies

development of the opposite consciousness of dualism. With the guidance of these two predecessors, Beauvoir inferred that women's subject could only be established in the opposition between men featured as the center and superior and women as the object and inferior. Therefore, in this opposition, the subjects of women are decided by the subjects of men. For this, Beauvoir realized, "Man can think of himself without woman. She cannot think of herself without man. … She is defined and differentiated with reference to man and not he with reference to her; she is the incidental, the inessential as opposed to the essential. He is the Subject, he is the Absolute–she is the Other." (Beauvoir, 1997: 16) The tragic fact is that when a woman hopes to be a subject she turns out to find that she desperately "lives in a world of the Other imposed by men."

In the combat between "being-for-itself" and "in-self" depicted by Satre, women's role is like "in-self" which is dependent and limited while men's role resembles "being-for-itself" which is independent and transcendent. "Now, what peculiarly signalizes the situation of a woman is that she–a free and autonomous being like all human creatures–nevertheless finds herself living in a world where men compel her to assume the status of the Other. They propose to stabilize her as object and doom her to immanence since her transcendence is to be overshadowed and for ever transcended by another ego (conscience) which is essential and sovereign." (Beauvoir, 1997:29) The tragedy of women lies in this conflict between the fundamental aspiration of every subject (ego)–who always regards self as the essential–and the compulsions of a situation in which she is the inessential. In other words, women are forever embogged in a dilemma where they feel the impulse of their internal "being-for-itself" yet are feeble to unshackle the position of "in-self".

Worse still, despite the downgraded status of women as the Other, according to Beauvoir, the scattered living state of women defines themselves as the accomplice of the Otherness.[1] They never, although the situation is improved today, unite together with the status of subjects or "us". Beauvoir emphasized that only through living like "being-for-itself", like transcendent subjects planning their own future could women be liberated and achieve liberty. In this sense, women's liberation movement is taken for an act of salvation not only of women themselves but also of the society as a whole. In this sense, the birth of the sisterhood of women betokens the future of the evolvement of the spirit of the humankind.

The combination of women's status of the Other and their usual desultory living state confines the judgment of black women to the racial features incompatible with the white's aesthetics. Manifestly, such a dimension descends from the substantial ontology of body studies, which is static under the gaze of the white world. This reduces women to a very dangerous existence of the "being-in-itself". In Morrison's first three novels, the focus falls on the racial dimension of body studies and their statuses as the Other and isolated beings. In her virgin novel *Bluest*, Pecola, the little black girl, with no requisite guidance except for the meager company of a compassionate white girl, Christine, fell a victim to the Other by blindly fantasying about a pair of blue eyes. In *Sula*, Sula, the young woman fighter, alone, challenged the dominant biased patriarchy with her sex-indulgent body. When Pilate, the protagonist in *Solomon*, attained her construction of self at her death to save her nephew Milkman and became a marker with her emblematic flight transcending the physical bounds of a black woman, this navel-lacking black woman broke the static existence of black women.

Afterwards, in the next three novels of *Tar*, *Beloved*, and *Jazz*, Morrison

---

[1] To some extent, Beauvoir condemns women as the accomplice of allowing themselves to have been defined as the Other. Michelle Ballet and Mary Daly also talks about this serious problem. In *Transcending the Holy Father* (Boston, 1973, p49), Daly attributes the phenomenon of accomplice to the external environment and the thoughts imposed on women. In *Contemporary Oppressed Women* (London, 1980, p85, p110), Ballet insists that this problem shall be further explored, yet she rejects the Marxist's opinion that this is merely a result of "false consciousness".

Chapter One　Self: a Theoretical Point of Departure of Body Studies

shifted her attention to the black women's body that turns out to be dynamic and initiative, which walks a further step on her way towards the construction of axiological subject.

1.3.2 Spatial dimension of somathetics in Morrison's novels

Largely, the way body exists in space reveals the way of humankind's existence. On the one hand, body is flexible in itself, on the other hand, it makes proper reaction to the environment. This results in the unity of body and the external space: body has integrated its environment into its own existence. Such integration comprises many contents of consciousness and spirit, which lays the foundation for the construction of social space. In the great leap from substantial subject to existential subject, as body has cast off the restrictions of the substantial subject, the spatial dimension of body becomes the expression of the phenomenological study of body. To trace the spatiality of body, it is necessary to clarify two concepts: space and body in space. First, space is the existing form of material. In the history of western philosophy, Plato has pointed out the complexity of the definition of space, claiming in *Timaeus* that as an almost indescribable "mixed concept", space can be understood in the definition of movement given by Aristotle: the realization of potential things in movement; space is not an empty box, it is closely connected with substances.

However, space cannot be equated with spatiality, for the stride from physical space to abstract space is realized from "space" to "spatiality". If Aristotle's definition of space belongs to the category of physical space, the space of social culture belongs to the category of abstract space. Soja once defined so, "Spatiality is society, which exists not as its equivalent in definition or logic, but in its specificity and formal constitution." (Soja 65) Nonetheless, as space had long been neglected and debased in the 19th century due to the long-predominant position of time in the realm of humanities and social sciences, it remained unchanged until "the turn of space" appeared in the 1970s as a result of Lefebvre and Foucault's interpretation and guidance of space theory (Zhou Hejun 66-68).

Humankind's basic feelings, including their perception of time and space through all their bodily activities, provide the basic framework for the development of their subjectivity. Such temporal and spatial framework, or its intuitive form is not readily inborn but gradually formed through complex bodily perceptual activities in humankind's infancy and childhood. This finds evidence in Heidegger in his *Being and Time* that our perception of space in daily life is obtained from the participation in various activities. For most of the time, our body, particularly when set in motion, is the medium for perceiving space; it is actually what fixes our position in the world. Heidegger reinforced that handlichkeit (ready to hand) is usually our mode of experiencing things, which implicates that except our eyes, our body, especially the moving body is an important medium of sensing space.

Henceforth, the trend of inextricable interweaving of body and space is set to continue. Bondi and Davidson expatiated: "To be is to be somewhere, and our changing relations and interactions with this placing are integral to understandings of human geographers." (Bondi and Davidson 338) This seems to contend that from the closet to the body, to the city, to the nation and to the globe, a variety of subjectivities are performed, resisted, disciplined and oppressed not simply in but through space. In contrast, today embodied subjectivities are more liable to be seen as possessing a "spatial imperative" (Probyn 282).

It is advisable to refer the spatial dimension of body to Henri Lefebvre's *Production of Space* (1974). In his masterpiece, Lefebvre disapproved of the conventional social theory's labeling of space as the vessel or platform of the evolvement of social relationships, pointing out instead that space is a rather important constitutive part. To him, space is produced, restructured and transformed with the development of history. By classifying space into three types of material, spiritual and social, Lefebvre is convinced that this classification

Chapter One Self: a Theoretical Point of Departure of Body Studies

helps unite these three spaces supposedly to have existed in the form of lonely and scattered knowledge and is now made easier for the subject's interpretation. (Zhu Liyuan, 2005:499)

Analogous to substantiality that studies the static and fixed features of body, spatiality, as a quality of existence, also belongs to body, yet with the focus on the body in movement and the body in relationships with the outside world. In fact, the spatiality of body is not only an important angle for man to perceive and manage body, but also endows him/her with the connotations of axiological subject in the sense of existence. To body, space is not an abstract noun but rather an equivalent to a verb of relation and production process, so in the behavior of creation and existence, space is produced and knitted together with the life process.

So, over time, the historically-constructed unique space constitutes social standards propelling people to comply with and reproduces social order, in which everyone finds his/her own position. Man's posture in space and his/her relationships with space therefore bear political and symbolic meanings. It is in this sense that man's attitude towards space is politics-oriented. Harvey averred that every social mode constructs its objective concepts of space and time to conform to the needs and goals of the reproduction of materials and the society, and to organize material practice according to these concepts. (Harvey 377)

To supplement the subordination of spatiality to body, Merleau-Ponty also affirmed "And indeed its (body's) spatiality is not, like that of external objects or like that of 'spatial sensations', a spatiality of position, but a spatiality of situation" (Merleau-Ponty, 1962:100). "By considering the body in movement, we can see better how it inhabits space (and, moreover, time) because movement is not limited to submitting passively to space and time, it actively assumes them, it takes them up in their basic significance which is obscured in the commonplaceness of established situations." (Merleau-Ponty, 1962:102)

In this sense, man's subjectivity or consciousness of himself/herself is spatial either in its origin or structure, i.e. the spatial elements are integrated into their own structures. Simply put, it is the surrounding space that molds a man whose consciousness of subject implicates spatiality. Such a process of implication and integration accompanies the growth of man's subjectivity, in other words, man's subject must be spatial before it is able to grow. (Tong Ming 117)

Going to the production of Morrison's middle-period novels, spatial narration is largely integrated and black women's bodies are set in types of moving and changed space. In the three novels of *Tar*, *Beloved* and *Jazz*, three independent yet interwoven and inter-penetrating spaces are highlighted: physical space, spiritual space and social space. As the first one stresses the effects of the materiality of changed physical space on people living in it; the second one emphasizes the psychological effects of the space conjured up in one's mind on people. To a greater or lesser degree, the last one concentrates upon the effect of changed social environment on people's personality development. In Chapter Three, physical space will be related to *Tar* in which Jadine's self-construction embarks on "transgressed" body in changed physical space, and spiritual space will be related to *Beloved* in which Sethe continues Jadine's unfinished self-construction in spiritual space via her daughter, *Beloved's* "traversing" body, and social space will be related to *Jazz* in which Violet accomplishes the construction of self in social space by means of "conflictory" body. Through these three spaces at deepening levels, black women's destinies in the complex social reality are surveyed in depth.

1.3.3 Discursive dimension of somathetics in Morrison's novels

From substantial subject in ancient ontology to existential subject in modern existentialism to the contemporary life-subject that highlights intuitive perception

Chapter One Self: a Theoretical Point of Departure of Body Studies

of body, a rough historical development of subject theory is outlined. The logic underlying this process is that theories move from the exploration of the external objects to the medium of consciousness to the internal subject of man. This gradual process demonstrates the human quality of philosophy as well as the value and contents of man's existence. Yet, the exploration of subject sees no end, unless it rids itself of the shackles of individuality that inevitably leads to self-centered subjectivity.

Humankind's consciousness of existence (which is called by Descartes "I think" or what she/he truly is, or the existence of thinking) is rooted in the initiative of pre-consciousness and pre-reflection. All the things of cognitive meaning such as words, terminology and signs must pass through his/her physical body before reaching man. This suggests that body plays a primordial role in fixing meanings: signs embrace tacit meanings, which are "spoken" out or perceived through the activities and body organs by the "listener". However, since the listener is facing towards the new space of the world and the location of his/her body, the individual man brings new meanings to words and the world as well. Merleau-Ponty contends so,

> The body's function in remembering is that same function of projection which we have already met in starting to move: the body converts a certain motor essence into vocal form, spreads out the articulatory style of a word into audible phenomena, and arrays the former attitude, which is resumed into the panorama of the past, projecting an intention to move into actual movement, because the body is a power of natural expressions. (Merleau-Ponty, 1962:181)

To comprehend the word "discursive" here, we need to trace the root of "discourse". The latter, in its closest meaning, is "written or spoken communication or debate"[1] and the former finds its adjective correspondent "of or relating to discourse or modes of discourse"[2]. Conspicuously, the discursive dimension of body studies by the author of this dissertation attends mainly to the effect of communication, which is further divided into two progressive parts of conveying or sharing of ideas and information.

As it is, in social practice, body plays the role of communicating with the outside world, as the facial countenances, gestures, or any movement of body may be suggestive of humankind's intention. In other words, body, like a sign, has performative quality, and conveys information, which, though is expressed in silence, passes on to others the psychological experiences in the vicissitudes of his or her life. Even in the extended field of history and society, body is still expressive in ways concerned with social production and distribution.

There are two categories of communications: linguistic communication and non-linguistic communication. Communication of body language is one type of non-linguistic communication. As linguistic communication is divided into two kinds of oral and written communications, non-linguistic communication encompasses body language communication and by-language communication and manipulation of objects, among which body language communication can be subdivided into the three types of body gestures, clothing & appearance, and spatial location.

With the above categorization, the relationship with the outside world by means of body language supplements the social practicality which language lacks, and therefore reinforces the study on humankind's subjectivity. With body-language communication, the study on humankind's Dasein has shifted from the immanence of individual subject to the reciprocity between subject and object, and has thus cast off the restriction of studying life-subjectivity merely within the abstract scope of individual subject. This not only considerably enriches the

---

[1] *The Oxford American College Dictionary*, published in Oxford University Press in 2002, p388.
[2] *The Oxford American College Dictionary*, published in Oxford University Press in 2002, p388.

Chapter One Self: a Theoretical Point of Departure of Body Studies

content of life-subjectivity, but also significantly expands the understanding of humankind's subjectivity to the development of inter-personal relations and the history.

In this inter-personal relationship, humankind is both subject and object, so his/her absolute subjectivity is attenuated and, by being self-centered, binds self-construction. Of the modern philosophers, Martin Heidegger's later thoughts, Jürgen Habermas's communicative theorie[1] and Hans-Georg Gadmer's *Philosophical Hermeneutics*[2], all value the dialogic and communicative nature of language, believing that language is indeed the mode of humankind's existence. Moreover, they believe that humankind's relationship with their existence and the relationships among subjects are the relationships between dialogue and communication. In such inter-subjective relationships, the absolute self-centered subjectivity of man as both subject and object is intensely lessened.

---

[1] Jürgen Habermas (1929—) thinks that the background of the living world provides the condition of consensus for linguistic communication. In analyzing the discursive quality of body, Habermas's communicative action theory may be helpful, as "this is an interaction of symbolic adaptation between subjects, which, with the medium of language and through dialogues, accomplishes mutual understanding and agreement among men. In mutual understanding which is the core of communicative acts, language plays a fundamental role." Though he admits the rational power of the speaker and behaviorist in achieving agreement in communicative acts, the rationality on which such agreement is be based on only implies that it is not imposed on each other by force or violence. Habermas always sticks to the moral ideal of humanity that equality and freedom can only be realized in communication.

[2] As for Gadmer (1900—2002), his philosophical project, as explained in *Truth and Method*, was to elaborate on the concept of "philosophical hermeneutics", which Heidegger initiated but never dealt with at length. Gadmer's goal was to uncover the nature of human understanding. To Gadmer, communication and understanding are the only routes to the perception of the existence of Dasein. He criticizes the methodologies of the natural sciences and the attempt to use these methodologies toward human sciences. He holds that human experience is situated in language and maintains a poststructural relationship to language in that it is the site of human experience. However, he does not agree with the poststructural or deconstructivist attitude that this indicates the failure of language to be able to convey meaning. Instead, he felt that this was the source of the success of meaning, arguing that humans are all constituents of language, which grows and changes with us; that we are in language as language is in us, and that this makes for understanding between people and across history.

To further elaborate on this, Merleau-Ponty stated as follows:

> The linguistic and intersubjective world no longer surprises us, we no longer distinguish it from the world itself, and it is within a world already spoken and speaking that we think. …It is however, quite clear that constituted speech, as it operates in daily life, assumes that the decisive step of expressions has been taken. Our view of man will remain superficial so long as we fail to go back to that origin, so long as we fail to find, beneath the chatter of words, the primordial silence, and as long as we do not describe the action which breaks this silence. The spoken world is a gesture, and its meaning is a world. (Merleau-Ponty, 1962: 184)

In this way, taken for a symbolic system of body that conveys a certain amount of information, the discursive dimension of body in a sense connotes history, which resides primarily in the communicative quality of different bodies and the practice of such communicative quality among different groups of people through different historical periods of the entire human existence.

As a matter of fact, the Dasein of subject lies not only in his/her utterances, but also in his/her deeds: there is no separation between how to say and how to do. Such discursive dimension of body may well be understood as the "performativity" (Nelson and Seager 342) of body, which has been influential to black women because it moves away from essentialist and static understandings of identity, and theorizes identity as constantly re-enacted through bodily performance. In Morrison's works, the black women's bodies do not exist as a "prediscursive"[1] site; instead, their bodies are constituted through compelled enactment and repetition of hegemonic discourses (of class, race, gender, and

---

[1] The term "prediscursive" refers to something "that comes before words, i.e. that which is not easily contained or assimilated into the symbolic domain of speech, language, signification". This brief definition comes from Derek Hook's "Pre-discursive' racism".

Chapter One   Self: a Theoretical Point of Departure of Body Studies

sexuality among others.) In other words, bodies are constituted by language–they are "texts" that bleed, eat, defecate, and so on, including lived-through experience more than linguistic terrains. As a result, bodies have a weighty and often "messy" materiality, viscosity, and fluidity, which is foreshadowed in the ontological study of self in the foregoing section.

There is no denying that Morrison's early six novels are also descriptive of black women's body experiences in spite of their racial or spatial features. Nevertheless, the body depictions in her last three novels demonstrate a more distinct tendency to discourse and the effect of communication, as in each novel there are varied encounters of male or/and female bodies: in *Paradise*, the black women's bodies which have undergone the transformation from exclusion to assimilation; in *Love*, the bodies of the two ladies after being alienated for years before finally ending up in harmony; in *Mercy*, a story concerns both the black and the white who are "re-enslaved" from liberty and forms a cycle in the history of mankind. Owing to their collective living state in those three novels, interactions are molded through dialogues conveyed by their bodies living in different groups, which are conducive to the ultimate construction of "reciprocal" self in black women.

Chapter Two

The Ethnic Body in *Bluest*, *Sula* and *Solomon*

In the year 1963 when Martin Luther King, Jr. (1929—1968) advocated his dream that his "four little children will one day live in a nation where they will not be judged by the color of their skin, but by the content of their character",[1] Morrison was already a member of an informal group of poets and writers at Howard who met regularly to discuss their literary works. She once attended one meeting with a short story about a black girl who longed to have blue eyes, which

---

[1] On October 23, 1963, Martin Luther King Jr., an American clergyman, activist, and prominent leader in the African-American Civil Rights Movement, organized and led the March on Washington in American history, where he delivered his "I Have a Dream" speech. In his speech, King expanded American values to include the vision of a color blind society. After winning the Nobel Peace Prize in 1964 for his work to end racial segregation and racial discrimination through civil disobedience and other nonviolent means, King was assassinated in Tennessee four years later on April 4, 1968.

was later developed into her first novel, *The Bluest Eye* (1970). Since then, the issue of racial discrimination had penetrated into her literary creation, including her succeeding two novels of *Sula* (1973) and *Solomon* (1977).

Despite her constant concern about racial discrimination in her writing career, Morrison placed a special premium on the racial dimension of body by portraying the black women images of Pecola, Sula and Pilate consecutively in the above novels and depicting the process of how a black woman is victimized and temporarily liberated from the gaze as the Other from the white-dominant patriarchal society.

2.1 Pecola: "lure of blue eyes" and the victimized self in the superior white culture

Pecola, the little black girl, was the protagonist in Morrison's virgin novel of *Bluest*. It was a poignant story of racial discrimination. In an interview in 1980, Morrison commented that her motive in *Bluest* was to write about the marginalized little girl who had never before been seriously treated in any place and by any person in literature (Taylor and Danielle 88). As Linden Peach extolled, "it was the first novel to give a black child centre stage; previously, the black child had not only been peripheral but doubly marginalized as a comic figure" (Peach 7). Antecedent to the publication of this book, the negative portrayal of black children and black people generally was a familiar theme within white fiction, so it bored viable symbolic meaning to take a little black girl for the protagonist, which was breakthrough in the creation of American black literature.

Ostensibly, *Bluest* is about a troubled, lonely, victimized, young black girl, Pecola Breedlove, who, together with her constantly fighting parents, lives in a black community in 1941 in Ohio where she is continually being told how "ugly" she is. As this fuels her yearning for blue eyes, she is finally driven insane by her fervent wish. In depth, the story implicates that how multitudes of black women fall victims to the internalized white aestheticism in the black community. The story begins with an instant introduction of the predicament of Pecola's life, which abounds in brutality from her parents, despise from her peers, and antipathy from other adults. Totally muddled, she attributes her predicament to her ugliness and dreams of pleasing others by transforming her physical appearance. To do so, she begins to pray to God for a pair of bluest eyes, assuming that so long as she possessed blue eyes, her parents would not quarrel or fight in front of her, the shop owner would be ardent to her, and her classmates and teachers would not spare their appreciation of her.

This initiates the first step of Pilate's victimization to "blue eyes", which embraces a psychological basis. From Freud onwards, psychoanalysts have held the view that a child's experience is not initially integrated or continuous, nor does it initially become experience of an individuated self. It is in the course of learning to understand itself as separated from its mother and being able to identify its own experience that a child is enabled to locate its experience in its own body.

In the black community where Pecola lives, the aesthetics of the white culture have been internalized: they liked light-skinned girls. The shop owner is distastefully indifferent to Pecola; all of Pecola's families and people in the community regard her as ugly and disgusting. This intensifies Pecola's blind belief in her ugliness and every day "long hours she sat looking in the mirror, trying to discover the secret of the ugliness, the ugliness that made her ignored or despised at school, by teachers and classmates alike". (*Bluest* 45) Still in the mirror, Pecola had compassion on herself and attributed her misfortune to her ugliness, imagining that with another beautiful look, her living condition might be disparate. That's why Pecola adores, "if her eyes, those eyes that held the pictures, and knew the sights–if those eyes of hers were different, that is to say, beautiful, she herself would be different." (*Bluest* 46)

Chapter Two The Ethnic Body in Bluest, Sula and Solomon

A number of feminists agreed with Freud and Lacan's description of a mental projection not of the actual body, but of the body as a kind of emotional map. Freud's ideas are elaborated in Lacan's argument that, during the mirror stage, the child forms an image of its own body by its own reflection in a mirror. This image of the body as a whole, forms a sort of provisional identity and presupposes conditions of the more stable symbolic identity. During the mirror stage, the child embarks on the process of coming to understand itself as situated in the space occupied by its body; or, to put it otherwise, embarks on the process of acquiring a stable emotional investment in its body and psychological continuity. Only when it has a body image can it understand its body as "mine" and possess a perspective on the world.

Likewise, the function of mirror in the process of objectification is expatiated by Beauvoir in *The Second Sex*. To Beauvoir, once a child becomes a young girl, she will reject her dolls for ever and find the miracle of a mirror, which moulds her knowledge of herself and the concretization of her own existence. To a woman, the image in the mirror is the self she perceives. Unlike men who need no mirror images to enhance their transcendental existence, a woman, having identified her passivity, sees a mirror as the society, the entire universe, and everything into which all her future possibilities are condensed. In this sense, any women so long as she can transcend the Other self reflected in the mirror, can dominate space and time and possess wealth, fame and joy just like men do.

Therefore, the self for whom psychological continuity is a possibility therefore has to be created through a series of interactions among the child, people around it, and the broader culture in which it lives.[1] Equally, psychological continuity has to be sustained, and social circumstances can either foster or damage it. In *Bluest*, all Pecola's interactions with the shop owner, her school teacher and classmates and the community she lived in constituted the emblematic

---

[1] For a non-psychoanalytic treatment of this theme, see Annette Baier, "Mixing Memory and Desire", in *Postures of the Mind* (London: Methuen, 1985)

mirror that offered her rudimentary knowledge of herself as a disgusting ugly black girl.

If the first psychological step predetermines the tragedy of Pecola, then the second step towards being objectified appears to be the real murderer in her life. Such objectification stems from the internalized white aesthetics that favors blonde hair, blue eyes, and creamy skins[1].

As her desire for beauty was certainly unable to be realized, Pecola's contempt and distaste for herself got intensified and uncontrollable to such an extent that she made outright denial of herself: in total desperation she hoped her physical body would disappear.

> "Please, God," she whispered into the palm of her hand. "Please make me disappear." She squeezed her eyes shut. Little parts of her body faded away. Now slowly, now with a rush. Slowly again. Her fingers went, one by one; then her arms disappeared all the way to the elbow. Her feet now. Yes, that was good. The legs all at once. It was hardest above the thighs. She had to be real still and pull. Her stomach would not go. But finally it, too, went away. Then her chest, her neck. The face was hard, too. Almost done, almost. Only her tight, tight eyes were left. They were always left. Try as she might, she could never get her eyes to disappear. So what was the point? They were everything. Everything was there, in them. All of those pictures, all of those faces. (*Bluest* 45)

According to Rae Langton, the author of *Feminism in Epistemology: Exclusion and Objectification*, Pecola's relentless obsession with the

---

[1] According to Trudier in *Fiction and Folklore: The Novels of Toni Morrison*, the mythology Morrison explores in the novel centers upon the standard of beauty by which white women are judged in this country. They are taught that their blonde hair, blue eyes, and creamy skins are not only wonderful, but they are the surface manifestations of the very best character God and nature ever molded.

Chapter Two The Ethnic Body in Bluest, Sula and Solomon

disappearance of her eyes makes the process of objectification. Different from objectivity which is about how mind conforms to world, objectification is "the opposite, …about some of the ways in which world conforms to mind". Langston reveals, "Objectification is a process in which the social world comes to be shaped by perception, desire and belief: a process in which women, for example, are made objects because of men's perceptions and desires and beliefs" (Fricker and Hornsby 138).

At a deeper level, except for the racial factor in Pecola's objectification, to say that women are made objects has something to do with how they are seen by men. MacKinnon says, "Men treat women as who they see women as being– Men's power over women means that the way men see women defines whom women can be." (MacKinnon 172) For such a suffocating eye from the perceiver and its suppression of women, Marilyn Frye denominates it "the arrogant eye" and its decisive role in the victimization of perceived women is described in the following excerpt:

> The arrogant perceiver…coerces the objects of his perception into satisfying the condition his perception imposes…He manipulates the environment, perception and judgment of her…, so that her recognized options are limited, and the course she chooses will be such as coheres with his purposes. …How one sees another and how one expects the other to behave are in tight interdependence, and how one expects the other to behave is a large factor in determining how the other does behave. (Frye 67)

Such "eye" is the forceful "gaze" of the white aestheticism projected by the condensed public opinion in the black community. In Satre's terms, it is the gaze towards the Other. Such a gaze consolidates the untrue nature of the gazed, allowing no existence of the gazed as true, independent individuals. Therefore, the gaze or concept towards the Other is internalized and facilitates the formation of "being-in-itself".

This internalized gaze as a conviction was revealed by Morrison in the novel: "…it (ugliness) came from conviction, their conviction. It was as though some mysterious all-knowing master had given each one a cloak of ugliness to wear, and they had each accepted it without question. The master had said, 'You are ugly people.' They had looked about themselves and saw nothing to contradict the statement; saw, in fact, support for it leaning at them from every billboard, every movie, every glance. 'Yes,' they had said. 'You are right.' And they took the ugliness in their hands, threw it as a mantle over them, and went about the world with it." (*Bluest* 39)

As Rae Langton reveals in *Feminism in Epistemology: Exclusion and Objectification*, "Instead of belief arranging itself to fit the world, it arranges itself to fit desire" (Ficker and Hornsy 139). No wonder that Pecola, as the product of objectification, fell a victim to the Other's gaze by arranging herself to fit her desire.

Each night, without fail, she prayed for blue eyes. Fervently, for a year she had prayed. Although somewhat discouraged, she was not without hope. To have something as wonderful as that happen would take a long, long time. …Thrown, in this way, into the binding conviction that only a miracle could relieve her, she would never know her beauty. She would see only what there was to see: the eyes of other people. (*Bluest* 46-47)

Merleau-Ponty has argued that body is the carrier of perception without which humankind's subject would be rootless and the experience, without which humankind's life, knowledge and meanings and even the mankind would disappear (Primozic 20). To a young child, body is a subjective projection, a tool

Chapter Two The Ethnic Body in Bluest, Sula and Solomon

with which he or she learns about the world. Through observing their own images, the child gradually views himself/herself as an object and accepts the aestheticism and judgment of himself/herself imposed by the outside world. In this case, when examining her "ugliness" in the mirror fully immersed in the superior white culture and their biased social judgment, Pecola blindly negated herself by detesting her bodily existence and desiring the disappearance of her "ugly" body and a substitution of beautiful blue eyes.

> Each pale yellow wrapper has a picture on it. A picture of little Mary Jane, for whom the candy is named. Smiling white face. blond hair in gentle disarray, blue eyes looking at her out of a world of clean comfort. The eyes are petulant, mischievous. To Pecola they are simply pretty. She eats the candy, and its sweetness is good. To eat the candy is somehow to eat the eyes, eat Mary Jane. Love Mary Jane. Be Mary Jane. (*Bluest* 50)

It is noteworthy that second to the gaze from white aesthetics, Pauline, Pecola's mother is an accomplice to Pilate's tragedy. The black girl's aesthetics was destroyed by her mother's acceptance of white masculine parameter of beauty: long, stringy hair, preferably blond; keen nose, thin lips; and light eyes, preferably blue. She, despite her original unsophisticated and kindness, unconsciously accepts the "gaze" of men and white aesthetics in the films she saw during her pregnancy and judged every face she saw by it. In her life, she loved to caress the white-skinned blond-haired little girl of her white host, and detested the ugliness of her own black children. Worse still, intolerable of her own blackness, she sedulously lavished her only money on clothes, cosmetics and even her hairstyle and molded some white characteristics on her own body.

As what body embodies is a biological type which needs to be interpreted in the society, a subject acquires his/her own body through perceiving the world. Yet, reversely, the society largely decides on the individual's attitude towards his/her body. (Scholz 59)

The conviction of "ugliness" consciously and unconsciously being imposed on Pecola, having bluest eyes means having everything–love, acceptance, friends, family–a truly enviable place in the society. So, Pecola's quest for bluest eyes, her magical talisman, has been interpreted as the "modern quest for a holy grail".[1] Such conviction tempts Pecola into abandoning freedom and becoming an object.

To such a quest of Pecola together with her mother, Satre held that it is a catastrophic self-deception which arises when self is, rather than to realize itself, but willing to be declined to the object, indulged in the existence of "being-in-itself". When trapped in self-deception, man usually "takes other's viewpoint to judge hisself", as held by existentialist theologian Paul-Tillich, "It is hard to choose a true life; most people would rather choose a life of self-deception, as the former requires the courage to be."[2] Women's self-deception actually happens when they accept their role as the Other or the object and abandon their potential as free and creative subjects.

The self-deception was explicitly pointed out by Morrison in the interview in 1994, "I thought in *The Bluest Eye*, that I was writing about beauty, miracles, and self-images, about the way people can hurt each other about whether or not one is beautiful" (Taylor and Danille 40). As it was, the image of the blue eyes permeated the entire novel, which informed the readers that what hurt the blind acceptance of white aesthetics could inflict on a young innocent black girl and the

---

[1] The mythological implication of Pecola's quest has been addressed by Trudier Harris in *Fiction and Folklore: The Novels of Toni Morrison*. According to Trudier, the mythology Morrison explores in the novel centers upon the standard of beauty by which white women are judged in this country. They are taught that their blonde hair, blue eyes, and creamy skins are not only wonderful, but they are the surface manifestations of the very best character God and nature ever molded.

[2] Refer to Erich Fromm's *Escape from Freedom*, (New York, 1941) and Paul Tillich's *"The Courage to Be"* (New York, 1952)

black culture as well.

As the last step to aggravate such hurt, Morrison intentionally culminated Pecola's life of tragedy in her rape by her own father. When the fact was mercilessly unchanged that her black body could not perish, and with the growth of her unrealistic desire, Pecola lost herself and spent all day and all night, envisioning the white skin and blue eyes. On a Saturday afternoon, she was raped by her habitually drunken father and later gave birth to a dead baby. So far, her dream was completely torn to pieces by the cruel reality. At that moment, the despair she received from the townspeople after the death of her baby, turned out to be the last blow to her: she was mentally disordered. The following were the whispers from the townspeople: "She will be lucky if it doesn't live. Bound to be the ugliest thing walking." "Can't help but one. Ought to be a law: two ugly people doubling up like that to make more ugly. Be better off on the ground." (*Bluest* 189-190) As a result, deeply entranced, Pecola "realized" her dream of owning a pair of beautiful blue eyes and talked to them endlessly in the illusory world. "She, however, stepped over into madness, a madness which protected her from us simply because it bored us in the end." (*Bluest* 206) Ultimately, Pecola's madness irritated everyone including the few who once had concern for her.

Morrison made a pointed remark at the end of the story: "So it was. A little black girl yearns for the blue eyes of a little white girl, and the horror at the heart of her yearning is exceeded only by the evil of fulfillment." (*Bluest* 204) From this, it was obvious that Pecola's tragedy was more the fulfillment of her dream rather than the dream itself: to Pecola, blue eyes were not the safeguard of happiness.

Therefore, judging from the sequence of steps leading to Pecola's tragedy, her loss of identity can be viewed as a process of "negative social construction": as a product of the community she lived in and the influence of her mother. In Pecola, this testifies that a black woman's identity is not one subject to essentialism, but rather one out of social construction. Of the two major theories of identity[1], some view identity as something essential, substantial and real existing somewhere within one's self; the others consider it variable, constructive with meanings created from the interactive society. Yet, with regard to Pecola, whose bodily aesthetics matters, integrity of the two views turns out to be plausible: her identity is an on-going formation of her fixed core consciousness of self in her interplay with the society. So, considering her social background, Pecola's identity is always in a process.

However, with the tragic story of Pecola in *Bluest*, Toni Morrison only set forth the issue: how can black women rid themselves, not momentarily, of the pervasive white aesthetics? Since Pecola's yearning for blue eyes to change her fate only turned out to precipitate her degradation, there must be some maneuvers in Morrison's later works to realize at least partially for the unfinished desire of Pecola for a better life. Further meditation on this is deeply reflected in her later two books of *Sula* and *Solomon*.

2.2 Sula: "unbridled sexuality" and the rebellious self against the patriarchal society

Morrison remarked in her interview in 1983 that as in her early works, both *Bluest* and *Sula* start from the childhood of the characters (Taylor and Danille 163). To some extent, *Sula* is a continuation of *Bluest*, which relays the girlhood

---

[1] Academic research on identity comes from a variety of fields: psychology, sociology, literature and other theories of social sciences and cultures. During the 40-odd years since the terminology of identity became a public discourse, it has been endowed with many meanings. Rosenberg (Morris Rosenberg 1987) listed ten different definitions of identity, From the long-standing self-consciousness to the consciousness of community to which an individual is affiliated to the consciousness of community co-possessed by an individual and others. In the current academic research, there are roughly two major kinds of theories: essentialism and social constructivism.

Chapter Two The Ethnic Body in Bluest, Sula and Solomon

of black women and extends it to their adult life. As a matter of fact, compared with *Bluest*, Morrison's *Sula* has a deeper insight into the life of black women. If Pecola is lost in the temptation of blue eyes of the white aesthetics and perishes in the values of superior white culture, then Sula, as her sharp contrast and pejorative of the conventions, takes her body for a weapon and revolts against male-dominated society by indulging in unbridled sexuality.

Markedly, with *Sula*, her second novel, Morrison switched her emphasis from black woman's victimization to resistance. Sula's act of fierce resistance can be interpreted by Mary Daly[1]. Daly favors existentialist theologians' reference of the sharp contrast between "being-in-itself" and "being-for-itself": the former lies at a fixed, specific, and "secular" level while the latter exists in a dynamic, intense, and "holy" relationship between fresh experience and feelings of other organic lives.

Daly regards women's movement as a "spiritual" revolution, in which women by rejecting the status of the Other, seek salvation and ignite the discovery of "transformation and transcendence", or transcending God. Such a revolution is a creative exhibition of existence, or an enlightenment of existence.

> The revolution of women–was an ontological, spiritual revolution, which was aimed at the worship of social idols which transcended sexual discrimination and intended to spark creative actions for transcendence. …It spared no efforts to seek the ultimate meaning and reality, or what was called "God" by some. (Donovan 177)

---

[1] Inferred from *Transcending God the Father* in 1973. Deeply influenced by Paul Tillich, and Martin Buber, especially Buber's *I and You* (1922), which was finished on the enlightenment from Heidegger's theory of institution. Martin Buber (1878—1965) was an Austria-born German philosopher of Judaism and translator of *The Bible*. According to Buber, the former of "being-in-itself"calls forth "I-it" relationship, or the dead nature conventionally interpreted by scholars; the latter of "being-for-itself" invites "I-you" relationship, or the relationship between a single I and a single you.

Daly denies the supposition that God is a "substantial transcendence" or a fixed, supreme male image. These conventional Gods' images which represented all forms of suffocating patriarchal system had to be destroyed and expelled, especially the "penis moral" in the raping culture: the evil trinity of rape, racial extinction, war. To Daly, if women persisted in their conflict status, such an evil trinity was bound to collapse.

So, women's liberation movement was viewed as an act of salvation not only for women themselves, but for the entire society as well. "The birth of women's sisterhood is the most typical anti-cultural phenomenon which predicts the future of mankind's spiritual evolution." To shatter the idols which hinder the formation of God, such a movement needed to drive the idols with internalized male priority out of the ideology and cultural system which have nurtured it.

To black women, the shattering of idols must start from the mechanism of their internal world: they must first reject and then dispel any d consciousness of being the Other that has been internalized. Such process assumes the meaning of salvation to the entire human society for the potentialities it has created for further new transformations. To Daly, the abandonment of objectification and affirmation of existence would create a new likelihood of "you and me", which will oblige those who degrade women as objects gradually to realize their existences as subjects.

Nonetheless, it is by no means an easy task to reject the state of objectification. To Daly, when a woman begins to see through the masks of the society with pervasive sexual discrimination and to face the horrifying fact, she has already deviated from her true self and gets alienated. In that case, out of all her unknown anxieties, she needs courage to "see" and to "be". Of all the possible solutions, her refusal to be affiliated to anyone whom she is to encounter will offer a new consciousness and awakening.

So, unlike other women living in Medallion, Sula becomes a woman to have seen through the "gaze" of patriarchal society and to dispel the internalized consciousness of the Other. She violates the conventional practice. Except refusing to marry and despising the accepted social morality, she goes to church without underwear and has "tried out" before discarding the husbands of townswomen, including the husband of Nel, her best friend. Despite the fact that all her "improper" behaviors "degrades" her with notoriety as the "witch" or "devil" in the townspeople's eyes, Sula never regrets her choice and sticks to her dissipated life opposed by the hostile community.

Sula's independence of the gaze of the townspeople and disregard of being the Other makes her a thorough-going or radical feminist, needing no other means to prove her own value. To free her true self from the patriarchal suppression, she steadfastly opposes any potential control, for in her eyes, men are trivial and are not and will never be the comrades of women. It is this resolution that drives Sula to have sex even with Nel's husband, which, as she holds, does no harm to her friendship with Nel at all. So, when Nel falls out with her, Sula is totally surprised, as to her, rather than an obstacle, men are merely an adornment to women, and the more a woman wants to confirm her own value through the outside world, the more easily she will be affected and lose herself.

Moreover, in Sula's eyes, Nel's parasitic life on her husband is tantamount to death. According to Daly, the life Nel was living is a self-deceptive one. To Daly, it is a great temptation to live in a self-deceptive way and therefore to refuse to prove one's life through shouldering the responsibility for it. As to housewives, their acceptance of a limited social role couldn't help them to "avoid nihilism" (in the words of Heidegger and Sartre), and their addiction to such a role will hamper them from being creative. This would make their existence an incomplete one.

That is why to Nel, the loss of husband means the loss of social status. To some extent, the loss of Jude means the loss of identity, the loss of life, and as a result, Nel becomes a woman without a man, and is deeply ashamed. In fact, what Nel cared about was not Jude, but the social symbol he stood for, without which Nel thought she would have been incompatible with the society and reduced to the object despised and compassioned by the convention. This is echoed in *The Second Sex*, in which Beauvoir declared women's subjection to the male-dominant society by saying, "Woman herself recognizes that the world is masculine on the whole; those who fashioned it, ruled it, and still dominate it today are men. … she has never stood forth as subject before the other members of the group", then implied the possible resistance in her following words, "Shut up in her flesh, her home, she sees herself as passive before these gods with human faces who set goals and establish values. In this sense, there is truth in the saying that makes her the 'eternal child'. …The lot of women are respectful of obedience. She has no grasp, even in thought, on the reality around her. It is opaque to her eyes." (Beauvoir, 1997: 609)

Against this yardstick, Nel is the woman "shut up in her flesh, her home" and Sula is a feminine image who can throw off the yoke of her flesh and move a vital step of growth out of the "eternal child". Therefore, to seek the still abstract and empty liberty in woman, what Sula could do is to exercise it only in revolt, which, according to Beauvoir, "is the only road open to those who have no opportunity of doing anything constructive". Moreover, other women, just like Sula, "They must reject the limitations of their situation and seek to open the road of the future." By contrast, Sula's obedience, or resignedness is only abdication and flight, and "there is no other way out for woman than to work for her liberation". (Beauvoir, 1997: 639)

When *Sula* was created in 1973, it was in the climax of the second-wave feminism. Dissatisfied with the call for equality in politics and social economy, radical feminists surpassed their predecessors and diverted their fight to the field of traditional culture, questioning the ideological and cultural system and social division in the male-centered society. Betty Friedan pointed out in her *The Feminine Mystique* (1963) that the society's division of women was wrong, which led to the oppression of women's destiny. To Friedan, the image of idealized women was restricted to the roles of homemakers and mothers, whose wishes of education and vocation are abandoned in this process (just like women represented by Nel in *Sula*). Kate Millett inherited the point in her *Sexual Politics* (1970) that sexual dominance was a pervasive ideology in the current culture, which provided the most basic concept of power (Millet 33).

Thus, women are confined to their roles of supplying sex, bearing children and managing house chores, and are thereafter denied opportunities of developing their identities. This has resulted in women's loss of self and unhealthy development of their families. Moreover, in *Sexual Politics*, Millett uncovered that the real gender distinction is not a biological but structural one and in the long history of mankind, the relationship between men and women is power-structured, which is a most deeply-rooted relationship of suppression.

As a solution, Foucault revealed that the relationship between power and individuals is a relationship between production and product, and that in a society of discipline, it is hard for an individual to rival power. Yet, when an individual creates power in his/her relationship with others, then rivalry would be launched between him/her and the power. Such a power relationships of inequity and mobility permeate micro social practice of all kinds. To an individual, only when such power structure is broken by his/her own force could it be possible for him/her to realize himself/herself. This conforms to the radical feminists' positioning themselves as male-oppressed "second sex" and taking "anti-social" means to realize their self.

Sula is such an "anti-social" individual and a black woman as well. During the four years between 1937 and 1941, she expressed her consciousness of self and conducted an uncompromising dialogue with the patriarchal society to counteract the effect of its disciplinary power. To Sula, her body is no longer a vessel lodging her single self, or a material existence carrying her substantial spirit, but rather it has been transformed to a place that integrates her somatic knowledge with community–representing personal identity (Lidinsky 191-192). Moreover, it was also a floating place where voices of self from different consciousnesses intervened and long-suppressed women's radical revolts against the conventional roles set by the patriarchal society assembled.

Consequently, Sula's combat against the patriarchal society, as an act in women's liberation movement, exerts an effect of salvation on her society. In her apparently "evil" and chaotic sexes with the townsmen, there was a power of kindness, which enormously enlightens in its own way the black community that is geologically remote, and economically isolated with deep-seated racial discrimination. It directs the intention of the black community towards kindness. Thanks to Sula's "destructive" effect, the townspeople have restored the long-lost virtues, like to "protect and love each other. They began to cherish their husbands and wives, protect their children, repair their homes and in general band together against the devil in their midst." (*Sula* 117-118)

After the death of Sula, the kindness-oriented kernel cohering the black community dies out with her perished body. Immediately afterwards, the newly-formed morals in the community disappeared all of a sudden: their caution and care for each other abandoned, mothers beating their kids again, reappearance of sons and daughters' grudge against the elderly, loss of wives' affection for husbands' injured vanity. The community in bottom was once more on the way to disintegration and extinguished in 1965 when the society underwent tremendous changes.

Despite the temporary kindness Sula has brought to the black community, in terms of Sula's unfinished construction of self, the author of this paper agrees with Zhu Rong-jie's viewpoint: "Although Sula fearlessly wages a battle against male domination and feminine 'sex roles', she lacks the knowledge of where to find an alliance to keep fighting against the social code, so that her lonely rebellion gradually brings about a physical deterioration and early death."[1] Sula's rejection of maternity, her promiscuous relations with townsmen, her disconnection with the African tradition all pose a challenge to black sexism.

In an interview with Robert Stepto, Morrison offered her critique of Sula: "(She) knows all there is to know about herself because she examines herself, she is experimental with herself, she is perfectly willing to think the unthinkable thing. But she has trouble making a connection with other people and just feeling that lovely sense of accomplishment of being close in a very strong way." (Taylor and Danille 14) In an interview with Anne Koenen (1980), Morrison called Sula "the one out of sequence" and construed as follows,

> I thought she had a serious flaw, which led her into a dangerous zone which is …not being able to make a connection with other people. …Sula's behavior looks inhuman, because she has cut herself off from responsibility to anyone other than herself. …Sula put her grandmother away. That is considered awful because among black people that never happened. You must take care of each other. That's more unforgivable than anything else she does, because it suggests a lack of her sense of community. Critics devoted to the Western heroic tradition–the individual alone and triumphant–see Sula as survivor. In the Black community she is lost. (Koenen 207-208)

Sula's discarding of her grandmother suggested her rejection of the sense of community as her behaviors violated the virtue of the black community that well

---

[1] See Mrs Zhu Rong-jie's doctoral dissertation entitled, "Wound and Healing–on the Theme of Maternal Love from the Cultural Angle"(p52), which is hinted by Morrison's words, "Contemporary hostility to men is bothersome to me. Not that they are not deserving of criticism and contempt, but I don't want freedom that depends largely on somebody else being on his knees." The statement is from Toni Morrison's interview with Anne Koenen, "The One Out of Sequence": An Interview with Toni Morrison, in *History and Tradition in Afro-American Culture*, Gunter H. Lenz, ed. (Frankfurt: Campus, 1984), p207-21. Quoted in Aoi Mori, *Toni Morrison and Womanist Discourse*, 1999, p25. note5.

treated the elderly. Unable to commit herself to a communal responsibility larger than her self-fulfillment, Sula's construction of self was incomplete. Just as Mori said, Sula's problem lied in the fact that she could not place and observe herself in a domain larger than her personal and limited experience (Mori 93-94).

Sula may have made her way but "she does not understand her past": and for Morrison it is the latter, and not the former, that empowers black women. Hirsch comments on the novel's ending, "for women who reject unconditionally the lives and the stories of their mothers, there is nowhere to go" (Hirsch 269). So, in some respects, Sula's struggle against the conventional society, though giving the conventional black women a promising direction, was nothing but a "criticism". Besides, such a temporary victory of self-construction obtained to some extent still is related to the men and at the expense of their wives, and hence an incomplete one.

> Toni Morrison demonstrates in Sula how black women do not automatically recover from the rupture …They may not achieve the spiritual wholeness they seek because in many ways the culture upon which they depend for definition is also ruptured. Morrison reveals the bankruptcy of both drastic existential atheism and a timid clinging to tradition. (Connor 174)

It is undeniable that Sula's failed efforts to truly construct her self has something to do with the radicalness and contradictoriness of predominant radical feminism then. Yet, anyway, at the end of the novel, Nel, after transcending the barriers of conventional moral and realizing the long-estrangement between Sula and her, sighed as though denoting something, "We was girls together." (*Sula* 174), and ended the novel with her acceptance of Sula, leaving much room for the construction of self for herself. Then how to reconstruct the self that was once partially established in Sula? Pilate in *Solomon* picks up where Sula stops and explores the potential consequences of body.

2.3 Pilate: "missing naval" and the constructive self of the black women

With regard to the construction of self, Pilate in *Solomon*, is perhaps the most eye-catching woman image in all Morrison's works: well-built, dark-skinned and short and disheveled hair, with a quilt to keep warmth in winter. Wild-natured, she has a great passion for nature and her body has "a smell of forest". After the death of her father, the twelve-year-old Pilate feels lonely and helpless; she is perplexed about her unknown future as the only relative she has in the world is her brother, Macon. To avoid feeling homeless, Pilate folds into her earring made of her mother's snuffbox a piece of paper with her name on it written by her father. The moment she puts on her earring, she has made up her mind to survive: her confidence to live on is given by the power of the name her father writes.

In addition to her black skin, Pilate's racial defect of having no naval further aggravates her character splitting. Despite her determination to survive, she is given numerous blows by the naval-lacking fact: men "called her mermaid" and women "swept up her footprints or put mirrors on her door" (*Solomon* 150). In this cold, careless, and contemptuous society, Pilate is limited to an isolated life, in which every other resource was denied her: "partnership in marriage, confessional friendship, and communal religion" (*Solomon* 149). Such life fills Pilate with pains and sufferings simply due to her physical defect of no navel. The ill treatments make Pilate exceptionally careful in her life to protect herself from further sufferings. For a long time, Pilate has been deliberately trying to cover her belly for living a common life as the ordinary people do. However, all her efforts are in vain except for her temporary success in getting pregnant and giving birth to Reba on the island. With no right attitude toward her own value of existence, to hide her belly or to isolate herself is on no account an effective solution to this predicament, which means destruction and disappearance rather than effective protection. As a matter of fact, Pilate's attempts to cover her belly are a revelation of her spiritual crisis: she is on the verge of a mental breakdown. This means the "self" in Pilate is about to split, since she cannot identify herself as an individual in the face of the misfortunes from her society. Overwhelmed by the agony imposed by her society, Pilate fails to know the essence of her life and accepts the wrongness of having no navel. In order to free herself from her split "self", Pilate has to go through the second stage of her internal conflict–"integrated self". Trapped in such a crisis of split mentality, all Pilate can do is to respond to all the inhuman treatments actively to reincorporate herself into her society.

Outside the novel, according to Anthony Giddens in his *Modernity and Self-Identity* (Bao Yaming 328), in the post-conventional order of modernity, "how my life shall be carried out" has become a question to be answered in people's daily life as to the secular exhibitions of how to take actions, how to get dressed and have food and water, as well as self-acquisition. In this way, individual self has become a reflective project in which the changed self will be excavated and constructed as a part of the reflective process of the changes of connected individuals and the society. Pilate's subsequent actions and reflections on her life value are efforts to acquire individual self. Since the fact of having no navel cannot be altered, her only way out is to "take offense." (*Solomon* 149) and throw away "every assumption" she has learned and begin at "zero" (*Solomon* 149). She abandons the assumption that it is wrong to have no navel and having no novel deserves punishment. She first cuts her hair that is one thing she doesn't want to have to think about anymore. Afterwards, she carries out her internal monologue by tackling the problem of trying to decide how she wants to live and what is valuable to her, "When am I happy and when am I sad and what is the difference?" "What do I need to know to stay alive?" "What is true in the world?" (*Solomon* 149) With her meditation on the predicament, Pilate is experiencing

Chapter Two The Ethnic Body in Bluest, Sula and Solomon

the integration of her split "self" through posing herself the basic questions in her mind: what is her true self? (When am I happy and when am I sad and what is the difference?), what is her own value? (What do I need to know to stay alive?), what is valuable to her in the society? (What is true in the world?) Such questions are both her inquiry into the essence of life and a reflective adjustment.

Pilate's handling of the above questions concerning the value of existence is enlightened by a note-worthy detail of a three-year-old child. By resorting to her memory of the daily life on "the crooked streets and aimless goat paths" (*Solomon* 149), Pilate ponders over sometimes on the "profundity" of the life, and sometimes on "the revelations of a three-year-old." (*Solomon* 149) Since she has not received much education and has no proper people at hand to console her, she can only talk with herself and extract answers to the demanding questions out of her understanding or encounters. How she gets the answers from the revelation of a three-year-old child is unmentioned in the novel. Yet, there must be some link between the joys and pains of the three-year-old child with her value of existence in the world, since children's joys and pains are valuably instinctive with no negative influence of the defective society. If a three-year old child is able to live a natural and placid life out of the deformities of the society, Pilate, as a grown-up, is also qualified for such a life.

That plus her alien's compassion for troubled people ripened her and–the consequence of the knowledge she had made up or acquired–kept her just barely within the boundaries of the elaborately socialized world of black people. Her dress might be courageous to them, but her respect for other people's privacy–which they were all very intense about–was balancing. She stared at people, and in those days looking straight into another person's eyes was considered among black people the height of rudeness, an act acceptable only with and among children and certain kinds of outlaws–but she never make an impolite observation. (*Solomon* 150)

So to some extent, the integration of Pilate's self has a direct relationship with her naval-lacking body, which, despite bringing enormous sufferings to Pilate, offers her opportunity of free expression as well. After overcoming her fear of despise and ill-treatments, Pilate, by exposing her naval-lacking belly, uses her "silent" body language to express her internal calmness: her singing and chewing things with her teeth is a further action to break the silence of women. "She chews things. As a baby, as a very young girl, she keeps things in her mouth–straw from brooms, gristle, buttons, seeds, leaves, string, and her favorite, …rubber bands and India rubber erasers. Her lips were alive with small movements."(*Solomon* 30) Moreover, knowing that Ruth, the mother of Milkman, is distressed as a result of the indifference posed by her brother Macon, Pilate considerately passes this habit on to her, as she perceives that rubbing lips, chewing teeth, and twirling tongue are all her body's touching and feeling herself. To her, in these close touches of tongue and teeth, a woman's pain, solitude, denouncement are endlessly released.

By means of those body "murmurings", Pilate, after acquiring her internal tranquility and contentment extends her love and care through doing good deeds in her community. This signals that her split "self" is gradually integrating. In addition to the effect of the warmth and satisfaction in Pilate's home on Macon and on the people in Pilate's neighborhood, she "mediated a peace" among quarreling drunks and fighting women in her community and allows "none of the activities that often accompanied wine houses…women, gambling and she more often than not refused to let her customers drink what they bought from her on the premises" (*Solomon* 151). In Macon's family, when she knows that her brother and Ruth are having no physical relations for ten years which is unbearable to Ruth, she gives Ruth "some greenish-gray grassy-looking stuff" (*Solomon* 125) to put in Macon's food and in this way makes Ruth pregnant. The birth of Milkman gives Ruth hope to live on. So Ruth concludes: "She saved my life. And yours, Macon. She saved yours too. She watched you like you were her own, until your father threw her out." (*Solomon* 125)

Chapter Two The Ethnic Body in Bluest, Sula and Solomon

Reflecting on Pilate's way of internal growth of self, it can well be assumed that if Pecola is victimized by the restrictions of "being-in-itself ", and Sula's sexual revolt in such restrictions against male-dominated society serves the transition, then Pilate realizes the great leap from "being-in-itself " to "being-for-itself ". Such a leap is made in nothing but the interaction between Pilate and Milkman. To a black woman, in order to leap from "being-in-itself " to "being-for-itself ", it is insufficient to have just transcended her own racial features and formed true aesthetics of beauty, but rather she has to interact with other people before she can possibly achieve such a historical leap.

In *Song of Solomon*, the difference between Pilate's selfishness and Hagar's is that Hagar is not a person without Milkman, she is totally erased. Pilate had twelve years of intimate relationship with two men, her brother and her mother, who loved her. It gave her a ferocity and some complete quality. Hagar had even less and was even more frail. It's that world of women without men. But in fact a woman is strongest when some of her sensibilities are formed by men at an early, certainly an important age. It's absolutely necessary that it be there, and the farther away you get from that, the possibility of distortion is greater. By the same token, Milkman is in a male, macho world and can't fly, isn't human, isn't complete until he realizes the impact that women have made on his life. It's really a balance between classical male and female forces that produces, perhaps a kind of complete person (Taylor and Danille 107).

In the novel, the last scene is enlightening in which Milkman is holding Pilate's dead body after she is killed mistakenly by Guitar. Only at that moment does Milkman realize the spiritual essence of Pilate's love. "Now he knew why he loved her so. Without ever leaving the ground, she could fly." (*Solomon* 341) So, in the end, following her aunt's suite, Milkman is able to sing and fly like his distant African ancestors, enjoying the momentary liberty as an individual. In the fierce violence, Pilate's crucified death connotes Milkman's achievement of self-construction in the flight which signifies a free will. Admittedly, so far Milkman has inherited the self-construction fulfilled by Pilate.

Pilate's attitude towards death is noteworthy in the last scene of *Solomon*, especially when it is combined with violence. Overtly, Pilate's attitude to death is a fearless one, as is shown in the story, "Throughout this fresh, if common, pursuit of knowledge, one conviction crowned her efforts: since death held no terrors for her (she spoke often to the dead), she knew there was nothing to fear. "(*Solomon* 150) To Georges Bataille (1897—1962), there are two kinds of taboos: one is about death and the other is about sex. The taboo about death reserves a distance between death and violence[1]. Yet Bataille took an interest in the dualism of death taboo, as he insisted on a truth about taboos: though the birth of taboos is to meet the need of driving violence out of daily life, there is always a temptation to break the limitations of such taboos. In this sense, reproduction and death are dialectically coordinated with each other. In other words, the death of one is always transformed into the birth of another; the former is the prediction and possibility of the latter. Life, as a negation of death, is the product of the dissolution of life, especially in mankind.

Besides the isolated transcendence on women's bodies, such transcendence is also embodied in the metaphorical combination of female and male bodies and their collective salvation. By portraying the male image of Milkman, Morrison seems to suggest that the continuation of the women's subject in male bodies is by no means accidental (which is hinted to varying degrees in Morrison's

---

[1] According to Georges Bataille (1897—1962), the primitive people thought that death is a disorderly state, which was opposite to the orderly labor. It was labor that subjected everything to order, and only through man's identification with labor that man broke away from violence. Yet, there are dual meanings of violence which signifies death: on the hand the horror of death distance people from it as they desire life; on the Other, the solemn and horrible factors in death fascinate and disturbed them.

following novels): as men's bodies are conceived in women's bodies, women's subject will never be complete and sound without the organic integration of men's subject. What's more, Pilate's acquired self-quest connotes that success of one's consciousness of self in fact lies with the recognition that she/he is both the object and subject, and that only when one is integrated into the existence of others can his/her quest for self be well-grounded and possible. This, of course, requires first of all, the transcendence over the "gendered" body that has objectified black women for so long.

2.4 Transcending "gendered" body in individualized black women

Gender is a range of characteristics used to differentiate between males and females. In addition to race, gender is one of the universal dimensions on which status differences are based. Sexologist John Money introduced the terminological distinction between biological sex and gender as a role in 1955[1].

Unlike sex, which is a biological concept, gender is a social construct specifying the socially and culturally prescribed roles that men and women are to

---

[1] However, Money's meaning of the word did not become widespread until the 1970s, when feminist theory embraced the distinction between biological sex and the social construct of gender. Today, the distinction is strictly followed in some contexts, like feminist literature, and in documents written by organizations such as the WHO, but in most contexts, even in some areas of social sciences, the meaning of gender has expanded to include "sex" or even to replace the latter word. Although this gradual change in the meaning of gender can be traced to the 1980s, a small acceleration of the process in the scientific literature was observed when the Food and Drug Administration started to use "gender" instead of "sex" in 1993. "Gender" is now commonly used even to refer to the physiology of non-human animals, without any implication of social gender roles (for example dogs or cats). In the English literature, the trichotomy between biological sex, psychological gender, and social sex role first appeared in a feminist paper on transsexualism in 1978. http://en.wikipedia.org/wiki/Gender Retrieved 2012-03-25

follow. *The Creation of Patriarchy*, Gerda Lerner deems gender to be "costume, a mask, a straitjacket in which men and women dance their unequal dance" (Lerner 238). As Alan Wolfe observed in "The Gender Question" (*The New Republic*, June 6:27-34), "of all the ways that one group has systematically mistreated another, none is more deeply rooted than the way men have subordinated women. All other discriminations pale by contrast". Lerner argues that the subordination of women preceded all other subordinations and that to rid ourselves of all of those other "isms" …racism, classism, ageism, etc. …it is sexism that must first be eradicated.

> Bodily existence which runs through me, yet does so independently of me, is only the barest raw material of genuine presence in the world. Yet at least it provides the possibility of such presence, and establishes our first consonance with the world. (Merleau-Ponty, 1962: 166)

Therein, just like the dependency of bodily existence on one's self expatiated by Merleau-Ponty, gender issue is not a simplified biological existence separable from the human history and social transformations. To Merleau-Ponty, the body may well be seen as "the hidden form of being ourself", or "personal existence is the taking up and manifestation of a being in a given situation" (Merleau-Ponty, 1962: 166). Behind its biological nature is the mystery of the history and society as well as humankind's natural yearning for an independent, equal and free life, which is exemplified in the first two waves of feminism. Such an appeal for life shakes women off the imprisonment of the Other as their first step towards such a goal.

Dualism–any system of thought that polarizes what we perceive is a narrowing world view, for it inevitably cuts the individual off from the "other", the not-I or the not-I or the not-good or the not-ordered. Dualism

Chapter Two The Ethnic Body in Bluest, Sula and Solomon

creates warring antitheses: the "other" is anenemy to strive with and ideally, to dominate. (Lauren Lepow, 165)

As the term "gendered body" in this paper is adopted to refer to body which is racially emblematized, to transcend "gendered body" is the very necessary step to bridge the gap between antithesized self and body, and a required precondition to convert "being-in-itself" into "being-for-itself". There are two consecutive steps of "transcend" as a verb: initially, "transcend" needs to move away from the original state of one's own existence, and then, after such departure, "transcend" ascends into another state of existence, in which she/he, while enjoying the valuable space of newly-obtained liberty, recasts relationships with other people around him/her. Such transcendence of gendered body is realized partially in Sula and fully in Pilate.

In fact, after identifying with the dynamic and historically-constituted body-subject by Merleau-Ponty, Johanna Oksala commented so, "There is no inhibited female corporeality and free and normal male corporeality in societies of sexist oppression, but rather two differently gendered and historically constituted experiences and modalities of embodiment." (Oksala 222)

Only when the existent is set in the negative can the transcending power surface in humankind's activities. As a feminist heroine, Sula seeks masculine-like power in a racist and sexist world which is in the negative. In addition to her unfettered sexuality, Sula rejects maternity as well, which means an assumption of masculinity or male liberty[1]. Sula, as Naama Banyiwa-Horne wrote, "protects herself against the mean world with a meanness which bristles against the

---

[1] In several interviews, Morrison has admitted fascination with Sula's choice, although it represents the ultimate evil for a woman as far as the community is concerned, "I guess I'm not supposed to say that. But the fact that they (men) would split in a minute just delights me···that has always been to me one of the most attractive features about black male life." See Robert Stepto, "Intimate Things in Place: A Conversation with Toni Morrison", from *Conversations with Toni Morrison*, Taylor-Guthrie, ed. 1994, p26

hostility of the world. Independent, adventurous, inquisitive, strong-willed and self-centered, Sula offers a welcome, if uncanny foil to Pecola's unquestioned acceptance and futile pursuit of those values which lead to her destruction." (Naama 31) Here, Sula's "destruction" functions as a crucial step towards her pursuit for "being-for-itself".

If Sula's rejection of maternity and indulgence in sexes with the townsmen are partial transcendence over "gendered body", then Pilate's death at the salvation of Milkman connotative as transcendence over immanence. Peculiar to the life-subject of existentialism, all concepts of solitude, vexation, fear, and anxiety, as presuppositions of death, are what differs life-subject from cognitive subject. This embraces the profound meditation of existentialism on the existential nature and future destiny of man. To this, scholars at home comment this way: "Our meditation and theories on 'death' are meager. Like 'life', 'death' is by no means a biological phenomenon, for it is a mental, cultural phenomenon involving such a series of fundamental and overall issues in human life as flesh and mind, self and others, individual and category, the world and nature, fact and value, existence and nihility, temporality and permanence, secular concern and ultimate care."(Zhang Shuguang 138) In fact, to existentialists, man is not God or any other infinite absolute being but an existence towards death as a finite existence. In this case, only their inner experiences are true, which is fundamental to the understanding of life-subject.

In *Solomon*, Pilate's death forebodes the transition of negating substantial metaphysical self and approaching existentialism. In Sula and Pilate, through breaking through the limitations of racial features of black women bodies, they are actually well on their way to acquiring the rights and status they deserve. Such an effort is an effort to "de-objectification". Evidently, the acquisition of self is still the obtainment of subject from the perspective of substantial thinking, so it is only accounted as the first step taken by the black women on their way to self-construction. Such a substantial self departs from "what man is" and views man

Chapter Two The Ethnic Body in Bluest, Sula and Solomon

as present, stagnant, solidified, so it will be trapped in reductionism and refer to a fixed quality of man as his/her nature.

Despite the male dominion in *Solomon*, Morrison summarized the momentum of all her first three novels in the her following interview with Taylor and Danille,

> But I think I still write about the same thing, which is about how people relate to one another and miss it or hang on to it…or are tenacious about love. … And about love and how to survive not to make a living but how to survive whole in a world where we are all of us, in some measure, victims of something. Each one of us is in some way at some moment a victim and in no position to do a thing about it. Some child is always left unpicked up at some moment. In a world like that, how does one remain whole–is it just possible to do that? (Taylor and Danille 40)

To some degree, gendered body is a type of substantial existence preset by Greek philosophy, which focuses on the form of existence. Aristotle's philosophy starts from a physical existent's transformation in form, and the perception of such an existent through senses complies with the nature of humankind's mind and body. Integrated in an existent's contact with the external world is the factor of space, body has cast off the restrictions of the subject of entity, body has integrated its surrounding environment into its own existence. Such integration comprises many contents of consciousness and spirit, which lays the foundation for the construction of social space. In the great leap from substantial subject to existential subject, and the spatial dimension of body becomes the expression of the phenomenological study of body. A body restricted by an absolute footing of racial and gender features is deprived of an open perspective, which can only be obtained in the realization of potential things in movement. In other words, the transcendence over gendered body unveils the historical movement of humankind's Dasein, which is in constant change and development and offers a space where we live.

The "body-subject" embraces the contradiction between transcendence and existence, which is primordial and hardly explicable. Different from object in the traditional philosophy, body is visible to others and perceives itself and the world and its "insight" mirrored in them as well. In other words, body resides in between the seers and the seen. As an interface between the perceiver and the perceived, black women's body is the merger of their flesh and soul. Despite its fundamental difference from consciousness-subject that is transparent, fixed and distinct, body-subject is opaque, unfixed, and anonymous, yet it is still endowed with pre-conscious understanding of the world and itself. By conducting activities of feelings and significance, body makes sense and forms the origin of objectivity. In the process of such activities, body shall not be objectified. With such activities, black women's gendered body rids itself of the "ontic" qualities, and embraces transcendence.

To black women, such transcendence over "gendered body" is an incipient effort towards "being-for-itself". In these three novels of *Blueset*, *Sula*, and *Solomon*, Morrison, however, shrewdly resists the temptations of a crude biological determinism. The biological facts are "insufficient for setting up a hierarchy of the sexes; they fail to explain why woman is the Other; they do not condemn her to remain in this subordinate role forever" (Beauvoir, 1997: 32-23). "It is not nature that defines woman; it is she who defines herself by dealing with nature on her own account in her emotional life." (Beauvoir, 1997: 38) "In human history grasp upon the world has been defined by the naked body" (Beauvoir, 1997:53); so "the facts of biology (must be seen) in the light of an ontological, economic, social and psychological context". (Beauvoir, 1997: 36) The human body, Beauvoir argues, is the malleable expression of a creature not entirely fixed or purely natural but significantly shaped by historical situations and societal conditions.

Chapter Two   The Ethnic Body in Bluest, Sula and Solomon

Yet, from Pecola to Sula to Pilate, the construction of self is finished in individualized black women. Though the construction of self is here temporarily finished, it is called "individualized" simply because all the three women are foregrounded or are singled out of a collective group of women who are still bound by their gendered bodies. In other words, they are singled out of the community they live in with the rest women like Pecola and Nel still blinded by racism. However, with the changed living space of black women, the construction of dynamic self is realized in the second stage of Morrison's novelistic creation, i.e. in novels of *Tar*, *Beloved* and *Jazz*, and black women finally transcend the primordial process of static corporeal development and prepares the process of spatial development of their body.

Chapter Three

The Spatial Body in *Tar*, *Beloved* and *Jazz*

As the statement goes "where there is space, there is existence." (Lefebvre 22), when an individual is situated in a space, his/her most direct experience is his/her consciousness of body and the space it occupies, and both his/her facial countenance and other bodily movements are immersed in the interactions between him/her and the outside world. Among mankind's basic senses, the spatial quality of body is demonstrated in the perceptual media that define his/her body's presence, so an individual's existence as well as his/her construction of self is inevitably affected by the three types of space: physical space, spiritual space and social space.

When Morrison began to create *Tar* in 1981, eleven years after the publication of *Bluest*, she had grown to be a mature writer, who, though never stop revolving the racial problems, cared more about the issue of "migration", which can be interpreted as "spatial displacement" and its marked influence on her characters. The three black women images of Jadine, Sethe and Violet respectively

Chapter Three The Spatial Body in Tar, Beloved and Jazz

from novels of *Tar*, *Beloved*, *Jazz* bear varied influences from their change in space. As such, the following will elaborate on the impacts of three types of space on black women's body and their contributions to their self-construction.

3.1 Jadine: "transgressed" body and self in "physical space"

As early as 1948, H.C.Darby stated in his paper " The Regional Geography in Thomas Hardy Wessex" published in *Geographical Comment*, "As a literary form, a novel is innately geological. As its world is composed of location, setting, boundary, perspective and vision, the characters of a novel are set in diversified places and spaces, so are the narrator of the novel and its readers" (Zhu Liyuan 2005: 499).

Despite the geological displacement apparent in *Tar*, the main characters' bodies experience fundamental displacement in space, breaking through the static bonds of racial features of body and entering into the realm of dynamic space. Serving as the transition between the first two stages of Morrison's novelistic creation, there is in *Tar* a dense description of Son's blackness as well as her profound reflection on the alien white culture adored by the black Jadine. The alienation of Son and Jadine is primarily attributed to the alienation caused by their conflictory values, which is closely correlative to the spatial displacement of their bodies.

Tar baby is a doll made of tar and turpentine used to entrap Br'er Rabbit in the second part of the Uncle Remus stories. The more that Br'er Rabbit fights the Tar-Baby, the more entangled he becomes. In modern usage according to Random House, "tar baby" refers to any "sticky situation" that is only aggravated by additional contact[1].

Another version of the tale (Wang and Wu, 2004: 102) goes similarly, yet with a more dismal ending: a farmer, vehemently harassed by a rabbit that steals the cabbages in his field, makes a baby with tar and erects it in the field to attract it. The rabbit, unknowing the truth, goes to tease it. Seeing no response from the tar baby, he turns outrageous and beats it. As a result, the rabbit gets stuck by the tar and loses his life.

The "sticky situation" and "death penalty" aside, the moral of the tale has also a lot to do with the effect of physical space. To the rabbit, the cabbage field is a space denied his intrusion; once he intrudes into the cabbage field and the road, he will be duly punished, regardless of the degree. In other words, the liberty of the rabbit can be guaranteed so long as the rule is obeyed.

Back in the novel, "tar baby" signifies Jadine and the physical space is embodied in the gigantic displacement of Jadine in Paris. "In many ways Jade (Jadine) is the descendent of Sula, who knows well before her short life ends that she has 'sung all the songs there are' (Sula 137)." (Lepow 37) Jadine is enabled to go to college in Paris with the financial assistance of Valerian, her uncle's white employer. Her success of becoming the cover girl of a famous fashion magazine in Paris endows her with a sense of accomplishment and growth. This suggests that she has become the product and appendage of white civilization, suffering

---

[1] In one tale, Br'er Fox constructs a doll out of a lump of tar and dresses it with some clothes. When Br'er Rabbit comes along he addresses the tar "baby" amiably, but receives no response. Br'er Rabbit becomes offended by what he perceives as the Tar Baby's lack of manners, punches it, and in doing so becomes stuck. The more Br'er Rabbit punches and kicks the tar "baby" out of rage, the worse he gets stuck. Now that Br'er Rabbit is stuck, Br'er Fox ponders how to dispose of him. The helpless but cunning Br'er Rabbit pleads, "but do please, Brer Fox, don't fling me in dat brier-patch," prompting Fox to do exactly that. As rabbits are at home in thickets, the resourceful Br'er Rabbit escapes. Using the phrases "but do please, Brer Fox, don't fling me in dat brier-patch" and "tar baby" to refer to the idea of "a problem that gets worse the more one struggles against it" became part of the wider culture of the United States in the mid-20th century. From .

unconsciously the "spiritual enslavement"[1] of the white culture.

During her years in Paris, Jadine "easily accepts the white values" and practices the white culture in practice: she despise the black woman in Paris for her "too much hip, too much bust" (*Tar* 45) unfavored by the white aesthetics. Moreover, on her initial encounter with Son, she doubts him "with rape, theft or murder on his mind" (*Tar* 91), and in subsequent conversations with Son, she looks on herself as a member of the streets and questions him about whether he is "a thief" or not, and what he wants "from us" (*Tar* 118).

Under the influence of higher education of white culture, Jadine is keen on self-pursuit and self-perfection, "She likes herself and is interested in self-realization, in which sense she is quite modern."(Birch 82) Her consciousness of self can be reflected in her quest for self at a Frenchman's running after her,

> I wonder if the person he wants to marry is me or a black girl? And if it isn't me he wants, but any black girl who looks like me, talks and acts like me, what will happen when he finds out that I hate ear hoops, that I don't have to straighten my hair, that Mingus puts me to sleep, that sometimes I want to get out of my skin and be only the person inside–not American–not black–just me? (*Tar* 48)

However, due to her deep immersion in white culture caused by the new physical space in Paris, Jadine is increasingly alienated from black culture, which forecasts her failure of self-pursuit. Later, when Son questions her about why she doesn't leave the streets family and live on her own, Jadine explicates, "I belong to me, but I live here" (*Tar*). Inside her words are contradictory connotations: on the one hand, she cherishes her independence per se, and she must belong

---

[1] American blacks underwent two slaveries in modern history: the first "bodily slavery" in which the African blacks were sold to America for being slaves; the second "spiritual slavery" in which the white maneuvered to extinguish the ancient and unsophisticated tradition of the black.

to nobody but herself; on the other hand, as she now lives in the streets, she gradually gets her culture rooted there.

Jadine's rootedness in white culture is antithesized in Son with his spatial displacement, too. As an African American, in addition to his intimacy with animals and plants, his body bears many primitive characters of nature: well-built and dark-skinned with a deep worship for nature, like "spaces, mountains, savannas–all those were in his forehead and eyes" (*Tar* 158). With "clipped and beautiful with spacious tender eyes and a woodsy voice. His smile was always a surprise like a sudden rustle of wind across the savanna of his face". (*Tar* 181)

Presumably, as his name hints, he is "the son" of Africa and a watcher of African conventions. In his eyes, the best society is the black community, and his hometown Eloe is a case in point. In Eloe, there are virtues of cooperation, unity, and equality while the industrial world as he perceives in Paris only teaches people "how to make waste, …how to talk waste, how to study waste" (*Tar* 203). Though he lives in the 20th century, he hates to learn about the advancements of white culture, and adheres to African conventions. One example is that obstructed by bigoted confidence, Son takes pride in the respect and equality enjoyed by the women in his hometown, totally neglecting the arduousness of their daily life. He holds: "Anybody who thought women were inferior didn't come out of north Florida." (*Tar* 268) His infatuation with the countryside increases his dislike for the city. To him, in New York city which Jadine likes, "all the black girls crying on buses, in Red Apple lines, at traffic lights and behind the counters of Chemical Bank" (*Tar* 216).

If in the antithesis between the two physical spaces of Paris and Eloe, Son and Jadine hold respectively opposite poles, the encounter of their bodies suggests the rivalry of the convention and modernity. At the one pole, there is Jadine, who is "a new capitalistic American black woman" as a product of the fusion of black and white cultures; at the other pole, there is Son representing the convention and ultimate possible salvation of Jade.

Chapter Three The Spatial Body in Tar, Beloved and Jazz

Though Son's salvation of Jadine fails, their body-to-body encounter offers a great temptation and shock to Jadine, just like what the tar baby in the cabbage field first appears to the rabbit. The abrupt appearance of Son's black body reveals the live, vivid and unique blackness to her. At such disclosure, she is oblivious of the effect of the fur coat in the mirror, and gets hit by the smell and "his skin as dark as a riverbed". "His hair looked overpowering–physically overpowering, like bundles of long whips or lashes that could grab her and beat her to jelly. And would. Wild, aggressive, vicious hair that needed to be put in jail. Uncivilized, reform-school hair. Mau Mau, Attica, chain-gang hair." (*Tar* 113)

To this, Jadine "struggled to pull herself away from his image in the mirror and to yank her tongue from the roof of her mouth" (*Tar* 114). Son seeks the cause afterward and sees his hair in the mirror,

> (It) spread like layer upon layer of wings from his head, more alive than the sealskin. It made him doubt that hair was in fact dead cells. Black people's hair, in any case, was definitely alive. Left alone and untended it was like foliage and from a distance it looked like nothing less than the crown of a deciduous tree (*Tar* 132).

Astounded at this direct body encounter representing the clash of two cultures of black and white, what Jadine instinctively does is to evade it: she struggles not to see him, which suggests her effort to resist what Son represents. Her maneuver is rejected by Son who desires to "breathe into her the smell of tar and its shiny consistency" (*Tar* 121). So it can be inferred that by distracting Jadine from the material temptation of the fur coat, Son hopes to awake her memory to the natural quality of black body and restore her blackness.

Underlying the bodily contact are heterogeneous natures assumed by Jadine and Son, as representatives of white and black cultures, which will, according to Tan Yingzhou, "arouse emotional responses of various degrees in people" (Tan

Yingzhou 250). If Jadine, immersed quietly in the white world for more than twenty years, is a homogeneous element, then Son, in contrast, together with his sudden appearance, is a heterogeneous existence that, by taking the form of a force or an impact, stirs the quietness of Jadine's living and passes his emotional energy to her. Under this circumstance, the appearance of Son, as a heterogeneous existence, becomes the Other, which, though violating the common criterion of the white judgment, has positive emotional value. To the interchangeability of the gender location of the Other, Morrison has wisely foreseen the same effect, "I could have changed it around and it could have been a man in Jadine's position and a woman in his. The sexes were interchangeable, but the problem is the same"(Taylor and Danille 105). Extensively speaking, just like Jadine's life is to some extent positively affected by Son, Son's blindly conservative life is also "awakened" by his encounter with Jadine.

Moreover, in the encounter between the two divergent characters of Jadine and Son, the function of an individual's emotion as a heterogeneous element is equally important with the substantial symbols embodied in his/her judgment. When Jadine and Son are interposed in the same physical space, their bodies spring up and supplant their natures as the protagonists of such an encounter. In their close bodily communion, a more profound communication between the two heterogeneous elements is conducted: they smell each other's body during their fierce conflict, although it is not the result of deep love or affection. In their bodily fight, the initial substantial symbol in the judgment of both characters is their smelling: while Son smells Jade for her vigor of life, Jade, under Son's compression, smells him, and, identifying his bodily smell not so bad as she has predicted, is enticed by him, and dissolves her prejudice against his skin of darkness.

> He had jangled something in her that was so repulsive, so awful, and he had managed to make her feel that the thing that repelled her was not in him, but in her. That was why she was ashamed. He was the one who smelled.

Chapter Three The Spatial Body in Tar, Beloved and Jazz

Rife, ripe. But she was the one he wanted to smell (*Tar* 123).

Unlike the indifference of tar-baby which infuriates the rabbit and incurs a hopeless fight, there comes after the thorough-going bodily contact, a positive and temporarily constructive emotional experience between the heterogeneous sides: Jadine sees in Son the primitive power of modern civilization to be injected while Son sees in Jadine's sophisticated beauty the demand of passion. Yet, both of them are aware that to Jadine, Son is a "transgressed" body that is refused by the territory of the streets.

In this case, to find a physical space compatible with their love, Jadine and Son choose to fly to New York after Christmas, where they hope to locate an atmosphere suitable for their life and careers. Their first arrival offers them a false perception that New York City is suitable for an "ideal love" without any outside pressure, and their life is desirable in contrast with others' life that is "ridiculous, maimed or unhappy" there (*Tar* 223). For four months in Dawn's apartment, being contented with their love and confidential, "She poured her heart out to him and he to her. Dumb things, secret things, sin and heroism. They told each other all of it. Or all they could" (*Tar* 224). They also care about each other: after Jadine sprains her ankle, Son gets up every half hour to wash her foot with liquid medicine; when Son's throat gets inflamed, Jadine, in order to cure him, lets him drink much brandy, and gets drunk with him. They find the needed security in each other's arms, and Jadine no longer feels being an orphan, "He unorphaned her completely. Gave her a brand-new childhood. They were the last lovers in New York City–the first in the world–so their passion was inefficient and kept no savings account" (*Tar* 229). In such temporary harmonious body caresses, they are totally forgetful of the outside world,

> They never looked at the sky or got up early to see a sunrise. They played no music and hadn't the foggiest notion that spring was on its way.

Vaguely aware of such things when they were apart, together they could not concentrate on the given world. They reinvented it, remembered it through the other. He looked at her face in the mirror and was reminded of days at sea when water looked like sky. She surveyed his body and thought of oranges, playing jacks, and casks of green wine. (*Tar* 30)

Such an "ideal love" breaks off when they leave New York: there is no eternal shelter for the existence of their heterogeneous love. "Son and Jadine departed out of their conflicting dreams." (Birch 175) Their following life gradually unveils the unconquerable contradictions. Despite their sexual life based on temporary gender equality, as Jade announces, "We're together. Nobody controls anybody" (*Tar* 255), the final separation is foredoomed by their cultural conflicts. The heterogeneous elements from their respective cultures develop into quarrels and fights: "Why do you want to change me?" Jadine asks, to whom Son kicks back the same question "Why do you want to change me? In their ensuing dialogue, Son on the one hand ridicules Jadine's affection for New York and her being "not from anywhere", on the other hand takes pride in declaring his black origin, "I'm from Eloe". This is refuted by Jadine, "I hate Eloe and Eloe hates me. Never was any feeling more mutual" (*Tar* 266). In fact, in Jadine's eyes, New York is not so hideous as demeaned by Son, neither is Eloe so wonderful as Son assumes.

To her, "New York oiled her joints and she moved as though they were oiled. Her legs were longer here, her neck really connected her body to her head" (*Tar* 221). Contrarily, Son's fascinating and enchanting Eloe could do little to endow black women with opportunities of developing their self-reliance. "Eloe was rotten and more boring than ever. A burnt-out place. There was no life there. Maybe a past but definitely no future and finally there was no interest. All that Southern small-town country romanticism was a lie, a joke, kept secret by people who could not function elsewhere." (*Tar* 259)

Chapter Three The Spatial Body in Tar, Beloved and Jazz

Jadine's trip to Eloe brings her to the reality of the extremity of Son's defense of black conventions, so she flees with the thought "but if ever there was a black woman's town, New York was it" (Tar 222). Each wants to liberate the other from the culture that is alien to his/her own, yet,

> This rescue was not going well. She thought she was rescuing him from the night women who wanted him for themselves, wanted him feeling superior in a cradle, deferring to him; wanted her to settle for wifely competence when she could be almighty, to settle for fertility rather than originality, nurturing instead of building. He thought he was rescuing her from Valerian, meaning them, the aliens, the people who in a mere three hundred years had killed a world millions of years old. ...Each knew the world as it was meant or ought to be. One had a past, the other a future and each one bore the culture to save the race in his hands. Mama-spoiled black man, will you mature with me? Culture-bearing black woman, whose culture are you bearing? (*Tar* 269)

Obviously, "Mama-spoiled black man" pertains to Son and "culture-bearing black woman" to Jadine. Due to the incompatibility of their heterogeneity, Son and Jadine are set apart, as Jadine farewells to Son, "You stay in that medieval slave basket if you want to. You will stay there if you want to. You will stay there by yourself. Don't ask me to do it with you. I won't. There is nothing any of us can do about the past but make our own lives better, that's all I've been trying to help you do. That is the only revenge, for us to get over. Way over. But no, you want to talk about white babies; you don't know how to forget the past and do better" (*Tar* 271).

Morrison, by exploring the ways in which past myths of "the folk" merge with significant events of the present, creates another variation on the theme of conversion, showing how the conflict between the wishing to be part of nature or society or a cultural tradition yet distinct from it reflects the inherent desire for growth in human beings. (Connor 181)

Jadine is also a tar baby in *Tar*, just as Son doesn't fit the white world, so is Jadine by no means willing to surrender to the backward black world. Their endeavors to break away from the tar-like adhesive force of each other bring the story of "tar baby" multiple connotations. If to some extent, Son's stubborn adherence to the black convention can be alleviated by Jadine, who, despite her success in the white world, is plagued with anxiety due to her disconnection with her black nationality. Hence the comment, "Indubitably, the combination between Son and Jadine is to be the best choice of the contemporary black race" (Wang and Wu, 2004: 124). However, the reality is adverse. The novel is left with an open and symbolic ending: Son returns to the Isle des Chevaliers to seek Jadine, and in futile efforts, runs away without "looking neither to the left nor to the right. Lickety-split. Lickety-split. Lickety-lickety-lickety-split" (*Tar* 305).

Some critics hold that what the characters in this novel are experiencing is not their emotional entanglements, but their choices over race and class-related ways of life faced by numerous blacks in modern society. Yet, I argue that this is also an issue closely connected with physical space. As it is, Son's predicament lies more in his failed fusion into the modern space than in his preservation of the black conventions represented by his hometown Eloe. In other words, when his body trespasses upon the boundary between conventionality and modernity, his heterogeneous element, without any needful adaptation, is doomed to rejection by the modern space.

So, by depicting the characters of Jadine as well as Son, Morrison aims to inform that the simple physical displacement of an individual, or a reduplication of his homogeneous element in a heterogeneous physical space like New York can produce nothing but an rootless, swaying self, apt to fall out at every moment. She once compared Jadine to a "cultural orphan" by making the following comment:

> She (Jadine) is cut off. She does not have, ...her ancient properties; she does not have what Ondine has. There is no reason for her to be like Ondine–I'm not recommending that–but she needs a little bit of Ondine to be a complete woman. ...There should be a quality of adventure and of nest. (Taylor and Danille 104)

As for the heterogeneous cultures underlying the two characters, Morrison, still in the same interview with Taylor and Danille, pointed out that the civilization of black people, which was underneath the white civilization, was there with its own everything. She further posed the question, "Everything of that civilization was not worth hanging on to, but some of it was, and nothing has taken its place while it is being dismantled", yet refuted the solution of producing a new, capitalistic, modern American black like Jadine by pointing out the danger in the production, "It cannot replace some essentials from the past" (Ibid, 105). Without effective communion between the two heterogeneous cultures, Jadine cannot nurture into a career woman and Son has nowhere to go either. In this case, the open ending of the story may well denote the potentialities of such communion, which is partly realized in the "spiritual space" in Morrison's next novel *Beloved*.

3.2 Beloved: "traversing" body and self in "spiritual space"

Edward Soja, the American postmodern physicist and Henri Lefebvre's student, comes up with three types of spatial epistemologies, in which the epistemology of "the second space" is simplified as the space constructed in mind rather than perceived by sense organs on the assumption that the production of knowledge is completed in the space constructed in discourses. According to Soja, in the epistemology of the second space, art rivals science, spirit overshadows material and subject dwarfs object. He presupposes that the production of knowledge is realized in the space of the construction of discourse, so the focus is on the conceived space rather than perceived space.

Morrison's fifth novel, *Beloved* (1987), sets in the periods of slavery and reformation after the American Civil War (1861—1865), spiritually investigates the restored self intrinsically tied to the horrors of slavery. As a black slave and the protagonist in the story, Sethe, in order for her two-year-old daughter to escape from being a slave, kills her daughter mercilessly and afterwards engraves her tombstone with a single word: Beloved. Eighteen years after the abolition of slavery, she is spiritually-tormented for her cruel act of infanticide. Her confrontation of the past with the present recurs in her new house 124 in Ohio which is continually haunted by the ghost of her baby: "124 was spiteful"; "124 was loud"; "124 was quiet" (Beloved 3, 169, 239). Through incarnating the dynamics of human relationships, the book aims to tell that some wounds cannot heal unless they are seen and manifested in the flesh, so that one's spiritual essence can be reconnected with its self. Beloved's presence, in particular, precipitates not only the familial and ancestral recovery of the enslaved, but also this reconciliation of morally and socially disassembled body and spirit of black people. For scholars on Morrison, the reconstitution of this yearning into an embodied configuration is the unspeakable through the flesh.[1]

In the larger sense, what *Beloved* aims to embody is not slavery but rather the problems of the black people's internal life, which is a rarity among books about slavery that cares about the evils of slavery and its abolition. Morrison's

---

[1] Many articles have been written on this aspect of Morrison's work. Some notable discussions include Mae G. Henderson's "Toni Morrison's *Beloved*: Remembering the Body as Historical Text" (1990); Rafael Perez-Torres's "Between Presence and Absence: *Beloved*, Postmodernism, and Blackness"(1999); and Linda Krumholz's "The Ghosts of Slavery: Historical Recovery in Toni Morrison's *Beloved*, 1999.

Chapter Three   The Spatial Body in Tar, Beloved and Jazz

purpose of creation is to "make up her life" (Taylor and Danille 248) and most important is to "deconstruct and reconstruct the reality via imagination" and exhibit "the internal world of the black slaves" (Taylor and Danille 252-253).

So, compared with the physical space, black women in this novel live more in the spiritual space, especially Sethe, whose spiritual space comprises two parts: one in the form of rememory and the other conjured up by the traversing body of Beloved. Both parts are conducive to the resultant construction of Sethe's self. What links these two parts is the infanticide, the most appalling expression of maternal love in the human society: she slays her beloved baby. Sethe chooses a way most unacceptable to all in expressing her topmost maternal love in the world.

When setting such a kid-slaying incident in the specific social and historical context of inhuman slavery, Morrison injects social and historical contents into Sethe's violence. Yet, regarding the fact that the majority of Beloved's story is given in the continual narration of Sethe, and the protagonist of the novel, the focus of the story is laid on the mother-daughter interaction and its impact upon the mother's growth in terms of self-construction. To this, Morrison so said,

> …because children will make you become the best thing you can possibly be, or the worst thing you can be. In other words, they put you to the test of being human, they look at you completely in terms of what's real, not whether your fingernail polish. (Christian, Mcdowell and Mckay 213)

Sethe's spiritual space in the form of "rememory" is a noteworthy element in *Beloved*. Despite her reluctance to recollect the past, Sethe is relentlessly preoccupied by the past experiences after her moving to 124, a lonely house abandoned by many for the haunting ghost of Beloved and is obliged to face her dual identities of slave and mother. As Sethe's spiritual space is mainly erected in 124, the physical space of 124 has served as the medium for the communion of Sethe and the spirit of her child. Beloved's presence is mentioned in close connection with 124 in the very beginning of the novel. "124 was spiteful. Full of a baby's venom." (*Beloved* 1)

Moreover, with Sethe's rememory of the past in 124, the physical space of 124–an incarnated component of the spiritual space, manifests itself as a dialogue between the "spirit" and one's "memory". To Sethe, rememory has become a rite of passage–a self-reflexive journey–allowing herself to reexamine the past in hopes of enjoining others to participate in this act of repentance and facilitate her individual healing. What's more, in a certain sense, such word of "rememory" is also the representation of the past activities and the reconstruction of the history. In a word, after the infanticide, it is in 124 that the spirit, by means of flesh, intervenes for the past to communicate with the present; it is in 124 that the reconciliation between the two is finally achieved.

To delve at a far deeper level, as Morrison has demonstrated in *Beloved*, the residue of slavery leaves an encoded rejection of the body embedded in the racial collective memory of African Americans. In Sethe's rememory of the past, her ensuing psychic battles results in a cycle of self-denial that prohibits self-knowledge to such an extent that the bodily experiences of slavery rearticulated in the spiritual utterances of rememory–a public and private ritual that combines the secular and the sacred, the flesh and the spirit, in a holy dance of submission to a being larger than the human self.

In the process of overcoming her deep-set terror of the slavery, Sethe sees her gradual spiritual growth. Originally, owing to her enormous fear of slavery, she is unwilling to bear another child with Paul D, which much perplexes him. Later, Stamp Paid, the one who helps his black fellows to flee to the "free land", tells Paul D that Sethe doesn't kill her daughter for lack of love. Paul D, despite feeling it hard to accept such a violent act, agrees with Sethe that "Your love is too sick." (*Beloved* 164) Sethe insists that she kills Beloved simply out of love, out of her unwillingness to see with her own eyes her dear child being enslaved in endless sufferings. Morrison thus depicted in the novel,

Chapter Three   The Spatial Body in Tar, Beloved and Jazz

The best thing she was, was her children. Whites might dirty her all right, but not her best thing, her beautiful, magical best thing–the part of her that was clean. No undreamable dreams about whether the headless, feetless torso hanging in the tree with a sign on it was her husband or Paul A; whether the bubbling-hot girls in the colored-school fire set by patriots included her daughter; whether a gang of whites invaded her daughter's private parts, soiled her daughter's thighs and threw her daughter out of the wagon. She might have to work the slaughterhouse yard, but not her daughter. ...And no one, nobody on this earth, would list her daughter's characteristics on the animal side of the paper. No. Oh no. Maybe Baby Suggs could worry about it, live with the likelihood of it; Sethe had refused– and refused still. (*Beloved* 251)

To her best knowledge, infanticide is Sethe's only way out of that emergency. Morrison concurred that this is the only way out for desperate mother slaves who love but dispossess their children, so the immorality of infanticide is attributable to the system of slavery rather than mother slaves (Wolff 417).

In his comment on Sethe's love for Denver, Paul D says "For a used-to-be-slave woman to love anything that much was dangerous, especially if it was her children she had settled on to love." (*Beloved* 45) So, when Paul D asks Sethe to bear a child for him, she feels impossible while believing that slaves' maternal love is a killer. After all the vicissitudes, they have outspoken the dualism of maternal love: love and the destructive force behind it. As such, the maternal nature under Morrison' pen is an ideology-implicating socialist system (Christian, Mcdowell and Mckay 215), which transcends the conventional logic of "love-equating" maternal nature and merges into it social and historical contents.

In the black slaves' lives, death has become an outlet and a choice over the foreseeable plight of being slaves, as has been alluded in the cruelty of slavery by

Morrison in the ensuing excerpt in the story,

> A whip of fear broke through the heart chambers as soon as you saw a Negro's face in a paper, since the face was not there because the person had a healthy baby, or outran a street mob. Nor was it there because the person had been killed, or maimed or caught or burned or jailed or whipped or evicted or stomped or raped or cheated, since that could hardly qualify as news in a newspaper. (*Beloved* 156)

Morrison thus, via her richly allusive prose, effects the spirit growth of Sethe on the superimposition of Beloved's "traversing" body. The latter's physical appearance may well be read as a blending of two forms of spiritual expression–African tradition and "Americanized" African tradition. In 124, the traversing body and self finally merge in spiritual space. If in some sense, the preliminary encounter of Jadine and Son's bodies in *Tar* end up in failed self-shaping "integration", then such a failed effort is relayed and proved to be a victory in integrating the past into the present via traversing body. At the end of the story, with the help of Paul D, Denver and other black people, Beloved as the shadow of the past is driven out of 124 for good. The moment she departs outright signifies that the past memory of agony dies and a "new" Sethe is born. As for Denver, she is also freed from Beloved's constraints and initiates a brand-new life as well.

In such superimposition of Sethe's spiritual grown upon the traversing body of Beloved in 124, Sethe's body functioning as a supplement cannot be denied. In her sexual relationship with Paul D, she is well on her way to acquiring self-dignity, which offers some peacefulness to her tortured life. As Paul D becomes the mirror of Sethe, she learns to regard her all-bruised body as the value of love, and by accepting the care of Paul D, she rids herself of anger and unloads the burden she has long been shouldering,

Chapter Three   The Spatial Body in Tar, Beloved and Jazz

He saw the sculpture her back had become, like the decorative work of an ironsmith too passionate for display, ...And he could tolerate no peace until he had touched every ridge and of it with his mouth, none of which Sethe could feel because her back skin had been dead for years. What she knew was that the responsibility for her breasts, at last, was in somebody else's hands. ...Maybe this one time she could stop dead still...and feel the hurt her back ought to. Trust things and remember things because the last of the Sweet Home men was there to catch her if she sank? (*Beloved* 18)

In illustrating the healing role of body to spirit, Morrison elaborates on Baby Suggs Holy, Sethe's mother-in-law, she cordially clarifies the imaginative function of spirit, which is enlightening to Sethe. In the story, instead of telling them to clean up their lives or to go and sin no more, she tells them that the only grace they could have is the grace they could envisage. That if they could not see it, they would not have it.

"Here," she said, "in this here place, we flesh; flesh that weeps, laughs; flesh that dances on bare feet in grass. Love it. Love it hard. ...Love your hands! Love them. Raise them up and kiss them. Touch others with them, pat them together, stroke them on your face cause they don't love that either. You got to love it, you! ...This is flesh I'm talking about here. Flesh that needs to be loved. Feet that need to rest and to dance; backs that need support; shoulders that need arms, strong arms I'm telling you. ... The dark, dark liver–love it, love it, and the beat and beating heart, love that too. More than eyes or feet. More than lungs that have yet to draw free air. More than your life-holding womb and your life-giving private parts, hear me now, love your heart. For this is the prize." Saying no more, she stood up then and danced with her twisted hip the rest of what her heart had to say while the others opened their mouths and gave her the music. Long notes held until the four-part harmony was perfect enough for their deeply loved flesh. (*Beloved* 88-89)

To appreciate each other's flesh with mutual care and dance under the magical treatment of spirit proves to be the best way to heal the historical wound of slavery and the undying hurt it leaves on the used-to-be slaves. This is what is described by Baby Suggs as love: the "necessity" of loving oneself and others. On the clearing, Sethe enters purgatory and descends into a psychical and emotional wilderness that reveals the close link between the flesh and the spirit.

Folk cries, hollers and shouts, work songs, and other secular songs, as well as dance rituals and ceremonials, became communal methods not only of expressing these longings but also of resisting racial oppression and spiritual depravity, through a reaffirmation of the flesh. (Henderson 153)

Morrison conceded two different levels of communication in *Beloved*, saying "There are times when she (Beloved) says things, what she's thinking, when she's asking something, responding to somebody. The section in which the women finally go home and close up and begin to fulfill their desires begins with each other's thoughts in her language, and then moves into a kind of threnody in which they exchange thoughts like a dialogue, or a three-way conversation, but unspoken–I mean unuttered. Yet the intimacy of those three women–illusory though it may be– is such that they would not have to say it." (Taylor and Danille 249)

With the permanent disappearance of Beloved, Sethe is able to heal her trauma and pull together a sense of herself over time. To this, Morrison conforms, "Yes, she does have a taste of liberty. And therefore she is able to scratch out something and then maybe more and maybe more. So she can consider the possibility of an individual pride, of a real self which says 'You are your best thing.' Just to begin to think of herself as a proper name–she's always thought of

Chapter Three The Spatial Body in Tar, Beloved and Jazz

herself as a mother, as her role." (Taylor and Danille 251) Sethe begins to accept herself as a woman and mother, as is confirmed by Paul: "You are your best thing, Sethe. You are." (*Beloved* 273)

> The difficulties Morrison encountered with *Beloved* came from the heights and depths she tried to conquer: The girl Beloved's voice at the end of the novel is wrenching testimony, not just her private suffering, but of all ravages of slavery. For Morrison, it was more than a personal triumph. (Taylor and Danille 244)

In this sense, there is a transcendent meaning with Sethe's rebirth as a grown-up. With the help of "rememory" incarnated in Beloved's traversing body, Sethe finally learns to recollect her fragmented self and get it integrated. To Sethe, transcendence of this kind is a "transcending birth", or the "second birth". Being a merger of spirit and body, transcendence is "perceptual".

Noticeably, from *Beloved*, though not elaborately dealt with, black women's construction of self has involved more than woman of Sethe, as in the story, such infanticide is unfortunately also the outlet of two other mothers: Sethe's own mother who throws away her own children one by one; the other is Ella who has "delivered , but would not nurse, a hairy white things, fathered by 'the lowest yet'" (*Beloved* 258-259). The reason for their abandonment is that the rejected children are the results of sexual slavery. Less radical and bloody than Sethe's infanticide, their behaviors still share the same nature of abandonment. Such a collective evil of "infanticide" calls for collective resurrection. To this Nellie once remarked, "Because although it is known that there were slave mothers who killed their children, the fact is that it's a story that has been covered up, that's a story that nobody really wants to talk about because it's the taboo, the black mother, certainly of all mothers, would not act in that way toward her child (Christian, Mcdowell and Mckay 213).

3.3 Violet: "conflictory" body and self in "social space"

From physical space in *Tar* to spiritual space in *Beloved*, the space in human society is apparently not the pure physical space that has the characteristics of homogeneity, permanence and incompressibility, etc. (Tong Ming 8) In spite of the fact that the natural space as the fountainhead of social process will not totally disappear, what dominates the human life is social life.

In *Jazz* published in 1992, Morrison probed the tension between a culturally-imposed collective and a socially-constructed individualized identity and detects how these opposing and potentially destructive forces are reconciled with each other. Its entire plot accounts with a difference how the murderous triangle of Joe, "Violent" and Dorcas is transformed into the familial love of Joe, Violet, and Felice.

The story happened in the 1920s, describing the experiences of a middle-aged couple in Harlem District in New York city. As migrants from the southern countryside, the husband lives on selling cosmetics while the wife is a hairdresser. The relationships among various characters are intensified due to jealousy, misunderstanding, hostility, etc. Their shattered marriage there leaves them at an even greater loss, which characterizes their consequent life in Harlem District with violence: Joe shoots his lover Docas and Violet tries to cut Docas's face at Docas's funeral. Yet, the violent accident was only a transition of the plot: it terminates the "silence" and starts the "communication" among the family members.

Chapter Three   The Spatial Body in Tar, Beloved and Jazz

As early as in Morrison's first novel *Bluest*, Polly[1], Pecola's mother, who after migrating from the South to the North, has undergone a loss of self. Such a stride in space, to some critics, bears strong social quality. "In the migration from the South to the North, the changes with entirely different territorial features soundly expatiates the social nature of space as well as the fall of Polly's fate." (Tang Hongmei 278) Likewise, Joe and Violet, when set in the chaos of the white-dominating city, are deprived of their inner tranquility and faced with an identity crisis in the marginalized space of living. Their identity crisis has a lot to do with their much-dwindled social space, which is rather complex and fully reflected in such a crisis. In other words, their identity crisis occurs under the influence of social space. According to Lefebvre, "Social space contains a great diversity of objects, both natural and social, including the networks and pathways which facilitate the exchange of material things and information. Such 'objects' are thus not only things but also relations." (Lefebvre 77) Such a definition lays stress on the relations in the society in which all social activities are interwoven with each other, and is therefore conceived as the "second nature" of the society.

In practice, two layers of social space exist in the society. The first layer of social space refers to a micro space, or the specific social environment for the characters' activities. In a novelistic creation, a micro space is the place that displays the inter-personal conflicts and plot, which plays a decisive role in the formation of the characters' personalities and the state of plot development in the novel.

The violence of body conflicts occur in the micro social space in *Jazz*. When Joe and Violet "train-danced on into the City, they were still a couple but barely speaking to each other, let alone laughing together or acting like the ground was a dance-hall floor." (*Jazz* 36) As Joe has nothing to talk about with Violet,

---

[1] In *Bluest*, Polly undergoes two shifts in space, the first shift with her families from her hometown in the Southern state of Alabama to the Northern state of Kentucky and the second shift with Cholly to farther northern Lorain, Ohio. The nearer she is to the racist capitalistic North, the more distant and alienated she is from the traditional African culture, which directly results in her self-debasement and her consequent adverse influence on her daughter Pecola.

he goes for Dorcas while Violet only talks with her parrot, which leads to the tragic accident. Joe shoots Dorcas dead after she loves someone else; Violet tries to defile Dorcas's face in her violent disruption of her funeral. In this plot, the funeral serves as a micro space displaying the inter-personal conflicts between Violet and Dorcas and relays the plot development, in which the characters' personalities are formed.

In the domain of social space, space is not the usual concept of geometric space or the traditional concept of geographic space, but a rearrangement of social relationships and a constructive process of social orders. In the story, Violet watches that Violet interrupts a funeral to defile the dead Dorcas's face and fights off the men attempting to stop her with a physical strength this Violet has long lost. Thus, here, the body is not simply a vessel for the self but changes in response to the role being played. This scene is not only telling in relation to Violet's divided sense of self, it also illuminates the underlying importance of the body and the dangers inherent in a racialized perspective that focuses on the body. As will be shown below, it also illuminates the potentially redeeming factors of a more unifying view. Violet knows that Dorcas is dead but feels she must destroy her face as well, for therein lies a threat tantamount to the live girl herself.

Rather than a homogeneous abstraction and logical structure or a presupposed transcendental order, it is a dynamic, contradictory, and heterogeneous process of practice.

> (Social) space is not a thing among other things, nor a product among other products: rather, it subsumes things produced, and encompasses their interrelationships in their coexistence and simultaneity–their (relative) order and/or (relative) disorder. It is the outcome of a sequence and set of operations, …(Lefebvre 73).

There is a diversity of social relationships involved in the conflicts in

Chapter Three The Spatial Body in Tar, Beloved and Jazz

the minor social space. Principally, the relationship from hostility to tolerance between Violet and Dorcas is a complex one. As for the relationship between Violet and Joe, they are alienated from and intimately related to each other, each reflecting and watching the performance of the other. To supplement these two relationships is the relationship between Violet and Alice, which is a beneficial one, too.

In these intervening relationships centering on Violet, a connection is erected between Violet and Joe. In terms of the social structure, according to Tong Ming[1], there are only two forms of "separation" and "connection" (The former is called "Space 1" and the latter is called "Space 2".). When the double "Space 1"s are connected with "Space 2", the simplest spatial structure is framed, on which all the other complex spatial structures are constructed (See Figure 1).

Space 2

(Space 1)———————————(Space 1)

Figure 1

With the core structure explicitly reflecting the basic situation of social formations, the function of Space 1 is to divide, separate, and extinguish at the level of social relationships while the feature of Space 2 is to connect and unite two Space 1s. In this situation, the connection of Space 2 exhibits a unique space process, through which the separate parts, though divided and independent, are united in the sense of their limitedness. (Tong Ming 150)

Nonetheless, in terms of the social space in *Jazz*, the nature of space is not solely decided by the feature of the structure, but also influenced by the methods of production, ways of living and complex social relations. Yet, what is in common

---

[1] Tong Ming's book: *Philosophy on Space*, Beijing, Beijing University Press, 2011, p9. In the book, Tong Ming has created the concepts of "Space 1" and "Space 2", commenting in the preface of book that "Space 1" and "Space 2" are the basic concepts of philosophy of space, and as trial concepts, they are of the uppermost importance in this research of ours.

between the physical space and social space is that Space 1 or "separation" corresponds to one's subjectivity and identity while Space 2 "connection" usually assumes the nature of commonness. As for the acting subject, she/he should first occupy a certain field (or usually in the form of field rather than of road) to exhibit his or her identity before forming his or her relationships with other subjects.

In constructing the connection, or "Space 2", two minor characters of Alice and Felice have played a supplementary role in reconciling the conflict between Violet and Joe. In *Jazz*, through constructing connections, inter-personal indifference is successively transformed into love and the hostility among major characters are reconciled. When identifying Violet's hostility towards others out of jealousy, Alice, Docas's aunt, a black woman who is aware of the importance of unity within the black community, dissuades her from the impending fighting."Fight what? Who? Some mishandled child who saw her parents burn up? Who knew better than you or me or anybody just how small and quick this little bitty life is? …Nobody's asking you to take it. I'm saying make it, make it!" (*Jazz* 113) With the help of Alice, Violet contrives to understand Dorcas. While her crazy jealousy is substituted with love, she gets the idea of taking Dorcas for her mishandled child, "Was she the woman who took the man, or the daughter who fled her womb?" (*Jazz* 109) In the end of the novel, Violet eradicated her envy, "Then I killed that me that killed her." (*Jazz* 209)

So is Felice in her reconciling with Joe and Violet. As a close friend of Dorcas, Felice, sympathetic and a witness of the whole process of Dorcas's getting hurt and killed, becomes the friend of Joe and Violet. She reveals it to Joe that Dorcas finally understands Joe's love to her and chooses to die for such love rather than being saved by the police or ambulance. Dorcas's last words at her death to Felice are, "There's only one apple. Just one. Tell Joe." (*Jazz* 213) Felice's words liberate Joe from grief, reestablishing confidence in him.

The story concludes in a peaceful and restful atmosphere with Violet accepting Alice's advice, "I'll tell you a real one. You got anything left to you to

Chapter Three The Spatial Body in Tar, Beloved and Jazz

love, anything at all, do it." (*Jazz* 112) It is at this moment that Violet really starts to love her husband and restores their long-broken emotional communication. In their final mutual understanding, forgiving, they have managed to love each other in their unique way. In their final emotional reconciliation, their preceding body reconciliation is decisive.

> It's nice when grown people whisper to each other under the covers. Their ecstasy is more leaf-sigh than bray and the body is the vehicle, not the point. They reach, grown people, for something beyond, way beyond and way, way down underneath tissue. …Breathing and murmuring under covers both of them have washed and hung out on the line, in a bed they chose together and kept together never mind one leg was propped on a 1916 dictionary, and the mattress, curved like a preacher's palm asking for witnesses in his name's sake, enclosed them each and every night and muffled their whispering, old-time love. They are under the covers because they don't have to look at themselves anymore; there is no stud's eye, no chippie glance to undo them. They are inward toward the other, bound and joined by carnival dolls and the steamers that sailed from ports they never saw. That is what is beneath their undercover whispers. (*Jazz* 228)

It shall be pointed out that before the final reconciliation of Joe and Violet's selves, the contradiction of their bodies is a by-product of the macro social space determined by the social and historical backgrounds of the story. Much larger than the micro social space, the second layer of social space expands to as far as the macro historical background, which provides and restricts the times and social conditions in which the character images move, and therefore is the mix of social relationships in certain times and on a certain scale. As a macro space determines and restricts a micro space, a micro space reflects and hints a macro space.

To trace American history at that time, after First World War (1914—1918),

America enjoyed relative prosperity in economy yet suffered from widespread detestation against war. With indifference growing and morality dying among Americans who were more practical and concentrated on money-making and enjoying themselves, a spiritual crisis broke out among people in the 1920s. According to the investigation of 1920, about 51% of American population lived in the cities with a large amount of technical inventions and the invention of household appliances, which liberated women from toilsome housework and engaged them into the social activities that could demonstrate their values. All the passion, romance, music and money in the 1920s' cities became an intensive appeal to Americans of all nationalities, including the Southern blacks who lived in dire poverty as a result of poor harvest. However, the phenomena of terrorist attacks deteriorated in the Southern and Southwestern parts of America, where racial segregation was practiced in public places and the black were occasionally sentenced to death stealthily. To augment their chances of improving life and escape such an environment suffused with violence, an increasing number of Southerners migrated to the developed northern parts after the Civil War.[1]

Set against this background, the conflicts between blacks and whites occurring in the major social space are distinct. Believing that "all the wars are over and there will never be another one. …At last, at last, everything's ahead", like their contemporaries, the characters in *Jazz* "train-danced to New York". (*Jazz* 7) However, as afore annotated, the America in the early 1920s was still an unequal society, both economically and politically. In 1929, the richest 1% of American population took possessions of 45% of the total wealth in America. As its aftermath, the wealth gap widened between the rich and the poor and the majority of minority nationalities, living on ill-paid jobs, found no free access to

---

[1] Statistics showed that between 1910—1920, as many as 3 % of Southerners migrated to the North. Till the 1920s, such a percentage mounted to 5 % as a result of ill-management of textile industry, decreased demand of cotton, and the gloomy agriculture in the South. Zhang Youlun, Xiao Jun, Zhang Cong's book: *Paradox of American Society*, Beijng, China Social Sciences Press, 1999, p260.

Chapter Three The Spatial Body in Tar, Beloved and Jazz

the white-dominant society like before, as has been shown in the marginalized survival of Violet and Joe in *Jazz*.

The above background to Violet and Joe's migration is not a representation associated or linked externally with their movement itself, but is immanent in the movement inspiring and sustaining it at every moment. To Violet and Joe, such a plunge into the macro historical background provides from their point of view, an original way of perceiving the situation.

Hence, the internalization of the historical background is in the fate of Violet and Joe, who live a marginalized life. In this case, the exploration of "connection" between the black and the white is significant, as is foreshadowed at the onset of the novel, "The quick darkness in the carriage cars when they shot through a tunnel made them wonder if maybe there was a wall ahead to crash into or a cliff hanging over nothing." (*Jazz* 30) In addition to their loss of original simplicity, the black's outright disillusionment in the 1920s was also reflected in the frustration of American dream held by the Violet and Joe. "It is from the uniqueness, contradiction and complexity of such marginalized living that the collective wounds on a larger social scale are identified in the individual psychological wounds." (Caruth 71) So, the final reconciliation between Violet and Joe not only serves as the "connection" in the divided body of Violet and Joe in the micro social space, but also forecasts the possibility of the "connection" between the segregated black and white, either for economic or racial causes.

The contribution of "Space 2" or "connection" also testifies to the poststructuralist view of self-construction. In *Jazz*, such a process of social construction overthrows the independent, rational subject philosophically set up by Descartes. Deriving from the independency of his rational self, Descartes's concept that individuals as subjects of free thoughts form the basis of politics and moral behaviors is labeled as "essentialism", which is not for long menaced by post-structuralism maintaining that subject exists in a complex network of social relationships. Rather than an existence prior to the socio-political structure, subject is a product constructed in a particular socio-political environment, and as the root of knowledge and actions, his/her behaviors in turn form the particular structure social and cultural (Namaste 132). In addition, essentialism is also denied by existentialists for approximately the same reasons. So, characters of the couple of Violet and Joe, as well as other people in the novel are such products molded by the environment and their emotional regression after all their physical conflicts in New York. As it is, the ending of the lingering affection and mutual desire between Violet and Joe forebodes the potential "connection" in the macro social space,

> That I have loved only you, surrendered my whole self reckless to you and nobody else. That I want you to love me back and show it to me. That I love the way you hold me, how close you let me be to you. I like your fingers on and on, lifting, turning. I have watched your face for a long time now, and missed your eyes when your went away from me. Talking to you and hearing you answer–that's the kick. (*Jazz* 229)

To sum up, from the two levels of the minor social space and macro social space, or the totality of social spaces have produced the "conflictory" body, in which the latter actually determines and restricts the former, a micro space reflects and hints a macro space. With *Jazz*, Morrison unfolds the entire process of the southern black's hard adjustments and accommodations in their lives in the northern cities at the turn of the 20th century. Among the indifference, estrangement and even hostility resulting from their lack of communication within the black community, black women's body also undergoes similar process of conflicts and reconciliation. "*Jazz* not only notices the existence of (social) problems, but also seeks the solution." (Wang Shouren, Wu Xinyun, 2004:168) This on the one hand explains why there comes the passionate and rhythmic appeal of love at the end of the novel, and on the other hand presupposes the transcendence over the "bound" body in black women.

3.4 Transcending "bound" body in the individuality of black women

In his *Modernity and Self-identity*, Giddens aired his view on the formation of self-identity and its involvement with body. Giddens's concept of self-identity is akin to that of self-construction. When expounding the sense of ontological security and anxiety in the modern society, Giddens remarked that instead of being a given fact or a result of the continuous activities of an individual's acting system, self-identity is always in a dynamic process of construction and "created and maintained in reflective activities of an individual" (Giddens 52). In this sense, self-identity refers not to a single character or a group of characters possessed by an individual, but to the self perceived in the evaluation of an individual's life experiences. Moreover, by being dynamic, such a process is characterized by constant change, activity or progress and hence assumes the "productive" nature that is fundamental to man's construction of self.

For man's inseparable role of body, Giddens further identified himself with the fact that in the dynamic process of self-identity formation, an individual body, more than boarding his/her "self" as a physical existence, is an acting system and a pattern of practice that must be directly engaged in the interactive process of daily life. Without constant interactions between man's body and the secular world, a consistent sense of self-identity shall never be retained.

Since body exists in a certain amount of space, the term "bound body" is correlative with the notion of space. Under the categories of physical space, spiritual space and social space, body's state of "being bound up" varies with distinct features. Different from physical space that forecasts the boundary menace of body, spiritual space values the convergence between physical space and the body, which makes their intercommunion possible. In light of social space, body on the one hand, becomes the signifier with dualistic significations with are both at the micro level and at the macro level, and on the other hand, functions as the second space or "Space 2" to organically integrate the two spaces. In spite of the rough categorization, the three spaces are actually juxtaposed with each other and intervene in their own ways. However, this is not the focus of the paper, whose purpose is to exhibit how body, sets in different states, and works its own way into the construction of self in the totality of black women. To solve this "enigma", Merleau-Ponty's following expatiation on transcendence might be a helping hand,

> Existence is indeterminate in itself, by reason of its fundamental structure, and in so far as it is the very process whereby the hitherto meaningless takes on meaning, whereby what had merely a sexual significance assumes a more general one, chance is transformed into reason; in so far as it is the act of taking up a de facto situation. We shall give the name transcendence to this act in which existence takes up, for its own purposes, and transforms such a situation. (Merleau-Ponty, 1962: 169)

Here Merleau-Ponty first pointed out the "indeterminate" nature or the quality of "being-in-itself" of existence and then emphasized the transformative function of transcendence in humankind's existence. To Merleau-Ponty, humankind's lived body is a transcendence that moves out from the body in its immanence in an open and unbroken directness upon the world in action. So, in a loose sense, black women's lived body as transcendence is pure fluid action and the continuous calling forth of capacities that are applied to the world.

Back in Morrison's middle-stage novels, the pursuit for self-identity is still a close concern in Toni Morrison's novels, yet it has some unique spatial quality related to American history of slavery. Just like the geographic separation of

Chapter Three　　The Spatial Body in Tar, Beloved and Jazz

Africa from America, the freedom of African Americans is also shattered. African Americans, on the one hand, long to enter the mainstream society of America, and on the other hand, have to try to sustain their black cultural tradition. So, African Americans' alienation of self is primarily due to their painful breakup from their own culture (mainly embodied in their forgetfulness of the past history), as well as their being permeated and reversed by the white culture.

Consequently, to restore the lost black culture, mend its permeation and remove the black's self-alienation, the black people should surpass the restrictions of their invisibly bound body. Clarified this way, the three women protagonists in *Tar*, *Beloved*, and *Jazz* become successors of Pilate who transcends "gendered" body with her redemptive fall and entangle themselves into the secular world in order to transcend their "bound" body.

So, from Jadine to Sethe to Violet in the three novels, their bodies are set in different levels of spaces: physical, spiritual and social, where their bodies play corresponding roles in forming their identities. In the process, a certain part of their "being-for-itself", of being transcendent, creative and promising, is realized. Dependent on "being-in-itself" as they innately are, their "being-for-itself" undergoes the everlasting process of self-realization and self-planning. This is endless lest "being-for-itself" be achieved once and for all, yet in which case "being-for-itself" will become "being-in-self" anew. It is in this process that an individual's potential of self-creation prepares humankind for their ultimate liberty or liberation.

Another point in this section is the apprehension of the "individuality" black woman and her causality with "bound" body. Ostensibly, individuality is already a leap over being "individualized", as the latter implicates the state of helpless passivity. In the first stage, black women are individualized with no company of the same sex. All of the three: Pecola, Sula, and Pilate are on their separate lonesome ways to pursue their self despite Pecola's meager help from little Claudia as well as the three whores[1]. Yet, in the second stage, Jade, Sethe as well as Violet are not as alone. With Margaret accompanying Jade, Denver, Sethe, Violet, two or more women come into the view of Morrison. Though the other three in company are also progressing as having been elaborated beforehand, the growth of the protagonists in the stage are also trapped in the individuality. In other words, their growth is still very limited as it exerts very little influence on the company. So theirselves, even if finished in Violet, are still largely finite, for they only transcend the static yoke of racial features and fail to attain a dialogic relation with What is unfinished in this stage is due to the two disadvantageous points: the finitude of self and individuality of black women. To this, Beauvoir points out in *The Second Sex*, "For the male it is always another male who is the fellow being, the other who is also the same, with whom reciprocal relations are established. …Women, therefore, have never composed a separate group set up on its own account over against the male grouping. They have never entered into a direct and autonomous relation with the men."(Beauvoir, 1977: 103)

As for the disadvantage of "individual salvation by solitary effort" and exigent necessity of women's collective liberation, she further elaborates in her comprehension of "transcendence",

> The liberation must be collective, … There have been, however, and there are many women trying to achieve individual salvation by solitary effort. They are attempting to justify their existence in the midst of their immanence–that is, to realize transcendence in the midst of their immanence. It is this ultimate–sometimes ridiculous, often pathetic–of imprisoned woman to transform her prison into a heaven of glory, her servitude into

---

[1] Of the many characters in *Bluest*, Claudia, a black girl together with her family and three whores who are sympathetic, tolerant and loyal stand out for their ignorance of the dominant white culture and adherence to the black culture. It is from them that little pitiable Pecola can get momentary mental relief and warmth.

Chapter Three　　The Spatial Body in Tar, Beloved and Jazz

sovereign liberty , ... (Beauvoir, 1977: 639)

In its spatial dimension, body is no longer viewed as an object or the bodily embodiment in the sense of conventional philosophy, which can not be explicated by objective physiology or reflective psychology. What connects the two is humankind's impulse to be Dasein, or to exist. Our experience of body exists in our "Dasein". In other words, our possession of body is realized in our worldly existence by means of body. With the medium of body, humankind involves and retains himself/herself in a variety of activities. As an indistinct, perceptual symbol, their body is thrown into the world. By doing so, humankind returns to their existence from the objective world and body no longer falls under the category of "being-in-itself" or "being-for-itself": the merger of body and soul recurs at every moment of the movement of existence. This "phenomenal body", by being both subject and object, forms a reversible cycle with the world.

To a large extent, "bound" body can be regarded as the "phenomenal" body, in which sense, body escapes being the object of epistemology. The visible body is not the bodily embodiment of "self"; the body is the self. Such a phenomenal body exhibits itself as the ultimate subjectivity of self. Noticeably, this subjectivity is set not in the objective state of time, but in the consciousness behind such time. Moreover, in such consciousness, the existence of body is nothing but the existence of "being-for-itself".

In the three novels, Jadine's "transgressed" body, Beloved's "traversing" body and Violet's "conflictory" body make up different body images, which, by embodying a capability of their bodies's interaction with the secular world, realizes the "way of stating that my (their) body is in the world" (Merleau-Ponty, 1962:101). In other words, to these three women, it is nothing but the motility of their bodies that help constitute their mode of living in the world. According to the concept of body schema proposed by Merleau-Ponty in his *Phenomenology of Perception* that embodies itself in body's motility, their different states of body suggest the way black women's body can exist in the world, or, a "situational spatiality", which refers to the spatiality belonging to their body. To Merleau-Ponty, it is body that outlines and decides the space rather than a body exists in space, i.e. without body there will be no space. As bodily space is the living space produced by our body, our situational spatiality presupposes the positional space.

Based on the bodily expression of humankind's intention in the world, in this second stage of Morrison's novelistic creation, Beloved's ultimate real "death", or permanent disappearance of her body is also noticeable (as has been elaborated beforehand in this chapter), for it has much to do with the dynamic construction of phenomenal self. Just like Pilate's salvation of Milkman at the expense of her life, Beloved ultimately passes her life on to her mother and Denver. Such disappearance is inseparable from the spatial dimension of body. "The world obtains a plurality of connotations from the perspective of body, which is the dynamic product of the rejection and obtainment of body." (Wang Min'an, 2004: 40)

In *Jazz*, what is in the micro space of black women's conflictory body is a reminder of the existence of the macro social space that constitutes a new perspective of history. When humankind's historical consciousness is set in different historical scopes, these historical scopes will merge into an intrinsically-moving macro scope featuring interaction and assimilation, which signifies the promotion to a higher commonality. Such commonality, if granted enough time, will overcome not only black women's individuality, but also the individuality of men.

Under the impact of the integration of historical scopes at various levels, black women's body, as a correlative of self, transcends their equally historically "bound" body and "projects" the world at the existential level from different angles. The moving function of body embodied in the displacement of space, is capable of offering meanings, which is a syncretism of living practice. It is in the motion that the black women's body, no longer being a subordinate to men, constitutes a "complicit" relationship with the others and the world as well.

Chapter Three The Spatial Body in Tar, Beloved and Jazz

As meaning is generated in its motion, body has become "phenomenal" body due to the primordial meaning it bears. While humankind perceives the world with their body and body is the real place where phenomena are embodied.

Taken as a whole, from Jadine to Sethe to Violet, the construction of self is achieved in the individuality of black women. Not slightly different from the passivity of being "individualized" in the three women of Pecola, Sula and Pilate in the first chapter, "individuality" is intended here to emphasize the unconscious distance from the community they live in. So, though these three black women finally transcend their "bound" bodies, the communal liberation of black women shall be observed in the women in *Paradise, Love, Mercy* in the next chapter.

Chapter Four

The Discursive Body in *Paradise, Love* and *Mercy*

As a secular existence, humankind is interposed in the integrated framework of interactions with objects in the world, which reflects the new features of existentialism's understanding of life-subject. In addition to the essentialist, stationary, racial quality and the transformative, moving, spatial quality, body has an undeniable discursive quality that belongs to non-linguistic communication, which, as a beneficial supplement to inter-personal communication, has been carried out in social practice and dedication to the reciprocity in constructing black women's subject. Besides the micro dialogues produced among black women's bodies, the tactical use of flashbacks Morrison adopts in the narration of her late three novels also forms a macro temporal dialogue between the present and past.

Bearing the feature of discursive function, black women's bodies play a decisive role in Morrison's novels of *Paradise, Love, Mercy*, in which the black

Chapter Four The Discursive Body in Paradise, Love and Mercy

women of the three novels live in communities of different kinds. Such communal lodging is a breakthrough of the scatteredness of black women's living situation. In accordance to this, their bodies are situated in changed spaces with different experiences in *Paradise*, *Love* and *Mercy*.

4.1 *Paradise*: collective self in the bodies from exclusion to assimilation

Paradise is based on a story Morrison heard while on a trip to Brazil in the 1980s about a convent of black nuns who took in abandoned children but who, regarded as an outrage, were murdered by a group of black men. Speaking about *Paradise*, Morrison stated that she "wanted to force the reader to become acquainted with the communities" and to replicate the experience of "walk(ing) into a neighborhood". "In *Paradise*, Morrison reflects on the value system of "collectivism" in the black community and discovers male chauvinism and black racialism concealed in it and their harms." (Wang Yukuo 174)

Paradise opens in 1976, the bicentennial of America's Declaration of Independence, in the South of America. Fifty years away from the story in *Jazz*, Morrison shifts the setting of the big northern city to a rarely-known town of Ruby in Oklahoma. The story starts directly with a stark disclosure "They shoot the white girl first."(*Paradise* 1) Afterwards, the novel elaborates only on parts of this revelation. "They" are nine armed men from Ruby, an all-black town in Oklahoma. Ruby models itself on Haven, which was established by the citizens' forefathers after they were rejected repeatedly by communities in 1890. This first "forbidding" was followed by another after Second World War, which promoted the founding of Ruby. The location of the shooting is the convent, which lies seventeen miles from Ruby and is a refuge of five women (Consolata,

Mavis, Gigi, Pallas, Seneca). "Ruby" is named after the sister of Deacon and Steward who died in the town. Despite their attempts to retain the purity of their community, with the transformation of the times, Ruby town undergoes the transformation of exclusion and assimilation.

Morrison does not return to the massacre until the end of the novel. Patching this splintered story are narrative lines involving the citizens of Ruby and the women who live at the convent. In *Paradise*, no single character dominates the entire novel since each of the nine chapters is entitled to one of the nine women's names. Their personal stories are entangled either with the history of all-black or with the larger world of "out there". However, the black men and women are kept apart. Part of the reason is that "The values are entirely different. The women are–you know–examples of the 70s. And the conservative black community is affronted and horrified by that."[1]

Another possible reason is "hyper-separation" or "racial exclusion" as the consequence of the Other. According to Plumwood, as the Other is considered not only different but also inferior, the Other is differentiated not by sheer difference but by radical exclusion, not by differentiation, but by hyper-separation. Radical exclusion is a core symbol of dualism (Plumwood 37).

This is evidenced by Morrison, who said so in an interview, "The isolation, the separateness, is always a part of any utopia. And it was my mediation, if you will, and interrogation of the whole idea of paradise, the safe place, the place full of bounty, where no one can harm you. But, in addition to that, it's based on the notion of exclusivity."[2]

Back to the novel, such exclusion of the Other is distinctly highlighted in the female bodies in the opening conflict in the story as well as the ensuing

---

[1] Conversation with Toni Morrison, March 9, 1998. The NewsHour with Jim Lehrer Transcript Retrieved 2012-1-8.

[2] Conversation with Toni Morrison, March 9, 1998. The NewsHour with Jim Lehrer Transcript Retrieved 2012-1-8.

Chapter Four   The Discursive Body in Paradise, Love and Mercy

narration of the women in the convent. Within the ninety-mile area, there are two places with only seventeen miles apart: one is Ruby where the black inhabit; the other is the convent that functions as some kind of refuge for the hurt and deserted women. Originally, the paradise of Ruby town welcomes no outsiders and construct a close-ended and patriarchal society in Ruby by the doctrines of Christianity, as it is a "unique and isolated" (*Paradise* 8) utopia with all its townspeople being solely black. In their eyes, an "outsider" and an "enemy", "… in this town those two words mean the same thing." (*Paradise* 212)

Comparatively, Consolata has been at Ruby the longest. She was raped as a young girl and rescued by a nun, Mary Magna. When Consolata was thirty-nine, she had an affair with one of Ruby's leaders, Deacon Morgan. She allows other women to stay at the convent, but after the loss of her lover and Mary Magna, she retreats to the basement, drinking wine and wearing sunglasses. Mavis has left an abusive husband and is traumatized by the deaths of her twin babies, who suffocated when she left them in the car. Grace/Gigi was involved in the civil rights movement. When her boyfriend Mickey was imprisoned, she headed for Ruby after hearing about a landmark of two entwined trees; sitting between them would generate an unimaginable "ecstasy". Gigi has an affair with K.D., the heir to the Morgan legacy. Seneca finds refuge in the convent from a history of abandonment and sexual abuse that has caused her to self-harm. The last to arrive is Pallas, or Divine, who has been betrayed by her mother and boyfriend. She ran away and, it is implied was raped by a group of men. These women's stories are not contained within their designated chapters, but are dispersed across the text. The novel's form counters the patriarchal ideology of the town; the experiences of Ruby's men are contained within the frames of the women's stories.

As the story proceeds, there forms a temporary community of the Ruby women and the convent women. "Women define themselves not only through their female roles governed by male authority, but through their memory of the predicaments and what to be healed by them." (Kearly 9) In the convent, the

Ruby women find temporal retreat for their sufferings. For instance, Arnette goes there to seek an abortion and finally delivers her baby. Billie Delia retreats there after the fight with her mother (*Paradise* 202): "What she saw and learned there changed her forever." (*Paradise* 52) In the midwife Lone's[1] meditation, there is a clearer idea of the special relationship between the Ruby women and the convent:

> It was women who walked this road. Only women. Never me. …Back and forth, back and forth: crying women, staring women, scowling, lip-biting women or women just plain lost. Out here …women dragged their sorrow up and down the road between Ruby and the convent. They were the Pedestrians. …But the men never walked the road; they drove it, although sometimes their destination was the same as the women's. (*Paradise* 270)

However, despite the alliance develops between the Ruby women and the convent women, to Ruby men, the presence of the latter poses a moral threat to their very existence. They disdain the "throwaway people" lodging there (*Paradise* 4), because they partly stand for what is "Out There," which the all-black town of Ruby must keep out. In Lone's words, they are "Not women locked safely away from men; but worse, women who chose themselves for company, which is say not a convent but a coven" (*Paradise* 276). Moreover, the older generation of Ruby people feels that the community is degenerating: disrespectful children, dissipated sexual relationships, abortions, and bareness, in addition to the many "broken" children.[2] Ruby's men project any fears of destabilization onto women, designating female sexuality as the site of potential deviation. Deacon and Steward Morgan base their paradigm of womanhood on an image

---

[1] Lone, the old midwife and wise woman, visits the convent regularly, and it is she, on the night before the shooting, who goes there to warn the women of the Ruby men's plot.

[2] Due to their exclusion of non-8-rocks to the community, the haven and later Ruby bloodlines are seriously inbred. For instance, all of the Fleetwoods' four children are suffering from congenital disease.

Chapter Four The Discursive Body in Paradise, Love and Mercy

they shared during their youth: the sight of nineteen nameless, smiling "Negro ladies" laughing and posing for a photograph (*Paradise* 109). Their sister Ruby, for whom the town is named, died in childbirth but has come to embody this ideal in the town's imagination. Those women who deviate from this ideal are designated a threat: the fairer-skinned women of the best family and Consolata, whose tea-brown skin fascinates Deacon. They thus put the blame on the presence of the convent women and eventually, for fear of losing control over them and "with God on their side", storm into the convent and massacre the five women living there.

Some women are recognized as legitimate members of the community, yet their sense of identity hinges on the men they are allowed to marry and the town offers few outlets for their private thoughts and yearnings. The ramifications of Ruby's gender ideology emerge not only in relations between the genders, but also in relations between the town's men.

It is consolata's story that ushers in the days leading up to the massacre. After emerging from the basement, she experiences an awakening that unlocks her from her malaise. She is approached by a man; when they address each other, she suddenly finds that he is standing beside her but does not seem to have moved. After this encounter, consolata addresses the women in the convent. She tells them to lie down on the floor and she traces the outline of each other's body.

The convent women "have been hurt profoundly by men, so that even they quarrel and fight most of the time, they're in what they consider a free place, a place where they don't have to fear that they are the people to be preyed upon, ..."[1] These women won't leave the convent partly because there they can escape their painful past, but more importantly, it is because of the tolerance and generosity of the hostess Consolata that endows them with a sense of security. "Ruby has the characteristics, the features of the Old Testament. It's patriarchal. The men...are

---

[1] Conversation with Toni Morrison, March 9, 1998. The NewsHour with Jim Lehrer Transcript Retrieved 2012-3-8.

very concerned about their role as leaders. The convent, as it evolves, becomes a kind of crash pad for some women who are running away from all sorts of trauma, and they don't seek the company of men."[1]

So, with the abandonment of women who are "hurt profoundly by men", the exclusion of body from the entire Ruby town at the macro level is unconsciously formed. Moreover, represented by the convent women, such "exclusion" also pertains to the outside world that is dynamic and develops with the times. In sharp contrast, there exists another bodily dialogue–the assimilation of body at the micro level, which is under the momentum of Ruby women's internal desire. The latter mainly happens between the four black women and Consolata in the convent who serve as each other's company and consolation.

Owing to the limitation of the space of this section, the analysis of the macro dialogue between Ruby men and women will ignore sparse body contact between them and only concentrate on the assault on the convent that appears at the very beginning of the story. As the convent is the epitome of the outside society, and the sufferings of women there echo the humiliations of the ascendants of the town: they are always denied opportunities of obtaining their desired things. "Scary things are not always outside. The most scary things are inside," Consolata so claims. (*Paradise* 39) They share much in common with the townswomen: just like the 14-year-old Arnette who doesn't want to bear a child, Pallas also tries to conceal her pregnancy; just like Arnette and Sweetie get mad for the deaths of their children, Mavis also fancies living with her two "revived" kids in the convent; Just like Divine, Seneca is also considered unbridled in sex, although both of them are innocent. Both Consolata's love for Deacon and Sonne's love for Deacon end up in failure, and so on. What's more, among Ruby's buried stories are those that involve engagement with the women of the convent: Billie Delia, a young woman erroneously suspected of promiscuity, seeks sanctuary there; Soane

---

[1] Conversation with Toni Morrison, March 9, 1998. The NewsHour with Jim Lehrer Transcript Retrieved 2012-1-8.

Chapter Four   The Discursive Body in Paradise, Love and Mercy

Morgan, awares that her husband is having an affair, asks Consolata to relieve her of the prospect of a third child; Sweetie Fleetwood, the devoted mother of sick children ignored by the Fleetwood men, goes to the convent for relief from the burdens of caring.

Luce Irigary, the postmodern French feminist, looked on her exploration and practice of the possibility of female discourse as a means of women's self-realization.

> If we don't invent a language, if we don't find our body's language, it will have too few gestures to accompany our story. We shall tire of the same ones, and leave our desires unexpressed, unrealized. Asleep again, unsatisfied, we shall fall back upon the words of men–who, for their part, have "known" for a long time. But not our body. Seduced, attracted, fascinated, ecstatic with our becoming, we shall remain paralyzed. (Irigary, 1985:214)

Such dim reconciliation is brightened up in the dialogue of body assimilation at the micro level: in her retrospect on her past life and all her questions, Consolata not only recollects herself, but also determines to accommodate these girls and guide them out of their nightmares. She is a woman of appeal: when she embarks on her business, she appears energetic and ever more beautiful with thick eyebrows, pearly white teeth; no-grey hair, pearly-smooth skin (*Paradise* 262). She instructs them to scrub the basement door, undress themselves and lie down. Here, in flattering light under Consolata's soft vision they've actually done as they were told.

> How should we lie? However we feel. They tried arms at the sides, outstretched above the head, crossed over breasts or stomach. Seneca lay on her stomch at first, then changed to her back, hands clasping her shoulders. Pallas lay on her side, knees drawn up. Gigi flung her legs and arms

apart, while Mavis struck a floater's pose, arms angled, knees pointing in. (*Paradise* 263)

When each finds the position she can tolerate on the cold, uncompromising floor, Consolata walks around her and paints the body's silhouette. Once the outlines are complete, each is instructed to remain there. Unspeaking. Naked in candlelight. Consolata speaks of the inseparableness of one's soul and flesh.

My child's body, hurt and soil, leaps into the arms of a woman who teach me my body is nothing my spirit everything. I agreed her until I met another. My flesh is so hungry for itself it ate him. When he fell away the woman rescued me from my body again. Twice she saves it. When her body sickens I care for it in every way flesh works. I hold it in my arms and between my legs. Clean it, rock it, enter it to keep it breath. After she is dead I can not get past that. My bones on hers are the only good thing. Not spirit. Bones. No different from the man. My bones on his the only true thing. So I wondering where the spirit is lost in this? It is true, like bones. It is good, like bones. One sweet, one bitter. Where is it lost? Hearme, listen. Never break them in two. Never put one over the other. Eve is Mary's mother. Mary is the daughter of Eve. (*Paradise* 263)

Evidently, Consolata briefs her crucial transition in her attitude towards the relationship between body and spirit. Originally, she believed in the spirit's superiority over body, and later she comes to realize the pivotal role of body in the existence of spirit. In other words, spirit is inseparable from flesh, or body; there is a symbiosis between the two like the kinship between mother and daughter.

Then, in words more explicit than her introductory speech (which none of them has understood), she tells them of a place where white sidewalks meet the sea and fish the color of plums swim alongside children. She speaks of fruit that

Chapter Four   The Discursive Body in Paradise, Love and Mercy

tastes the way sapphires look and boys using rubies for dice. Of scented cathedrals made of gold where gods and goddesses sit in the pews with the congregation. Carnations are tall as trees. Dwarfs with diamonds for teeth. Snakes aroused by poetry and bells. Then she tells them of a woman named Piedade, who sings but never says a word. "The convent, as it evolves, becomes a kind of crash pad for some women who are running away from all sorts of trauma, and they don't seek the company of men. They have been hurt profoundly by men, so that even though they quarrel and fight most of the time, they're in what they consider a free place, a place where they don't have to fear that they are the people to be preyed upon, but the values are different."[1]

In this case, Consolata's words seem to wield mesmerism on the four women boarding there; they begin to speak out their hurts in the form of nightmarish dreams loudly. Mavis witnesses her child dying in the car; Gigi talks about tear bomb and her cut finger; Seneca, after being abandoned, runs around in the hall and sleeps with the light on at night; Pallas's pain after being raped by a strange grievance when her mother becomes her rival in love. In loud dreaming for the first time, they are "exhausted and enraged" (*Paradise* 264). As they cannot resist the temptation of "telling dreams", which helps release their suppressed pain, they still go to the basement and speak out their pain.

Enlightened by the dialogue, Pallas insists they shop for tubes of paint, sticks of colored chalk. "Paint thinner and chamois cloth. As a response, they understood and began to begin. First with natural features: breasts and pudenda, toes, ears and head hair. …They spoke to each other about what had been dreamed and what had been drawn." (*Paradise* 265) In this way, their bodies' silhouettes on the cellar floor have become the substitutes of each of them, which helps them relieve their mental burden and care about their real live bodies. At this moment, all the five women in the convent have changed:

---

[1] Conversation with Toni Morrison, March 9, 1998. The News Hour with Jim Lehrer Transcript Retrieved 2011-8-12.

A customer stopping by would have noticed little change. May have wondered why the garden was as yet untilled, or who had scratched SORROW on the Cadillac's trunk. May even have wondered why the old woman who answered the knock did not cover her awful eyes with dark glasses; or what on earth the younger ones had done with their hair. A neighbor would notice more–a sense of surfeit; the charged air of the house, its foreign feel and a markedly different look in the tenants' eyes–sociable and connecting when they spoke to you, otherwise they were still and appraising. But if a friend came by, her initial alarm at the sight of the young women might be muted by their adult manner; how calmly themselves they seemed. And Connie–how straight-backed and handsome she looked. How well that familiar dress became her. …unlike some people in Ruby, the convent women were no longer haunted. (*Paradise* 266)

By co-circumscribing their tender bodies on the floor, a discourse among the black women comes into being, which, with its multiple connotations, flexibility, and tension, rivals the steadiness of phallogocentrism[1]. At this time, the convent women's action of delineating their bodies forms their "body schema" or little narratives, which highlights simultaneously the relationship between their body and the outside world and implicates their concept about such a relationship. To those women, their body is far more than an instrument or a means; it is the expression of their existence in the world and the visible form of their intentions. Such expressive function of body was revealed by Merleau-Ponty as follows:

---

[1] This term "phallogocentrism" focuses on Derrida's social structure of speech and binary opposition as the center of reference for language, with the phallic being privileged and how women are only defined by what they lack; not A vs. B, but, rather A vs. A (not-A). The term was the coinage of Hélène Cixous and Luce Irigary who combined Derrida's logocentric idea with Lacan's s symbol for desire. In modern grand narratives, phallogocentrism laud men and reason to extremes and practice sexism and racism.

Chapter Four   The Discursive Body in Paradise, Love and Mercy

> The body's function in remembering is that same function of projection which we have already met in starting to move: the body converts a certain motor essence into vocal form, spreads out the articulatory style of a word into audible phenomena, and arrays the former attitude, which is resumed, into the panorama of the past, projecting an intention to move into actual movement, because the body is a power of natural expression. (Merleau-Ponty, 1962: 181)

In addition to the function of communication, the bodily dialogue among the convent women subverts the male dominance and foregrounds their female features or sexual differences. Complying with post-modern feminism in the 1980s that is anti-essentialist and emphatic of the process of existence, such bodily dialogue by centering around body rather than reason, functions as "little narratives" to assert difference and generates existential ontology.

Jean-François Lyotard, the primary representative of post-modern discourse and post-structuralist philosophy, professes a preference for this plurality of "micro-narrative" that competes with each other, and supplants the totalitarianism of grand narratives with the importance of difference. To oppose the unjust application of generality and values, he encourages people to take the side of difference when they are buried in totalization. In his *Discours, Figure*, Lyotard overturns the dominance of reason represented by discourse, emphasizing the effect of figure, as is a defense of eyes or vision and signification of the body's existence. To Lyotard, "seeing" is an intuitive activity of perception, and figure and image are equated with a power that can strengthen humankind's life and stream of desire. In this sense, the body graph of the convent women is a certain kind of figure or image that buffets the intangible patriarchal society, and conducts its own discourse of difference.

Just like Pilate's easy tranquility towards death, Consolata in the face of the assaulters, looks up towards them, as if smiling at some beautiful scenery and says before the gunshot, "You are back." (*Paradise* 289) Here, "you" might refer to Deacon who she hasn't seen for a long time, or Mary who depends on her for survival, or Big Daddy who resembles her, "The bullet enters her forehead." (Paradise 289) In the story, Consolata takes off her sunglasses to face up to the dismal life, which resembles Pilate in her undaunted disclosing of her naval-lacking belly to the public. According to the narration of the story, Consolata seems to be the only victim to the Ruby men's assault on the convent and is probably shot dead by her former lover Deacon or her brother Steward. It is remarkable that Consolata's last word before her death is the word of "holy". "In a word, through the description of the rational standpoint of women in Ruby town towards the Oven, the openness, tolerance and assistance of the convent women, Morrison stresses the telling and healing functions of the women in the convent and demonstrates the value and effect of women."(Wang Yukuo 193)

Such constituting are the micro dialogue among the Ruby women and the macro dialogue between Ruby men and women, the reconciliation between black feminists and white feminists are equally enlightening. Despite the divergences between them, many black feminists stick to their opinion that the two groups should detect the underlying cause and try to assimilate their differences through negotiation, turn them into a power and liberate themselves in communities.

Gloria Joseph maintained that the destiny of black women was intimately bound to that of black men.[1] She, together with her group wrote in their declaration in 1977 to the effect that despite their being feminists and lesbians, they disagreed with the notion of separation proposed by the separatists in white women, and felt the close tie between them and the black men with the decision to fight with them against racial discrimination side by side.

The influence and consequence of the assault is left untouched upon until

---

[1] When the white women won the right to vote in 1920, the black women and men in the South were still forbidden to vote, which lasted till the passage of Voting Rights Act in 1965.

Chapter Four The Discursive Body in Paradise, Love and Mercy

the last chapter of the story, though very indirectly. The ending is as follows: four months afterwards, the Ruby town makes a funeral for a little girl called Sweetie, symbolizing the ending of an old life and the beginning of a new one. Moreover, though unexpectedly, the whereabouts of Mavis, Gigi, Pallas, Seneca who formerly lived in the Convent are revealed as well.

The symbolic meaning of the bodily dialogues among the Convent women is multiple. On the one hand, communications are indispensable within the black community; on the other hand, racial segregation should not be the excuse of the black's seclusion from the outside world, as such seclusion, while keeping the white out of Ruby town, turns down the entry of newborn things and possibilities of the black race's development. This could only aggravate backwardness of the black race. Under the circumstances, their open communications with the outside world and self-improvements are the only way out to promoting the status of the black race.

> Living in a town that is preoccupied with replication, the citizens of Ruby cultivate an unhealthy kind of division in order to secure their place in the community and attend to deviant personal needs. The convent is a site for an empowering kind of dualism. The unidentified man who approaches Consolata functions as a questioning, relativizing twin self. (Lister 65)

The dialogues at both levels jointly point to the implied theme of the novel, i.e. a religious love beneath the exclusion and assimilation of bodies. Paradise is the third part of Morrison's trilogy (*Beloved* for maternal love, *Jazz* for love between lovers, *Paradise* for religious love) and anatomizes the complexities involved in loving God. Speaking about Ruby's citizens, she states: "(t)hese people really believe that their lives are structured by and glorified by God …I wanted to try to describe that and try to describe how that love can go away."[1]

In *Paradise*, almost all the people are pious Christians and they have repeatedly mentioned Jesus or God. Ever since the colonial period, the black have been placed outside every opportunity and political administration, in which case they could do nothing but appeal to God for guidance to release their internal suppression in church practices. Their yearning for religious love is revealed in the definition of love by the priest:

> Love is divine only and difficult always. If you think it is easy you are a fool. If you think it is natural you are blind. It is a learned application without reason or motive except that it is God....Love is not a gift. It is a diploma. A diploma conferring certain privileges: the privilege of expressing love and the privilege of receiving it. (*Paradise* 141)

Consequently, it is not hard to reckon the importance of communication from the connotations of the title of the novel, "Paradise". Without communication, be it bodily or non-bodily, any paradise-like places will be unavoidably destructed. For this, Morrison once corresponded in her redefinition of "paradise" that the original concept taking God's chosen people for the essence of paradise and alienating them from the others shall be doubted and added an implicit question mark. (Mori 88)

As a matter of fact, such a love for God embraces Morrison's unfulfilled wish for the requisite communication and assimilation between the black men and the black women. Such a concealed love is later elaborated in Morrison's next novel entitled *Love*.

---

[1] "An Hour with Nobel Prize-Winning Author Toni Morrison." Interview with / Charlie Rose, March 16, 1998.

Chapter Four   The Discursive Body in Paradise, Love and Mercy

4.2 *Love*: collective self in the bodies from alienation to harmony

"To some extent, *Love* can be viewed as the continuation of *Paradise*." (Wang and Wu, 2004: 199 As the title suggests, the theme of the novel is "a further variation of love: that which is shared by children." (Lister, 69) Threaded together by the alienated love, the novel amplifies on race, sex, family, abandonment, and horror and the human nature as well. "In terms of theme, *Love* can be traced back to the same origin with Morrison's former love trilogy of *Beloved* (about maternal love), *Jazz* (about lovers' love) and *Paradise* (about religious love) as has been afore-mentioned, all of which place high premium on the importance of communication." (Wang and Wu, 2004: 199) In this novel, the focus is tactically extended to a group of women, or the Cosey women, despite the ultimate condensed reunion of Heed and Christine at the end of the story. This time, Morrison, following her politically-engaged method, narrates a big story on a small scale of a family with her exceptional aptitude.

Just like *Paradise*, the historical element concerns the entire Civil Rights Movement in *Love*. The novel starts 25 years after Cosey's death in the 1990. Yet, despite his death, Cosey's influence lingers to influence the relationship between Heed and Christine as well as every other one in the family, just like the Civil Rights Movement. When Cosey's career was in prosperity, racial discrimination was rampant and people cherished strong reminiscence for the Civil Rights Movement. When the black were deprived of their voting rights in the 1990s, their discontentment was on the rise for the post-Civil Rights Movement.[1] As a result of the disillusionment of post-Civil Rights Movement, what is implied in *Love* is the black's intact social status and their consciousness of self in the post-Civil Rights Movement.

The story of *Love* takes place in an eastern coast town called Silk in a house at 1 Monarch Street, the home to Bill Cosey, a rich prodigal and proprietor of a hotel and resort. The italicized commentary of a woman named L, which stands for love, frames the novel, traces the history of the resort and provides a coda to some of its parts. L used to be the chef at a seaside resort owned by Cosey. The resort was constructed in the 1930s as a playground for folk who felt the way he did, who studied ways to contradict history. Converted during the Depression, the resort became the "best and best-known vacation spot for colored folk on the East Coast, but the 1950s and 1960s brought new conditions, and people began to opt for Hilton or cruise ships."(*Love* 6)

In the 1990s, Cosey's resort is no longer a destination but a stop-off point for commuters. When the novel opens, only the youngest members of the family are alive: Cosey's granddaughter Christine and his second wife Heed. Heed was Christine's best friend until 52-year-old Cosey bought her from her destitute family for two hundred dollars to be his bride. Heed was an uneducated 11-year-old child. Cosey's mentally unsound daughter-in-law, May, seemingly jealous of Heed, does everything in her power to keep her away from her own daughter, Christine. The two, so similar in age, have already connected and simply can't be friends. Christine and Heed now live in the house that Cosey apparently left to his "sweet Cosey child" in a will, which was hastily written on a menu. This ambiguous wording has provoked an ongoing battle between the women. Junior

---

[1] The Civil Rights Movement in the 20th century brought far-reaching influence upon America. From then on, the open racial discrimination has been legally forbidden and morally despised by the public. The scholars on racial problems term the period after the Movement as "Post-Civil Rights Movement. In the rising black pollution in America, the 1990s American society witnessed no substantial improvement in the living conditions of the black but the regression of racial discrimination.

is hired by Heed to write the Cosey family history and Heed sees something of herself in Junior and finds their common link.

The novel moves backward and forward in time, revisting pivotal encounters between the characters and unveiling secret gestures and connections: Heed's affair with a hotel guest, Sinclair; L's forging of the will on a menu to ensure protection for the Cosey women; Cosey's ongoing relationship with Celestial, a prostitute and the recipient of his original will; the burial of the hotel deed by May. Seeking definition outside the Cosey family, Christine leaves the resort as a young woman and joins the black nationalist movement. Involvement in the movement becomes an outlet for her personal needs and grievances. However, her enthusiasm diminishes by 1970, when it is "sapped by funerals" (*Love* 163-164).

In her opening commentary, L expresses wonder that her people have "forgotten the beauty of meaning much by saying little" (*Love* 3). In specific, the novel highlights the misunderstanding that further estranges the two girls after Heed's marriage: Heed returns from her honeymoon desperate to tell Christine of all that she has seen but is greeted with scornful laughter at her new clothes; she makes a peace offering of her wedding ring to Christine, who calls her a slave; when Christine corrects Heed's grammar and Cosey spanks his wife, Heed sets fire to Christine's bedroom; at Cosey's funeral, Heed stops Christine from placing rings on her husband's fingers and screams "in recognition that she would never hear the word (love) again" (*Love* 163-164).

The importance of communication is foreshadowed in the long indifferent bodily separation between Christine and Heed, which is revealed in the very beginning of the novel. When Junior first comes to the Coseys for job interview, she finds that "each woman lived in a spotlight separated–or connected–by the darkness between them." (*Love* 25) Worse still, there is no vocal communication between Heed and Christine, even when Christine downstairs sends food to Heed who lives upstairs, "no knock preceded her and no word accompanied her."(*Love* 27) she simply "entered carrying a tray", and "placed the tray on the desk where

Heed and Junior faced each other and left without meeting a single eye."(*Love* 28)

As early as in an interview in 1977, Morrison had talked about love being her basic theme, "all the time that I write, I'm writing about love or its absence."(Bakerman 40) After twenty odd years, what she cares about in *Love* relays the basic feeling of love under the complex effects of history, race, and sex, etc. As has been pointed out, "Morrison's redefinition of love in this novel attracts wide attention to love, exploring how the black women should love, how they should dispel the shadow in life, and how they should hinder love from being alienated." (Wang and Wu, 2004: 210) As Ernst Cassirer comments,

> There are no other means to know humankind except their life and behaviors. Yet, any attempts to integrate the findings in this field into a single and simple formula are doomed to fail. The basic element of humankind's survival is contradiction: having no "essence", they have no single or homogeneous existence and are posited in between the opposing poles of existence and non-existence. (Cassirer 16

What's more, if in *Jazz* and *Paradise*, her preceding two novels, Morrison has made calls for love, then in *Love*, she ponders over to what extent love can change characters' destinies and the way love changes the destiny of women is Morrison's purpose of writing. It is noteworthy that at the beginning of the novel, the two ladies are located in the same house, yet on separate floors, which sets obstacles for their communication. As the story continues, their deadlock is aggravated by their psychological alienation. Worse still, for a long time afterwards, they take each other for enemies with curses. This incurs years of tragic misunderstandings between the girls, who vie endlessly for Cosey's love and affection, even after his death, and ultimately develop a deep and dark hatred for one another.

Chapter Four   The Discursive Body in Paradise, Love and Mercy

It was impossible that no one knew of the fights between them when Christine returned to take up permanent residence. Most were by mouth: quarrels about whether the double C's engraved on the silver was one letter doubled or the pairing of Christine's initials. It could be either, because Cosey had ordered the service after his first marriage but long before his second. ...But there were also bruising fights with hands, feet, teeth, and soaring objects. For size and willingness Christine should have been the hands-down winner. With weak hands and no size, Heed should have lost every match. But the results were a tie at the least. For Heed's speed more than compensated for Christine's strength, and her swift cunning anticipating, protecting, warding off–exhausted her enemy. Once-perhaps twice-a year, they punched, grabbed hair, wrestled, bit, slapped. Never drawing blood, never apologizing, never premeditating, yet drawn annually to pant through an episode that was as much rite as fight. (*Love* 73)

Different from the temporary bodily fight between Jadine and Son in *Tar*, in this process of reaching a tie in the vocal fight, Heed's and Christine's lived body has been "phenomenalized", as it exhibits a phenomenon not from the level of pure consciousness but from the crevice between "non-being-for-itself" consciousness and "non-being-in-itself" object. What exists in such a "phenomenal" body is the perceptual subject of body. When vocal language is inappropriate and abrupt in their deadlock, their body becomes a medium of efficacious communication to each other, and at this moment, the way people use their bodies is decisive as it evokes a simultaneous patterning of body and the world in emotion. What's more, to comprehend the transcendent meaning of body-expressed anger in the case of Heed and Christine can refer to Merleau-Ponty's analogy, "The use a man is to make of his body is transcendent in relation to that body as a mere biological entity. It is no more natural, and no less conventional, to shout in anger or to kiss in love than to call a table 'a table'. Feelings and passional conduct are invented like words." (Merleau-Ponty, 1962: 189) In expressing anger, the body is no longer a physical entity, but a natural way of embodiment of an individual's intention that can be prophetic of the future development of the situation.

In the ensuing years of silence between Heed and Christina, their scanty communication is conducted by their "phenomenal" body, which is a tacit, yet direct expression of their perception of the world. To them, body, instead of words, turns out to be more connotative and commutative as well, just as their reticence has always been. The sense of their reticent gestures is not given, but understood, that is, seized upon by an act on the spectator's part. The communication or comprehension of gestures comes about through the reciprocity of one's intentions and the gestures of the other, of one's gestures and intentions discernible in the conduct of the other.

> Finally they stopped, moved into acid silence, and invented other ways to underscore bitterness. Along with age, recognition that neither one could leave played a part in their unnegotiated cease-fire. More on the mark was their unspoken realization that the fights did nothing other than allow them to hold each other. Their grievances were too serious for that. Like friendship, hatred needed more than physical intimacy; it wanted creativity and hard work to sustain each other. (*Love* 73-74)

The posture of body makes sense per se, which is an ability of expressing feelings and emotions. In this way, body is set in the reversible cycle of being the seer and the seen, which constitutes an expressive relation between the body-subject and the perceived world and lets the two know each other through their inter-connection. If it is body that makes it possible for the production of meaning, then meaning is also expressed in body. Body thus becomes a signifier since meaning is produced and comprehended in body posture, i.e. through its own behaviors in perceptual experience, body makes it possible to convey the primordial perceptual meanings. To Merleau-Ponty, "Action doesn't remind me of anger: action is anger." In a word, meaning exists in action; the implementation of bodily actions is the process of the expression of meanings.

In *Love*, the fight between the two women breaks the deadlock that has been there for many years. To them, such fight is the outlet for their long-suppressed hostility resulting from misunderstanding, in which their alienation starts to dissolve. Through the fight, they realizes a much-awaited communication, though not a peaceful one, which is a key step towards their final harmony.

Extensively speaking, in the world-wide patriarchal society, such autonomous expression of women, regardless of their skin color, breaks the long-suppressed historical silence, becomes a mode of living by which they resist "aphasia", and defies the dual shelters of power discourse and male discourse. In the historical movement, this is women's generative process from the subordinate Other to an individual of independent subjectivity. Moreover, this process was received by Beauvoir in *The Second Sex* as the transformation from the state of essence to that of existence. She also noted that as such process sees no end, it requires women's vigilance. In the eyes of modern feminists, women's restoration of their lost discourse solely through their autonomous expression is only an inalienable start for their social existence. In this case, to accomplish women's social existence, the "reciprocity" proposed by Beauvoir may well be the potential solution to the confrontation between the subject of women and that of the other sex.

After the break-up of the frozen sisterhood between Heed and Christine, it is the increasing approach of their bodies that gradually narrows their psychological distance and dissolves their accumulated grievance. Admittedly, there is only a thin line between love and hate, yet after years of hatred, the solution of the Coseys' conflicts resorts to the bodily communication between Christine and Heed.

When they searched for more interesting means of causing pain they had to rely on personal information, things they remembered from childhood. Each thought she was in charge. Christine because she was strappingly healthy, could drive, go about, and run the house. Heed, however, knew she was still in charge, still winning, not only because she had the money but because she was what everybody but Papa assumed she was not: smart. Smarter than the petted one, the spoiled one miseducated in private school, stupid about men, unequipped for real work and too lazy to do it anyway; a parasite feeding off men until they dumped her and sent her home to gnaw the hand she ought to be licking. *(Love* 74*)*

Furthermore, in the long preparation for the final unity of Heed and Christine, the latter serves as the link between the Civil Rights Movement and gender problem, which is also the very first image of the Civil Rights Movement portrayed in Morrison's works. Through her, *Love* depicts the dedication of black women to the Civil Rights Movement, pointing out that sex oppression is still a serious problem in the Movement, and that to reverse their doom, black women have nobody but themselves to rely on. Along with this, the importance of the inner unity of black women is foreshadowed as well. This can be inferred from the tactical installation of the final harmonious reunion of Heed and Christine.

At the end of the novel, due to a signified "encounter" of their bodies, a positive communication is realized between Heed and Christine. In the attic, Heed instructs Junior to forge a will leaving everything unequivocally to the latter. Christine arrives at the funnel, and as the women confront each other, Junior stealthily pulls the carpet under Heed's feet. The floorboards give way, and Heed falls. Christine instinctively goes to save Heed while Junior flees the scene. Such a help denotes Christine's intention of reaching a possible reconciliation. Under this circumstance, for the first time since Heed's marriage, the women talk honestly. Heed reveals that she married Cosey to be near Christine; Christine tells Heed

Chapter Four   The Discursive Body in Paradise, Love and Mercy

that she wanted to go on her honeymoon with her. When Junior tells Romen what has occurred, he leaves her to help the two old women. To Christine and Heed, though one of them has been dead by the end of the novel, their selves have been translated from alienation to harmony in their bodies. In this sense, their "body subject" is constitutive in the process of the diminish of their hostility, just as Oksala commented as follows,

> The body is not a surface or a site on which psychic meanings are played out. Neither is it a mute container of subjectivity. The body subject is constitutive in the sense of being generative of meanings that are preconscious and preconceptual: subjectivity means embodied capability to creatively respond to the existing norms. (Oksala 224)

Accordingly, the subjectivity of Heed and Christine, cultivated in their unconscious bodily communication exhibits their potentiality of "creatively" or "positively" solve their long years of feud. To further exemplify the significant role of communication, what functions as a counter-example is the successful communication between Romen and his grandparents Sandler and Vida Gibbons. Romen, a true and upright soul, owes much of his decent behavior to his grandparents, Sandler and Vida Gibbons's guidance. Knowing how to communicate effectively with his grandson, Sandler plays a significant role in Romen's development into a strong person. Moreover, in the end, in addition to the harmony between Christine and Heed, Romen and his actions become an example of the goodness that can evolve when people take the time to carefully and lovingly express themselves. Just like what Sula and Nel have found in *Sula*, such love is a potentially liberating love for it is untainted by societal expectations. Romen thus performs two of the novel's great acts of love, which manifests itself through quiet acts of protection: he foregoes his reputation among his friends to rescue a girl from a gang rape, and overlooks his infatuation with

Junior to attend to Heed and Christine at the end of the novel.

Reflecting on the recovery process of Heed and Christine, it is not difficult to identify the decisive role their bodies play in it, which can be referred back to Chapter One, There are two progressive parts in unveiling the discursive dimension of body: the conveyance of ideas and information and the sharing of them. For the further embodiment of discursive function of body, Morrison's novel of *Mercy* will proves to be another case in point.

4.3 *Mercy*: collective self in the bodies from freedom to "re-enslavement"

Morrison's ninth novel, *Mercy*, cites numerous instances of brutality and deprivation, making adaptations of American slavery in *Beloved* in a very early, seventeenth-century form. What may well throw them for a loop is the redemptive tone: a pristine landscape, a compassionate white Northern farmer, and a notable absence of racial animosity–felt even more keenly in an election year with a full deck of race cards. In *Mercy*, Jacob Vaark's collection of laborer-charges (a Native American, a black child, an orphan, and two indentured servants) is united by and against a spreading culture of servitude that has little to do with skin color.

In *Mercy*, a dialogue of the humanity's living existence takes place, which transcends the dialogues between men and women, regardless of skin color. Assuredly, in *Paradise* and *Love*, from exclusion to assimilation, from alienation to harmony, female bodies have partially striven into liberty and self has transcended the nature of individuality. With liberty being the ultimate state of self, Morrison reverses in *Mercy* the direction of arriving at the reciprocal self and returns to her point of departure, yet this time at a much higher level–the concern for the entire humankind.

Chapter Four The Discursive Body in Paradise, Love and Mercy

Being Toni Morrison's ninth novel published in 2008, *Mercy* was set in the 1680s in American colonies, approximately two centuries prior to the year of 1873 when the story of *Beloved* was fixed. This historical work allows Morrison to return to the subject of slavery, which she surveyed to popular and critical success with *Beloved*. In *Mercy*, Except for alluding it to the inerasable black skin, Morrison extended the concept of slavery to everyone and over the context of the African American experience, which, to some extent, interprets why slavery reemerges in Morrison's works in her latter years of creation, for slavery is a historical trauma in her heart.

Apart from seeking self, feminists also have the restoration of the forgotten history as part of their tasks. To them, the restoration of the forgotten history is "to find the useful past" which has gradually become the kernel of the process of black women's liberation. In proof of that, Alice Walker argues in her doctoral dissertation "In Search of Our Mothers' Garden" (1974) that the salvation image which surpasses the identity of the Other should be rooted in the true and ascertainable living experience of a certain group or community.

As has been exhibited in Morrison's later works, such enslavement gradually loses distinction of color or gender. "The color and gender demarcations of contemporary fiction have begun to blur in the last decade, in part due to writers such as Morrison, whose contributions stand tall against any literary standard."(Taylor and Danille 244). In *Mercy*, Morrison's handling of issues of slavery and liberty is more multi-faceted than in her foregoing novels by tracing the origin of slavery in America of the late seventeenth century. The setting and the characters are complex and diverse in *Mercy*. The novel includes Portuguese, Dutch, English, Native American, African, and mixed-race characters, all vying for a place in this new world, where there is an Eden-like quality in the beauty and richness of the vast land despite the rampant diseases of measles and smallpox.

Before analyzing the discursive dimension of body in the enslaved women, it is imperative to outline the slavery of varied forms in the story. Each of the "servants" of the Vaark household is somewhere on the continuum between slavery and liberty, in the form of bondage that is not necessarily race-based. Sorrow is "mongrelized" of mixed race parentage with curly red hair and does not appear to be considered black by anyone. She is an unpaid servant, though, who is threatened with sale. Lina is a Native American slave, and Will and Scully are white indentured servants. These slaves, to complement Florens' first-person narration of enslavement, are each given a chapter in the third-person narrative in the novel to enhance the enormous difficulty of unshackling the widespread trans-racial, trans-sexual slavery (Wang and Wu, 2009: 43).

Among all the forms of slavery in the book, however, Florens' slavery is highlighted, as she is the main character as well as the main narrator of the story. Florens opens the story with a monologue, as she is addressing a young African blacksmith on a journey that is both literal and figurative. Florens is a slave born in America of an African mother, originally owned by Portuguese plantation owners. Through an act of mercy, she becomes part of the household of the Vaarks, who are a farming and trading couple.

No better than the pitiable little girl Pecola in *Bluest*, Florens is also a seven or eight year-old child when abandoned by her mother and receives no education from her mother. Though she is unaware of the "important thing" (*Mercy* 8) that her mother wants to tell her when she is taken away by Vaark Jacob, she confesses "…mothers nursing greedy babies scare me. I know how their eyes go when they choose. How they raise them to look at me hard, saying something I cannot hear."(*Mercy* 8) Florens' mother might not have known the fact that though her act of "mercy" had protected her daughter's body against the usual humiliation of black woman slaves, a shadow is long cast down upon her daughter's heart. So, to some extent, Florens' mind is still enslaved even when she arrives at the house of her new owner of the Jacobs. "That all this time I cannot know what my mother is telling me." (*Mercy* 161)

Unquestionably, in the new house, Florens is vehemently self-abased.

Chapter Four The Discursive Body in Paradise, Love and Mercy

"Florens would have been his prey. It was easy to spot that combination of defenselessness, eagerness to please and, most of all, a willingness to blame herself for the meanness of others." (*Mercy* 152) Despite self-abasement, Florens is rather "quiet, timid" for the ever-lasting horror of abandonment she has suffered when young. So, in the Jacobs' eyes, she is so humble that "Not only was she consistently trustworthy, she was deeply grateful for every shred of affection, any pat on the head, any smile of approval." (*Mercy* 61)

In fact, not only Florens but also women of other skin color are under the yoke of slavery, too. Lina is the native Indian who has survived a fatal attack of smallpox in her tribe and her original name of Messalina is shortened to "Lina" to signal a sliver of hope. "Afraid of once more losing shelter, terrified of being alone in the world without family, Lina acknowledged her status as heathen and let herself be purified by these worthies." (*Mercy* 47) Nevertheless, she is still an alien and "a praying savage" (*Mercy* 5) in others' eyes.

Rebecca, as the white mistress of Florens and Lina, is vexed by her parents' abandonment and the "enslavement" that permeates her life. At the age of 16, she is sold by her parents to the new world to save the money to foster her. Since her real marriage to Jacob is better than her expectation as Jacob treats her as his counterpart and calls her "my northern star" (*Mercy* 87), she retains seclusion after the consecutive death of her children and husband. To her, Jacob's death is an abandonment. "However well she loved the man in life, his leaving her behind blasted her." (*Mercy* 153) After recovery, she is changed outright, "underneath her piety was something cold if not cruel." "What both husband and wife had enjoyed, even celebrated, she now despised as signs of both the third and seventh sins." "Refusing to enter the grand house, the one in whose construction she had delighted, seemed to him a punishment not only of herself but of everyone, her dead husband in particular." (*Mercy* 153) She thus indulges in the maltreatment of everyone and the hurt of wanton "spiritual enslavement".

Different from *Paradise* and *Love*, in *Mercy*, the discursive dimension of body is produced primarily at three levels: one taking place between Florens and the blacksmith, another taking place between Florens and herself, and the last taking place among Florens, Lina and Rebecca. These interwoven dialogues centering around Florens prove the social quality of humankind, as "Humankind is essentially a social existence inalienable from their community. As the abandonment by the society is the cruelest punishment, humankind can only survive in their coexistence with the society." (Zhu Liyuan, 2006:121)

All I'm saying is simply this, that all life is interrelated, that somehow we're caught in an inescapable network of mutuality tied in a single garment of destiny. Whatever affects one directly affects all indirectly. For some strange reason, I can never be what I ought to be until you are what you ought to be. You can never be what you ought to be until I am what I ought to be. This is the interrelated structure of reality. (Warren 174)

In the bodily dialogue between Florens and the blacksmith, Florens has been objectified, and become a "spiritual" slave. Surely, if Florens's abandonment by her mother made her self ignored, then her fascination for the blacksmith's body at her age of sixteen deprived her of self. Her extreme thirst for love enslaved her to her affection for the blacksmith. "…seeing the shine of water running down his spine", "I have shock at myself for wanting to lick there, …My eyes not my stomach are the hungry parts of me. …My stomach is open, my legs go softly and the heart is stretching to break." (*Mercy* 37-38) Only rarely did she confess having tasted liberty for the first time when she saw a stag moving up the rock side. "I wonder what else the world may show me. It is as though I am loose to do what I choose, the stage, the wall of flowers. I am a little scare of this looseness. Is that how free feels? I don't like it. I don't want to be free of you because I am live only with you."(*Mercy* 70) Deep in her heart, the blacksmith was her "protection" (*Mercy* 69), her "shaper" and her "world" as well. (*Mercy* 71)

Chapter Four   The Discursive Body in Paradise, Love and Mercy

Such subordination of Florens to the blacksmith prophesizes a failure in her love for him. When Lina tried to enlighten her, saying, "You are one leaf on his tree," Florens shook her head, closed her eyes and replied, "No. I am his tree." (*Mercy* 61) To this she stuck until she was sent on an errand for the blacksmith (who was supposed to have some medical knowledge as he had cured a dying woman slave) to cure the dying mistress after Jacob had been dead. When she tried hard to find the blacksmith, she found that he had taken an orphan called Malaik. To save time, Florens was left at home to take care of the boy while the blacksmith rode a horse to heal the mistress. At this moment, the scene harassing her appeared in her mind, "A minha mae leans at the door holding her little boy's hand, my shoes in her pocket. As always she is trying to tell me something." (*Mercy* 137) When she sees the hate in the eyes of Malaik who wants her leaving, her is jealous and fears that Malaik might get more love from the blacksmith makes her pull his arm to stop his screaming for the doll which has been hidden by her. Seeing Malaik still and limp on the floor, the blacksmith gets furious and knocks Florens off her feet. Each word of the following crucial dialogue hurts Florens when she inquires for the reason why she is to be driven away by the blacksmith,

> Why are you killing me I ask you.
> I want you to go.
> Let me explain.
> No. Now.
> Why? Why?
> Because you are a slave.
> What?
> You heard me.
> Sir makes me that.
> I don't mean him.

149

Then who?

You.

What is your meaning? I am a slave because Sir trades for me.

No. You have become one.

How?

Your head is empty and your body is wild.

I am adoring you.

And a slave to that too.

You alone own me.

Own yourself, woman, and leave us be. You could have killed this child.

No. Wait. You put me in misery.

You are nothing but wilderness. No constraint. No mind.

(*Mercy* 141)

Evidently, despite being a black like the blacksmith, Florens has, in sharp contrast with the blacksmith, "no mind" or thoughts. As a free black, the blacksmith has a strong consciousness of self and values the independence of individuals. Florens's "You alone own me." is a romantic and passionate profession of love, which uncovers the truth of her loss of self and the enslavement of his unconsciousness. The great disparity at the level of spirit of the blacksmith and Florens cannot be mended by their skin color, so they cannot end up being lovers. "Through the blacksmith, Morrison shows that enslavement, besides in physical body, could exist at the level of spirit. Enslavement at either side will means the loss of liberty, and even the enslavement in romantic passion will jeopardize one's soul." (Wang and Wu, 2009: 40)

Different from the internal dialogue, the dialogue between Florens and her self takes a visible form and occurs mainly in a secret room. Florens' choice of carving words on the wall with a nail in a secret room other than storing them in her heart is a form of dialogue between her body and self. After her frustrated

Chapter Four   The Discursive Body in Paradise, Love and Mercy

love for the blacksmith, Florens became mature with a deep understanding of love and her self. There is a crucial detail concerning Florens's final spiritual liberty or growth. After a big quarel with the blacksmith, Florens strode back to her master's house. Her original "feet of a Portuguese lady" (*Mercy* 4) which were "too tender for life" and never had "the strong soles, tougher than leather, that life requires" (*Mercy* 4) were finally changed, as she now ran with bare feet, "the soles of my feet are hard as cypress" (*Mercy* 161).

To Florens, the primary aim of writing is to kill the pain of losing her lover, yet the process of writing is equally painful to women. "Confession we tell not write as I am doing now. I forget almost all of it until now. I like talk." (*Mercy* 6) "The walls make trouble because lamplight is too small to see by. I am holding light in one hand and carving letters with the other. My arms ache." (*Mercy* 160) However, the bigger ache was in her heart, "You won't read my telling. You read the world but not the letters of talk. You don't know how to." (*Mercy* 160) However, it was writing that got Florens back to the way of "returning her self", as she realized, "If you never read this, no one will. These careful words, closed up and wide open, will talk to themselves." (*Mercy* 161) She envisioned that these words needed the air outside so that they could dance in it, "through clouds cut by rainbow and flavor the soil of the earth." (*Mercy* 161) At last, her "monologue" on the wall, as another form of little narratives, has become a sublimation of her consciousness of herself,

I am become wilderness but I am also Florens.
In full. Unforgiven. Unforgiving. No ruth, my
love. None. Hear me? Slave. Free. I last. (*Mercy* 167)

With the above words of "In full" and "Free" inscribed on the wall or through her bodily talk with her mind, Florens, despite her enslaved status left unchanged, finally acquires her true self in her mental liberation after the tough process of being "unforgiven" (by the blacksmith) to "unforgiving" (to the blacksmith as well). To unconsciously echo such a paradox, the blacksmith once asserts "slaves are freer than free men," "One is a lion in the skin of an ass. The other is an ass in the skin of a lion." With the double paradoxical metaphors, he puts special premium on the potentials of the enslaved people, which is also what Morrison hopes to convey. To his words, Florens resonates, "That it is the withering inside that enslaves and opens the door for what is wild. I know my withering is born in the widow's closet." (*Mercy* 160) Rather than the external world, true enslavement comes from the mind, so Florens's problem lies with her "empty mind", her lack of judgment, in which case she has to eradicate the concept of "women belonging to men and for men" before she could obtain liberty.

Unlike Pilate in *Solomon* whose meditation of how her life shall be led is still a vague query on her self, Florens, though a few years younger, is conducting a clear-cut self-reflection with the help of her bodily writing, which is a noticeable improvement compared with Pilate and crucial to her consciousness of self. In Florens, a complete elucidation of her self is rendered in a thoroughgoing reflection after she arrives at awareness of itself as well as of its results. To transcend Descartes's impregnable Cogito, one needs to not only adopt a reflective attitude, but furthermore reflect on this reflection, and understand the succeeding situation as a part of its definition and realize the transformation which she/he will bring with it in the spectacle of the world and in humankind's existence.

When little Florens first comes to the farm, Lina gives her maternal love. "Mother hunger–to be one or have one–both of them reeling from that longing." (*Mercy* 63) Lina tells Florens experiences and her understanding of life, "They had memorable nights, lying together." (*Mercy* 61) "Rebecca had confidence in Florens… And she felt a lot of affection for her, although it took some time to develop." (*Mercy* 96) After the successive death of her children, when Florens newly arrived, instead of pleasing her as supposed by Vaark Jacob, Rebecca feels

Chapter Four The Discursive Body in Paradise, Love and Mercy

more melancholic than ever, "Nothing could replace the original one and nothing should." (*Mercy* 96)

On a far larger scale, the dialogues between women and men are launched simultaneously in the story. "In *Mercy*, 'enslavement' is taken by Morrison for the metaphor of the living state of the humanity, with no exclusion of men." (Wang and Wu, 2009: 43) On the side of women there are Florens, Lina and Rebecca; on the side of men, there are the Willard and Scully, two white indentured servants, as well as the blacksmith. "As the man of mercy, Jacob has for the time being 'stabilized' the helpless world of women, while the blacksmith obsessing Florens has 'upset' the women's world and facilitates their changes." (Wang and Wu, 2009: 43) Before the arrival of Rebecca, she tries her hard to assist Jacob in managing the farm and afterwards she sincerely helps the new mistress Rebecca and forms deep friendship with her. "They became friends. Not only because somebody had to pull the wasp sting from the other's arm. Not only because it took two to push the cow away from the fence. Not only because one had to hold the head while the other one tied the trotters. Mostly because neither knew precisely what they were doing or how." (*Mercy* 53)

Based on the dialogues centering around Florens and dialogues between sexes, Florens as well as Lina gradually constructs their subjects. Just like Florens' physical mother, Lina is originally a shackled slave with the thought that "We never shape the world...The world shapes us."(*Mercy* 71) While she is rendering help and warmth to Florens, she is also a typical character who manages to redeem herself in that narrow and suffocating living environment, even with the help of fragments of religion and belief. "Relying on memory and her own resources, she cobbled together neglected rites, merged Europe medicine with native, scripture with lore, and recalled or invented the hidden meaning of things." (*Mercy* 48) In Willard's eyes, there is a certain kind of "purity" in her and "Her loyalty...was not submission to Mistress or Florens; it was a sign of her own self-worth–a sort of keeping one's word. Honor, perhaps." (*Mercy* 151)

The relationship between the blacksmith and Florens, or the relationship between man and woman is one of dialectic between the "being-for-itself" and "being-in-itself". If women's transcendence is re-trapped into immanence and stagnancy, the degenerated existence will be reduced to "being-in-itself" and become the savage life dominated by the specified environment. In this case, the degenerated freedom will become coercive and accidental, which, if agreed by the subject, will lead to a moral error.

> The core of philosophy is no longer an autonomous transcendental subjectivity, to be found everywhere and nowhere: it lies in the perpetual beginning of reflection, at the point where the individual life begins to reflect on itself. Reflection is truly reflection only if it is not carried outside itself, only if it knows itself as reflection-on-an-unreflective-experience, and consequently as a change in structure of our existence. (Merleau-Ponty, 1962: 62)

Therefore, what young Florens has internally experienced is clearly nothing but reflection-on-an-unreflective-experience, or a kind of "awakening enlightenment", which is a must-be and perpetual in the long process of women's liberation. Moreover, as has been afore-illustrated, such enlightenment takes place in Florens' social practice, which is based on her intercommunication with people in her community. In contrast, Rebecca is one who is still trapped in her own spiritual enslavement, as she rejects communications from people around her. Worse still, she abruptly turns rather cruel and merciless after Jacob's death, "she beat Sorrow, had Lina's hammock taken down, advertised the sale of Florens." (*Mercy* 155) Treated this way, both Florens and Lina are inflicted by such "hurt" (*Mercy* 155).

To wind up the "freedom" hardly sought and represented by Florens out of her "re-enslavement", Morrison pointed out in her motivation of novelistic creation, "I really wanted to get to a place before slavery was equated with race.

Chapter Four   The Discursive Body in Paradise, Love and Mercy

Whether they were black or white was less important than what they owned or what their power was."[1] By these words, Morrison's sincere prospects on a society where everyone is equally treated, though carried out in subjunctive mood is prophetic of the possibility of the collective transcendence of the black community and the white as well.

4.4 Transcending "individual" body in the community of black women

Ever since Toni Morrison entered her third stage of novelistic creation, she began to break through the "finite" self imprisoned in the individuality of black women. Rather than being isolated in some way, black women live in communities in *Paradise* and *Love*. Though in *Mercy*, black women's living situation, via being fixed in a time almost at the distant genesis of American history, is much more complex.

To Walter Benjamin[2], historical time is not a piecing together of the objective past, present and future, i.e. not evolving through objective time. Though time is condensed in Jetzet (now), the past displays new meanings in retrospection. In other words, there is a "retrogressive" time in human history, as resounded by Jaspers who pointed out that just like the previous two eventful

---

[1] Kachka, Boris. "Toni Morrison's History Lesson." New York Guides.
[2] Walter Benjamin (1892-1940) was a German-Jewish literary critic, philosopher, social critic, translator, radio broadcaster and essayist. Combining elements of German idealism or Romanticism, Historical Materialism and Jewish mysticism, Benjamin made enduring and influential contributions to aesthetic theory and Western Marxism, and is associated with the Frankfurt school. Benjamin was especially sensitive to the concept of space and to the living state of man in certain space. He was interested in super-realism, which he believed has translated time into space and converted the historical transformation into the present world. In the sense of time, man is passive while in the sense of space, man has initiative due to is/her imaginations.

centuries which were marked not by sheer upward progress but by occasional destructions, the progress of the future is also of multiple possibilities. In this sense, the progress of human society and history is exceptionally complex and tortuous, which has been evidently noticed and observed by Morrison.

In 1996, the National Endowment for the Humanities presented the Jefferson Lecture to Morrison, the U.S. Federal Government's highest honor for achievement in the humanities. Morrison's lecture, entitled "The Future of Time: Literature and Diminished Expectations", began with the aphorism, "Time, it seems, has no future."[1] Cautioning against the misuse of history to diminish expectations of the future, Morrison sets a counter-example in her latest creation of *Mercy*.

1680 was the time of "New Eden" on the Northern American continent, it was still the feudalist period back in Europe. The individuals, according to Ceorg Lukacs (1885—1971), were still objects rather than subjects, for people at that time failed to realize themselves as social existences as a result of their narrow-minded regionalism and nationalism, small-scale farming, as well as ill-communication and backward science. The background aside, this is true of people enslaved in *Mercy*, which raises the question of what on earth leads to human slavery, is it their skin color or their ignorance or even obscurantism?

Regarding the historical background, the year 1680 was also a time of reconstruction after deconstruction by posing a challenge to the symbolism of "Eden", destroying its false totality and by incorporating it into the formation of newly-constructed meaning. By reversing the temporal arrangement of the novel, Morrison seems to caution that social gender is not born of unitary, common, non-historical root, but should be placed in the specific class, race, history and culture, with the 1990s feminists' consensus. They held that the meaning of the change

---

[1] Denise Hawkins, "Marvelous Morrison - Toni Morrison - Award-Winning Author Talks About the Future From Some Place in Time," *Diverse Online* (formerly *Black Issues In Higher Education*), Jun 17, 2007.

Chapter Four   The Discursive Body in Paradise, Love and Mercy

of social gender occurs in a series of intersections and interactions, and that the initiative function of women in history and reality shall be sought to supersede the simple and stalemated mode in which women are portrayed.

Parallel to Pilate and Beloved's deaths, at this stage of Morrison's novelistic creation, Consolata also embraces her death with composure in *Paradise*. There are at least two significances of Consolata's death. Firstly, different from the previous two individual black women whose deaths only help one family member achieve their selves (in the case of Pilate, that is Milkman; in the case of Beloved, that is Sethe), Consolata's death is far more beneficial: by posing the profound question of the meaning of life (Wang Gang 115), it is a salvation of several other black women, or a sacrifice to the awakening of the community of black women. Secondly, as a white woman, Consolata's death is even more connotative than the two black females of Pilate and Beloved; it in some way symbolizes the long-yearned unity of the white and the black and the prospect of reciprocal relationship between sexes, which is also the wish of Morrison in her later years of literary creation as well as modern feminists like Beauvoir who hoped so after retrieving the loss of matriarchy,

> These facts have led to the supposition that in primitive times a veritable reign of women existed: the matriarchy. It was this hypothesis, proposed by Bachofen, that Engels adopted, regarding the passage from the matriarchate to the patriarchate as "the great historical defeat of the feminine sex". But in truth that Golden Age of Woman is only a myth. To say that woman was the Other is to say that there did not exist between the sexes a reciprocal relation: Earth, Mother, Goddess–she was no fellow creature in man's eyes; it was beyond the human realm that her power was affirmed, and she was therefore the outside of that realm. Society has always been male; political power has always been in the hands of men. (Beauvoir, 1997:102)

Not coincidentally, such an effort that transcends race and sex paves the way for humankind's ultimate realization of self, which overlaps "androgyny"[1] as concurred with by some feminists. To understand black women's Dasein, it is imperative to know that on the one hand, black women exist in their relationship with nature, but more in their relationship with the society and their daily contacts with other people. It is their interactions with the other people, i.e. their daily practical activities, grants them opportunities to acquire self-transcendence with their perception.

Luce Irigary, when criticizing Hegel for his exclusion of women in constructing his theory of absolute spirit, points out that the possible sole solution to the reconciliation between objective spirit and absolute spirit is to reconsider the concept of gender, different genders and the ethical relationship between different genders. (Irigary, 1993: 141-142). To Irigary, the reconsideration of the concept of gender means that gender shall not be limited to its biological sense. As for the relationship between different genders, it entails transcendence over the gap of communication between different genders, which is partially realized in the transcendence over individual body in the community of black women, like what is elaborated in this section.

An example of such transcendence in the practical relationships with others and his/her self is embodied in the blacksmith in *Mercy*, as agreed in the following remark,

---

[1] Androgyny refers to the combination of masculine and feminine characteristics. This may be as in fashion, sexual identity, or sexual lifestyle, or it may refer to biologically inter-sexed physicality, especially with regard to plants and human sexuality. An alternative to androgyny is gender-role transcendence, the view that when an individual's competence is at issue, it should be conceptualized on a personal basis rather than on the basis of masculinity, femininity, or androgyny. Some existential feminists like Virginia Woolf (1882—1941) welcome the second point as it is anti-essentialist.

Chapter Four   The Discursive Body in Paradise, Love and Mercy

> As a free black, the blacksmith seems to be the only one who can fully control his body and soul. Just like in a fable, the blacksmith's occupation requires him to forge, mold, mend others' souls and be a man who can reveal the truth and awaken the humanity of the enslaved. (Wang and Wu, 2009: 43)

In transcending "individual body" in the community of black women, the discursive function of body plays an indispensable role, which in the postmodern sense, undermines the hegemony of grand narratives or meta-narratives legitimized in modernism and criticized by Lyotard. Likewise, Lyotard's postmodern theories reevaluate the legitimacy of knowledge and status of intellectuals to dissolve the generality and totalitarianism. The objective truths of "sagas", or "salvation" in patriarchal society described by grand narratives are no longer adored, only little narratives are plausible in the secular world of postmodernism and potentiated to endow the humankind with new meanings and values.

Besides the convent women in *Paradise*, Heed and Christine in *Love*, Florens's guidance of her consciousness to her self through her body writing in *Mercy* can be labeled as self-recognition, and turns object into subject through her introspection. In such introspection, Florens is constructing her self in a sense. As a subject of growth, Florens embodies her unique characters as a conscious existence or driven by her unique self. The realization of her unique independence transcends the mirror-like reflection of her surroundings and encounters, or even the objective realization of self that has been influenced by the surroundings or encounters.

> The sense of the gesture is not given, but understood, that is, seized upon by an act on the spectator's part. ...The communication or comprehension of gestures comes about through the reciprocity of my intentions and the gestures of others, of my gestures and intentions

discernible in the conduct of other people. It is as if the other person's intention inhabited my body and mine his. (Merleau-Ponty, 1962: 185)

Though diachroneity is lacking in Merleau-Ponty's "reciprocity", considering such "reciprocity" in the bodily interactions among people, if the above black women are taken as a whole, their body can be understood as the "reciprocal body" in that the actions made by their body make sense and are taken either by themselves or by others. What's more, the meaning of their body receives varied feedbacks from the others in the process of reciprocation, and hints that an individual shall never alienate himself/herself from their black community for any reason since his/her self-quest or self-realization has never been independent, but closely connected with the community where she/he harbors. Nor is such self-quest or self-realization separable from the black history, for the past, inclusive of both Africa and the old South of American continent under Morrison's pen, is the gem of black culture and the shelter for their souls.

Chapter Five

The Construction of Self in Black Women's Body

To some extent, Heidegger's late thoughts, Habermas's intercommunicative theory and Gadmer's philosophical hermeneutics all contributed to the "linguistic turn". Due to their dialogic and communicational qualities, their theories break through the limitations of the nature of individuality for humankind and their subjectivity, and shifts instead to their relationships, communication and interactions. This not only provides innovative perspectives and significant contents for humankind's life-subject, but reveals the all-roundness of their existence in the process of real life and history.

As to black women's self-construction, transcendence over their body, regardless of their physical states, is a representation of the construction of axiological subject. Regarding the transformation from "being-in-itself" to "being-for-itself", the construction of axiological self comprises three stages throughout Morrison's novels: static construction of "ontic" self, which is finished based on the individualized black woman; dynamic construction of "phenomenal" self, which is finite on the basis of the individuality of black woman; spiral construction of "reciprocal" self which is grounded on the community of black women.

5.1 Static construction of "ontic" self vs. "finished" self

In Morrison's early three novels, the judgment of black women from the substantial ontological perspective is stifling, for it deceives black women into believing that the separate self must be antithetical, representative of simply defined polarities of good and evil. Dualism is a logical mode behind the marginalized groups who are constructed as the Other, which in many feminists' eyes, is notorious for being viewed as an endless abstract domain contending for the dominance over the Other.

In *Bluest*, Pecola defines her world in terms of gender antithesis: the perfect, blond, blue-eyed, much-beloved Shirley Temple versus the ugly, un-blue-eyed, much-despised Pecola herself. Intoxicated by her fancy of possessing a pair of blue eyes, she is victimized in such deadly antithesis. Nel's tragedy in *Sula* is also a product of her determinedly dualistic view: she sees her subordination to her husband Jude as an inseparable part of her self until this blind belief is crucially torn apart by her discovery of her husband Jude's infidelity with her best friend, Sula, a purportedly dissolute woman. At that moment, Nel, for the first time in her life, is forced to define a self on her own. Only near the end of the novel is she required to question her tidy morality and finally to recognize all that she has deprived herself of by choosing not to be Nel but rather Sula.

So, if, under the impact of Sula's audacity, Nel's awakening is black women's self-construction in embryo, Pilate in *Solomon* pushes such construction into more profound dualistic thinking. In her presentation of Milkman's quest, she

Chapter Five   The Construction of Self in Black Women's Body

begins to suggest that the trap of dualism is not inescapable. Milkman spends his first thirty years of life in a void, like Nel's. Though he tries to choose between good and evil (represented by his mother Ruth and his father), or between order and disorder (represented by his father and his aunt Pilate), he just fails. Only when he labors in his quest does he gradually come to realize that the lines he has so darkly drawn between perceived dualities have not helped but hindered him in his research for identity. In the novel's final paragraph, when life and death, victory and surrender all merge, Milkman truly triumphs.

To black women, to "transcend" is to surpass their racial features, as the ontic self is primarily limited to their racial features. From the subordinate Other to an independent self, women with a "finished" self are born in the historical movement. In *The Second Sex*, Beauvoir remarked that when one declared to have transformed from the state of essence into that of existence, she/he had acquired true morality, and that such transformation shall be maintained with his/her constant alertness. "The true problem for woman is to reject these flights from reality and seek self-fulfillment in transcendence. The thing to do then, is to see what possibilities are opened up for her through what are called the virile and the feminine attitudes." (Beauvoir, 1997:83)

However, the self in the process of construction from the objectification of Pecola to Sula's recognition of her existence then to Pilate's unshackling the status of the Other is regarded as static. The loss of, quest for, and acquirement of their subjectivity of these three types of women along the way mainly relies on their own knowledge of their gendered bodies. Such a construction is virtually free from interaction with other people, men especially. However, this, for the most part, is still categorized as the existence of "being-in-itself", a long way to go before realizing the existence of "being-for-itself" except when it is momentarily realized in Pilate's ultimate salvation of Milkman.

In fact, there is an ontological meaning attached to black women's body, since their skin color and curled hair, except for their rather slow physical evolution, are much unlikely to be changed within a visible period of time, in which sense, black women's self is inextricably chained to the unchangeable physical features they are born with. In the three stories exhibited in Pecola, Sula and Pilate, such a self, though completed temporarily in the first three females, is only a static one, concerned merely with the recognition of their external black bodies. In other words, the finished self in Pilate is still an ontic one, which is related to the entities, or the undeniable racial features of the black women.

Even in feminist theology, Rosemary Radford Ruether, a feminist theologian suggests that Christianity[1] embodies a dualistic world view that leads to authoritarianism and sexism[2] which is also one root of black women's nightmarish sufferings, as is illustrated in the following,

> All the basic dualities–the alienation of the mind from the body; the alienation of the subjective self from the objective world; the subjective retreat of the individual, alienated from the social community; the domination or rejection of nature by spirit–these all have roots in the apocalyptic-Platonic religious heritage of classical Christianity. ... from the feminine is the primary sexual symbolism that sums up all these alienations. The psychic traits of intellectuality, transcendent spirit, and autonomous will that were identified with the male left the woman with the contrary traits of bodiliness, sensuality, and subjugation. (Ruether 44)

Ruether argues that male subjugation of the female is "the primary psychic model for…oppressor-oppressed relationships between social classes, races and nations" (Ruether 46). For black women who are afflicted with sexism as well as

---

[1] In feminist theology, Christianity is taken as "the heir of both classical Neo-Platonism and apocalyptic Judaism."
[2] Sexism is a disapproving word, referring to the idea or belief that the members of one sex are less intelligent, able, skilful, etc. than the members of the other sex, esp. that women are less able than men, and that particular jobs and activities are suitable for women and others are suitable for men.

Chapter Five The Construction of Self in Black Women's Body

racism, the projection of the Other–easily adaptable to national, racial and class differences–has basically and primordially been directed against women.

As a result of the projection of the Other, the self based on black women's "ontic body" can well be regarded as "ontic" self, which while resting mainly on biological determinism and tragically restrained by the absence of liberty, is rather static and limited. When the basic living state of a single black woman with limited subject is outlined in a static mode without touching on the temporal dimension of her life or without relating to the profound contradictions implicated in the finitude of the woman from the perspective of history, the actual life of hers is destined to be limited in essence.

"Neither body nor existence can be regarded as the origin of the human being, since they presuppose each other, and because the body is solidified or generalized existence, and existence a perpetual incarnation." (Merleau-Ponty, 1962: 166) To Merleau-Ponty, body and existence are an inalienable integrity; the essence of the humankind can not be reduced to any isolation of body from existence or of existence from body. "…the body expresses total existence, not because it is an external accompaniment to that existence, but because existence comes into its own in the body." (Merleau-Ponty, 1962: 166) Without the incarnation of existence in the secular world, self that is primarily based on the bodily features can only be static and much limited.

Therefore, to retain their existence, a certain transcendence is pressing for black women. In the contradiction between the limitedness of black women and their ideals for equality and liberty, transcendence as a possibility of existence is born. Surely, in such transcendence from the state of essence to that of existence, "being-for-itself" is transcendent, creative and towards the future while "being-in-itself" is specific, accidental, subjective self which is internalized without any possibility of change and growth. As a reified substance, "being-in-itself" is formed under the meditative look of "being-for-itself" or the supervision of other consciousness.

To such transcendence, Beauvoir admits women's physical weakness by saying, "Woman is weaker than man; she has less muscular strength, fewer red blood corpuscles, less lung capacity; she runs more slowly, can lift less heavy weights, can compete with man in hardly any sport; she cannot stand up to him in a fight. "(Beauvoir, 1997:34) Yet, she also refutes that "…in fact, when a woman does a task worthy of the effort of a 'human being', she can well be as active, efficient, cautious and restrained as men." (Beauvoir, 1997:391)

That may well justify why in *Solomon*, the falling death of Pilate at the gunshot of Guitar is of critical significance. To a large extent, Pilate's death is a turning point of black women's construction of self. According to Levinas, "bodily feeling is composed of the five basic senses, or the primary information. Our possession of body merges in the conglomeration of multiple experience and cognition. I am my pain, my breath, my organ; what I possess is more than a body and I myself am a body." (Levinas 86-87) To Levinas, body should be regarded as the way humankind exist and posit himself/herself rather than an existent, and it is in the actions of body that humankind accomplishes his/her existence at large.

Despite the corporeal helplessness when rivaled by Guitar's gun in the chaotic wrestling in the cave, Pilate's physical action of falling and her resultant death in the arms of Milkman achieves a lived form of transcendence, which on the one hand finishes Pilate's construction of self, and on the other hand signifies the unended construction of black women's self, even if in men.

5.2 Dynamic construction of "phenomenal" self vs. "finite" self

Instead of racial or gender concerns, Morrison's middle three novels explore black women's body from the perspectives of physical space, spiritual space, and social space, i.e. black women are viewed as a multi-level conglomerate of body

Chapter Five The Construction of Self in Black Women's Body

and non-body activities in the secular world.

In *Tar*, a story of temptation, entrapment, and failed redemption, Morrison attacked dualism as it had pieced together her first three novels on every front. Centering around the afflicting obsession of ghost as a result of infanticide, *Beloved* launches a spiritual exploration of the restored self intrinsically tied to the horrors of slavery after the American Civil War. In *Jazz*, Morrison probed the tension between a culturally-imposed collective and a socially-constructed individualized identity and explored how these opposing and potentially destructive forces are reconciled with each other.

In these three books, the three black women of Jadine, Sethe, Violet undergo successively the interaction of bodies with their selves, which is though invisible yet perceptible either by the senses or through immediate experience and casts constructive meaning on each. So the self achieved in the process may well be understood as a "dynamic" one, though it still has its limitations, which lies in its individuality of black women. In other words, the self that black women have always been attempting to construct should be collective before it is ultimately accomplished. Due to the individuality of subject, the achievement of self is still finite.

Despite the relay of life in both the individualism and the individuality of black women (for the former, see Pecola, Sula, Pilate and for the latter, see Jadine, Sethe, Violet), one of Morrison's first six novels' intentions is still upon the sense of community. Positive or negative, those black women exist behind the white boundary that has tried to define them through phallogocentrism and transcend it with the help of their bodies. Nevertheless, those women are limited by their scattered living. Aware of that, Morrison, despite her interest in notions of community, solidarity and ancestry, and the history among them, she shifts her novels frequently into these areas through examples of displacement and disunity before moving towards endorsement of communal values. The deliberation of this technique is detectable from her essay "City Limits, Village Values: Concepts of the Neighborhood in Black Fiction" where she argues:

> While individualism and escape from the community was frequently a major theme in Black writing, it should be regarded for what it was: A devotion to self-assertion can be a devotion to discovering distinctive ways of expressing community values, social purpose, mutual regard or... affirming a collective experience. (Jaye and Watts, 38)

Closely related to disadvantages of the individuality of black women's self, Beauvoir once condemned women for being the accomplices of permitting themselves to be defined as the Other. She further gave its reason of women's living situation being scattered, i.e. they have never (now, of course, the situation is somewhat improved) been united as subjects or "us" (Donovan 173). However, such individuality in self-construction is resolutely reversed in Morrison's three novels of *Paradise, Love, Mercy*, in which the sense of community and collective growth of black women are explicitly delineated.

Opposed to "ontic" self which is concerned with entity or physical determinism in the sphere of black women study, "phenomenal" self refers to self which is born in phenomena and "perceptible by the senses or through immediate experience" (*The Oxford American College Dictionary*, P1023). For black women, their "phenomenal" self rests mainly of the layer of living experience through which other people and things are first given to them, or the system "Self-others-things" (coined by Merleau-Ponty, 1962: 57) as it comes into being rather than the reception of black women's physical features.

> The abstract movement carves out within that plenum of the world in which concrete movement took place a zone of reflection and subjectivity; it superimposes upon physical space a potential or human space. Concrete movement is therefore centripetal whereas abstract movement is centrifugal.

Chapter Five   The Construction of Self in Black Women's Body

The former occurs in the realm of being or of the actual, the latter on the other hand in that of the possible or the non-existent; the first adheres to a given background, the second throws out is own background. (Merleau-Ponty, 1962:111)

Extensively, modern society seems to be faced with a historical paradox: the external loss of subject co-exists with the internal seclusion of the subject. On the one hand, the expansion of commodity economy and technical autocracy accelerates the process of their reification; On the other hand, the infiltration of various life-and-death competitions, power and money in social life widens the psychological distance among subjects, which aggravates the estrangement of modern people and leads individuals to seclusion. Under these circumstances, if the lost subjectivity of individuals is redeemed by existentialists, then late philosophers like Wittgenstein[1], Levinas, Habermas, etc. will reject such secluded self from different perspectives.

Along with their life practice, black women's intersubjectivity gradually takes shape and makes up the content of their spatial existence. As it is, from black women's individual subject to their intersubjectivity, the first thing they encounter is the secular world where they contact and form relationships with others. Their mutual understanding, communication and adaptation are the prerequisites for the working of the living world. And the living world, while harboring humankind's self, offers possibilities for the embodiment of subjectivity: only when one's

---

[1] As an Austrian-British philosopher who worked primarily in logic, the philosophies of mathematics, of mind, and of language, Ludwig Wittgenstein's philosophy is often divided between his early period, exemplified by the *Tractatus*, and later period, articulated in the *Philosophical Investigations*. The early Wittgenstein was concerned with the logical relationship between propositions and the world, believing that by providing an account of the logic underlying this relationship he had solved all philosophical problems. The later Wittgenstein rejected many of the conclusions of the *Tractatus*, arguing that the meaning of words is constituted by the function they perform within any given language-game. Wittgenstein's influence has been felt in nearly every field of the humanities and social sciences, yet there are widely diverging interpretations of his thought.

subject is no longer faced with a strange and alien world, can she/he achieve true self-realization. So, it's improper to regard inter-subjective existence as the loss of subject.

> It is never our objective body that we move, but our phenomenal body, and there is no mystery in that, since our body, as the potentiality of this or that part of the world, surges towards objects to be grasped and perceives them. (Merleau-Ponty, 1962:106)

According to Merleau-Ponty, the body in motion is not the "objective" body but the "phenomenal" body which is intelligible and potential. So, with black women's bodies in motion, their secluded selves bound by "ontic" selves are transcended and become "phenomenal" ones. Moreover, as inter-subjective relationship is both intrinsic and extrinsic, its intrinsicality implies the necessity of transcending secluded self and moving from subject to inter-subject. For the extrinsicality of inter-subjective relationship, it requires the endorsement of the significance of existence by the subject so as to avoid the dissolution of self in such relationship. It should be noticed that mere adherence to the externality of inter-subjective relationship usually lead to self-centeredness, and the one-sided emphasis on the internality is very prone to the alienation of subject. To reconcile the two qualities of inter-subjective relationship, the recognition of the subject's value of each other is imperative, which in practice is embodied in mutual understanding, mutual communication and respect towards each other.

To black women, with the historical leap from subject to inter-subject, such dynamic construction of "phenomenal" self can well be deemed as the crucial transition from "being-in-itself" to "being-for-itself". They become conscious of what they hope for and how they shall work for that aim. Without spatial movement, an individual's dialogic relationships with other people can hardly be established, and she/he will be deprived of her/his social quality. Conversely, with inter-subjective relationship with the outside world realized in her/his moving body, her/his subjectivity, logically related intersubjectivity, is reinforced by the latter.

To sum up, in the middle stage of Morrison's novels, black women, though quite well on their ways to inter-subjective communication, their motile-body-based "phenomenal" selves are still confined to individuals, which needs to be further transcended in Morrison's late novelistic stage where a spiral construction of infinite, reciprocal self is accomplished.

5.3 Spiral construction of "reciprocal" self vs. "infinite" self

With regard to black women's body in Morrison's late three novels, the antithetic dualism that despises women as the Other is transcended. To banish it, the only way out is to supersede it with an unhierarchized concept of difference[1], which transcends their "colonized" identity and the adoption of a "pure" identity of women. For this, Alice Echols contends that whether feminism must transcend sex or testify the female qualities has become a new gap in the field of feminist theories.[2] To her, such dualism is a false proposition and needs revision; it should incorporate factors of transcendence and endorsement.

In *Paradise*, gender quality and assimilation are what Morrison always

---

[1] Plumwood Note: In both sense of predictive and propositional logics, dualism shall be regarded as a rather particular division or dichotomy: in the sense of predicative logic, dualism and extreme exclusion signifies the maximum of non-common features; in the sense of propositional sense, dualism signifies a very peculiar negation or the notion of the Other. A solution to the predicament of dualism is the replacement of it with an unhierarchized concept of difference. From Val Plumwood's *Feminism and the Mastery of Nature*, 1993 trans. By Ma Tianjie and Li Liyi, Chongqing Publishing Group, 2007. p45-50.

[2] Echols, Alice, Daring to be Bad: Radical Feminism in America 1967-1975, Minneapolis, MN: University of Minnesota Press, 1989.

intends to achieve. From their exclusion to assimilation by the black men and the white, the living state of the group of convent women is drawn in the little narratives of their body drawing in the basement. So is true with *Love* where Heed and Christine, after years of their "cold war", break their deadlock through their reticent bodies hint, and with *Mercy* which by portraying how the black girl of Florence, despite her identity as a slave, obtains her psychological liberty through her body writing out of her entanglement with the blacksmith. Considering the publishing years of those three books almost at the turn of the twenty-first century, the advocacy of difference and multiplicity, opposition to hegemonic discourse are the real connotations of "the end of subject" in post-modernism.

The deconstruction of subject in post-modernism is to dissolve the rule of hegemonic culture by restoring in the society true liberty and social justice. The latter point can be referred to the theory of "field equality" of John Rawls[1], which can help base the interpretation of equality on the natural qualities of the entire humankind. Provided a circle is drawn on a piece of paper, all the dots within the circle (which is what the "field" covers), despite their varied distances to the center of the circle, possess the quality of being inside the circle and hence with equality. (Singer 19)

Supposing in Rawls's theory of "field equality", the circle center signifies phallogocentrism and each dot stands for an individual black woman, then the collection of the dots, signifying the women living in the community in *Love* and *Mercy*, regardless of their varied distances towards the circle center, are "identical" and share the equality of being in the circle.

---

[1] John Rawls (1921—2002), was an American political philosopher in the liberal tradition. His first book, *A Theory of Justice* (1971) revitalized the social-contract tradition, using it to articulate and defend a detailed vision of egalitarian liberalism. In the book, his theory of justice as fairness envisions a society of free citizens holding equal basic rights cooperating within an egalitarian economic system His *Political Liberalism* (1993) addresses the legitimate use of political power in a democracy, aiming to show how enduring unity may be achieved despite the diversity of worldviews that free institutions allow.

Chapter Five   The Construction of Self in Black Women's Body

> Morrison is suggesting a vision that has been evidenced throughout the writings of black women, an awareness that culture and religion collaborate in creating worlds and selves. Religious faith provides a framework and structure, while cultural forms allow for variation and diversity. (Connor 181)

As a matter of fact, besides black women, there are still poor laboring women, and colored women, who have been concerned about in feminist theories, which is a beneficial extension of the focus of white middle-class heterosexual women in the first two waves of feminism. The complexity and multiplicity of the current feminist experience is amended by the third-wave feminism that tolerates the differences in race, nationality, class, sexual tendency, as well as the internal differences within the female groups and their uniqueness in history and culture. This may be an inheritance of Beauvoir, who proposed,

> I shall pose the problem of feminine destiny quite otherwise: I shall place woman in a world of values and give her behavior a dimension of liberty. I believe that she has the power to choose between the assertion of her transcendence and her alienation as object; she is not the plaything of contradictory drives; she devises solutions of diverse values in the ethical scale. …to be a woman would mean to be the object, the other–and the other nevertheless remains subject in the midst of her resignation. (Beauvoir, 1997:82-83)

Noticeably, from *Mercy* onwards, the construction of self is "spiral" in two ways: one is the "retrogressive" time of 1680 in which the story is set; the other is the "renewed" construction of self against the historical background of "re-enslavement" in *Mercy*. Such a spiral itinerary conforms with the construction of "absolute self" proposed by Fichte[1], which is the absolute unification of subject and object. It is neither experienced self nor transcendental self, but the transcendental element of all self-consciousness that exhibits absolute freedom and unity. Such self-consciousness provides transcendental basis for all knowledge and experiential substantiality. Fichte's "absolute self" merges theoretical reason with practical reason, and grants a considerably high status to self with possibilities of creative actions.

The spiral construction of "reciprocal" self in Morrison's late novels exemplify the fact that humankind is, by nature, an existence in practice, which determines that their existence per se is immanently unfixed, historical and generative, and that the world they live in can be nothing but unfinished, fluid and open as well. (Zhu Liyuan, 2006:108) The syncretism of the two aspects can well be comprehended in the construction of self.

Ever since the death of Pilate after the completion of black women's static construction of "ontic" self, the axiological perspective of self, as a general category of relation, is already under way. When reciprocity of self unveils in their life in Morrison's late novel, black women shall be viewed as an issue of "how" and evaluated in the process of changes and development towards the future. The construction of axiological self is a developing, generative process featuring equality, liberty and transcendence, which embraces different values, forces, sexual tendencies and skin colors and integrates black women's multiple

---

[1] As a German philosopher, Johann Gottlieb Fichte (1762—1814) is often perceived as a figure whose philosophy forms a bridge between the ideas of Kant and those of the German Idealist Hegel. Recently, philosophers and scholars have begun to appreciate Fichte as an important philosopher in his own right due to his original insights into the nature of self-consciousness or self-awareness. Fichte did not endorse Kant's argument for the existence of "things in themselves", the supra-sensible reality beyond the categories of human reason and saw the rigorous and systematic separation of "things in themselves" (noumena) and things "as they appear to us" (phenomena) as an invitation to skepticism. He made the radical suggestion that we should throw out the notion of a noumenal world and instead accept the fact that consciousness does not have a grounding in a so-called "real world". In fact, Fichte achieved fame for originating the argument that consciousness is not grounded in anything outside of itself.

Chapter Five The Construction of Self in Black Women's Body

identities of humans, females as well as their dark skins. "...everything in man is contingency in the sense that this human manner of existence is not guaranteed to every human child through some essence acquired at birth, and in the sense that it must be constantly reforged in him through the hazards encountered by the objective body. Man is a historical idea and not a natural species." (Merleau-Ponty, 1962: 170))

In such a historical process of human child's growth, released in the transformation from "being-in-itself" to "being-for-itself" is liberty, which translates substantial ontology into relation-based ontology, i.e. a new ontology that is based on equal and dialogic relations. In fact, between these two stages of self-recognition, there is a middle area: consciousness of self, i.e. the consciousness of the situation of "being-in-itself", which, just the same as "being-for-itself", has a nature of liberty. The difference is that while the former represents epistemological liberty of consciousness, the latter emphasizes humankind's free will of actions. To Beauvoir, each person is the source of his or her own meaning; to obtain consciousness of self is to realize that one is both object of the world and subject that can endow himself or herself with meaning. In a word, self-consciousness is an organic mix of object and subject in him or her. That's also why Kant declares that liberty is the ultimate definition of humankind's nature, and the paramount value of man as an existence of subject. Merleau-Ponty also revealed the quality of value assumed in the presentation of "empirical" self rather than "phenomenal" self, which is a transitional stage between "phenomenal" self and "reciprocal" self. "Starting from the spectacle of the world, ...it looks for the conditions which make possible this unique world presented to a number of empirical selves, and finds it in a transcendental ego in which they participate without dividing it up, because it is not a being, but a unity or a value." (Merleau-Ponty, 1962: 62)

To Marx, liberty displays the supreme human relationship, or the unification between subject and object. Marx once described the overall development of free personality in this way, "Such communism equals humanism as accomplished naturalism, and equals naturalism as accomplished humanism. It is the real solution to the contradiction between man and nature, between man and man, the real solution to the struggle between existence and nature, between objectification and self-confirmation, between liberty and necessity, between an individual and the category. It is the key to historical myth." (Marx 81)

Still in *Phenomenology of Perception*, Merleau-Ponty set aside a chapter expatiating freedom deduced from the intersubjectivity among humans. He rejects the envisaging of one's existence (or Dasein in Heidegger's terms) as absolute contact with oneself or as an absolute density with no internal fault, but instead, as "of subjectivities by each other in the generality of a single nature, the cohesion of an intersubjective life and a world". (Merleau-Ponty, 1962: 452) Therefore, to Merleau-Ponty, (t)he present mediates between the for oneself and the for others, between individuality and generality.

> I must apprehend myself immediately as centered in a way outside myself, and my individual existence must diffuse round itself, so to speak, an existence in quality. The for-themselves–me for myself and the other for himself–must stand out against a background of for Others–I for the other hand and the other for me. My life must have a significance which I do not constitute; there must strictly speaking be an intersubjectivity; each one of us must be both anonymous in the sense of absolutely individual, and anonymous in the sense of absolutely general. Our being in the world, is the concrete bearer of this double anonymity. (Merleau-Ponty, 1962: 448)

He even redefines "reflection" with emphasis on the intervention of intersubjectivity in the following remark, "True reflection presents me to myself not as idle and inaccessible subjectivity, but as identical with my presence in the world and to others, as I am now realizing it: I am all that I see, I am an inter-subjective field, not despite my body and historical situation, but, on the contrary, by being this body and this situation, and through them, all the rest." (Merleau-Ponty, 1962: 452)

With freedom being released in the transcendence over body and construction of finite self, humankind has become potentially capable of pursuing the infinite. However, the unifying process of finitude and infinitude consists in humankind's practical activities as held by Marx afore. That is one of the exact connotations of the "re-enslavement" in *Mercy* on black women's itinerary of self-pursuit.

Conclusion

After retrieving the philosophical concepts of self and body and the inalienable "kindred" between them, the paper reevaluates the philosophical evolution of "ontology" from the period of "ontic" self, to "phenomenal" self, and to "reciprocal" self. During this long historical period, self has undergone roughly two major periods: one of "substantial" subject and one of "non-substantial" subject. In such historical transformation, body plays a pivotal role, which assists the construction of the axiological self in the community of black women.

Toni Morrison as a Nobel Prize winner, has produced a multitude of women characters in her works. As early as Morrison's creation of her first novel *Bluest* in 1970, she has already mentioned that her writing of the novel is to display to the world "how to have an integrated existence in the world where everyone is hurt to varying extents" (Bakerman 60). Such existentialist perspective of self

Conclusion

conforms to the non-substantial principle[1]. This move, by shifting the exploration of ontology from the prescriptions of self to the value and meanings of it in the historical context, from the descriptive language of self to the axiological judgments of self, achieves the purpose of entering and transforming human life and makes preparations for the human liberation.

Based on the historical needs of humankind, the dissertation proposes that axiology, while pertaining to the meanings of the real world and the ideal state, entails common criteria of judgment and certain orientation of value and influences the evolution of culture. It is the correlative principle of value that constitutes the value system of culture. In the historical development, traditional Chinese culture, through prescribing the relationships between Heaven and man, community and self, justice and benefit, reason and desire, unveils its axiology in the blended schools of Confucianism, Taoism, Mohism[2], Legalism[3], Buddism, which, predominated by some schools of value, are characterized by

---

[1] There are two basic tenets of modern ontology: the tenet of rationality and the tenet of non-substantiality. The former refers to the rational evaluation of humankind's behaviors and the results from the perspective of their purpose. Moreover, they emphasize the effectiveness, legality, and validity of ontological prescriptions. The latter requires that the way of raising questions about ontology should be changed. In other words, the question should be transformed from "what substantia is" to "what substantia should be" (here "substantia" is a Latin word, which derives from the Greek word "ousia" and equals "to be" in English. It is the core of ontology), from the thinking mode of objects to that of reflection, and from the concern about the prime state of ontology to the axiological connotations of ontology and their prescriptive functions on humankind's activities.

[2] Mohism was a Chinese philosophy, developed by the followers of Mozi, and is best known for the concept of "impartial love" or "universal love". It evolved at the same time as Confucianism, Taoism and Legalism, and was one of the four main philosophical schools during the Spring and Autumn Period (from 770BC to 480BC) and the Warring States Period (from 479BC to 221BC).

[3] In contrast to Taoism's intuitive anarchy, and Confucianism' s benevolence, Legalism is a classical Chinese philosophy that emphasizes the need for order above all other human concerns. The political doctrine developed during the brutal years of the Fourth century BC. To the Legalists, attempts to improve the human situation by noble example, education, and ethical precepts were useless. Instead, the people needed a strong government and a carefully devised code of law, along with a policing force that would stringently and impartially enforce these rules and punish harshly even the most minor infractions.

perceptual experience of body (Xu Zong), dynamic balance of contradiction and supplementation as well as orientation of multiple values[1].

As for the relations between individuals and their community, similar to Habermas's intersubjectivity, Confucianism in Chinese philosophy holds that humankind can only develop to the full in interpersonal relationships. (Feng Youlan 68) Moreover, just like Aristotle, Mencius also conceives that humans are "political animals", and that all their ethical relations could only be developed in their country and society. So, in a sense, Confucianism is the embodiment of intersubjectivity in Chinese philosophy.

If the understanding between subjects involves the principle of reason, then the mutual respect for and affirmation of each other's value and meaning of existence embodies the principle of humanity. Evidently, an appropriate positioning of inter-subjective relationship unfolds, in essence, as a unified historical process of reason and humanity, which on the one hand, internalizes the pursuit of truth, the tendency for good, and the orientation towards beauty in the inter-subjective contacts in the living world, on the other restrains the encroachment on the inter-subjective relationships by power and capitalist commodity relations and free the subjects from degradation.

Regarding the importance of communication and in this epoch of fierce tension, the Pope of John Paul II accounted the tolerance and love in the larger sense as follows: in the shift from violence to peace, from conflict to tolerance and coordination, power is conducted through edification and justice is ultimately achieved through love.[2]

All this considered, the author reckons that to black women, their construction of self falls under the category of axiology, which is a beneficial

---

[1] It is widely acknowledged that traditional Chinese culture is characterized by precedence of human relations over nature, precedence of community over individuals, precedence of justice over advantage, precedence of doctrines over instruments.

[2] John Paul II, "Address at Puebla" Origins, VIII(N. 34, 1979), I, 4 and II, 41-46.

approach of reunderstanding black women's multi-factors-based complex self. As has been expatiated in the above chapters concerning Morrison's black women stories, the three consecutive stages of selves synthesize themselves into the overall notion of axiological self. Since humankind's existence is uncertain, historic and generative in social practice, their nature is not a preconditioned, static or solidified entity and the world they live in is unfinished, floating and open, too. In this case, black women's construction of axiological self must break through the simplified epistemological dualism of subject/object and delve into their social activities, which will help them maintain their difference, turn them to "being-for-itself " from "being-in-itself ", and approach them to liberty in the infinite state of generation. Predictably, in the integrated existence of humankind and the world, the existential meanings of the world are unveiled, which in turn embodies humankind's transcendence and infinitude in the perennially spiral process of development.

In African culture that adores the family, community, an individual can interpret the world with his/her life and capacity to shoulder responsibilities. Rather than being degraded to the status of objects in isolation and opposition, the Africans, black women included, are more willing to have their body viewed as the place where their contents of character are acutely felt and their mode of living and behaviors as existents are comprehended. With their inherent yearning for open-minded communication with the outside world, they are especially eager to be generous and share with the world their fruits of civilization, just like people from other nationalities.

Extensively speaking, the entire humankind on the earth descends from and sharing and worshiping one self, especially the self of supreme goodness or "mercy" as hinted by Morrison. Covering the transcendent values of freedom, love and harmony, these virtues are created and shared in their life practice. When all cultures share the goodness in their associations with each other, the complementarity serves the tenet of relationship in the sharing process of different cultures. Being a social existence, an individual's life can rely not solely on his/her own efforts, but on his/her communications with people from different cultures. In such cultural communications, one can not only see the elements of his/her own life, which are the basic modes of the key values, but also the more profound meanings of his/her daily life.

The inter-subjective and inter-cultural communications can help transcend each other's limitation and enrich themselves, which is the basic root and common goal of the humankind. Living in the contemporary epoch, increased communication and deepened cooperation as the completion will distance humankind from desperation and activate their infinite creativities preserved in their life experience. Yet, to realize it demands a true sharing that not only cares about the common needs but also the particular requirements of every individual.

Moreover, the three black women's deaths (specifically, Pilate, Beloved and Consolata), in other words, the disappearance of their bodies is significant to the living people around them. To Heidegger, existence towards death is the true state of Dasein, as death signifies the end of existence or non-being that can be measured by the standard of equality. It is actually the case in the novels, however, what Morrison concerns most is not the enlightenment of death to the living, but how blacks and even whites shall live their present life. Indeed, contrasted with unbiased equality before death, diverse opportunities of developments are embraced in living and it is in the continuation of self-affirmation that the formation and development of subjectivity acquires its practical basis.

The inter-subjective and inter-cultural communications can help transcend each other's limitations and enrich themselves, which is the basic root and common goal of the humankind. Living in the contemporary epoch, increased communication and deepened cooperation as the completion will distance humankind from desperation and activate their infinite creativities preserved in their life experience. Yet, to realize it demands a true sharing that not only cares about the common needs but also the particular requirements of every individual.

Moreover, the three black women's deaths (specifically, Pilate, Beloved and Consolata), in other words, the disappearance of their bodies is significant to the living people around them. To Heidegger, existence towards death is the true state of Dasein, as death signifies the end of existence or non-being that can be measured by the standard of equality. It is actually the case in the novels, however, what Morrison concerns most is not the enlightenment of death to the living, but how blacks and even whites shall live their present life. Indeed, contrasted with unbiased equality before death, diverse opportunities of developments are embraced in living and it is in the continuation of self-affirmation that the formation and development of subjectivity acquires its practical basis.

In the recent ten years or so, Morrison published her two newest novels, *Home* (2012) and *God Help the Child* (2012) consecutively. *Home*, just like the contradictory connotations in the title of *Mercy*, is "beautiful", "brutal" and "cumulatively powerful" (commented by *Publishers Weekly*), delineates with a moving tone about an apparently defeated man finding his manhood and his home. In the novel, Morrison extends her profound take on history with the twentieth-century tale of redemption: a taut and tortured story about how Frank Money, the psychically-damaged veteran's desperate search for his self in a world disfigured by war and rediscovery of his courage to undertake his responsibilities. In the light of the theme embodied in protagonist, *Home* can well be a sequel of *Mercy*, yet with a male protagonist, and an inheritance of *Solomon* against a changed temporal and spatial background.

Interrogating the war trauma in the new historical setting, *Home* still forms inter-textual discursive relationships at least with the former two novels of *Solomon*, *Beloved* and other novels of Morrison's as well. Via such dialogues among texts, Morrison's undying maneuver on the one hand testifies to the spiral construction of "reciprocal" self and on the other relays such a constructive process and matters in its own way in the world until in her last novel *God Help the Child*, published four years before her death, in which she rewrites a childhood trauma–the lost parental love of a young girl called "Bride" with blue-black skin abused by her light-skinned parents who are ashamed of her child. Bride grew up without love, tenderness, affection or apology in a world that group people by their skin color, and a world where the lighter one's skin is, the higher one might climb. Yet, fortunately, she finally reconstructs her self through communications with her boyfriend.

Taken as a whole, Morrison's existence aesthetics is based on the reconstruction of the meaning of individual life, focusing not on the essential thinking of "what is" but on the existential thinking of "how to live" and "how well the black women live". It advocates the generative pluralistic symbiosis dialectical mode of thinking based on the theory of inter-subjectivity. In addition, through the aesthetic examination of the death of black women, it reflects the transcendence of the body and the black women's pursuit of infinite and perfect life existence state as well as longing for the strong life intention to surpass themselves out of their dissatisfaction with the limited and imperfect living conditions. In this sense, Morrison's aesthetics of existence expresses man's conscious understanding of the nature of his own life in the form of fiction: not only for survival, but also for a kind of life value and meaning. Existence aesthetics is a requirement from existence to ideal as well as from the reality to the future. To a great extent, Morrison's last two works, *Home* and *God Help the Child*, reflect her broader aesthetic realm of existence, which transcends the limitations of individuals, nations, countries, ideology and historical reality, moving from a closed aesthetic sense of self-existence to an open and universal value of existence, i.e., from the basic microscopic state of existence criticism to the high dimensional perspective of the ultimate existence concept.

Works Cited

Primary Sources:

Morrison, Toni.

---. *The Bluest Eye*, New York: Alfred A. Knopf, 1993.

---. *Sula*, London: Vintage, 1998.

---. *Song of Solomon*, Knopf Doubleday Publishing Group, 2004.

---. *Tar Baby*, New York: Alfred A. Knopf, 1981.

---. *Beloved*, New York: Alfred A. Knopf, 1987.

---. *Jazz*, New York: Random House, 1992.

---. *Paradise*, London: Random House, 1998.

---. *Love*, London: Vintage, 2004.

---. *A Mercy*, New York: Random House, 2008.

References

[1]RUSHDY A. "Rememory: Primal Scenes and Constructions in Toni Morrison's Novels"[J]. Contemporary literature, 32:2. 1991.

[2]Bakerman, Jane S. "Failure of Love, Female Initiation in the Novels of Toni Morrison," American Literature, 1981.

[3]DE BEAUVOIR, S. A Very Easy Death[M]. New York: Pantheon, 1985.

[4]Beauvoir, Simone de. The Ethics of Ambiguity, Bernard Frechtman. Secaucus, NJ: Citadel Press. 1948.

[5]Beauvoir, Simone de. The Second Sex, Vintage, Random House, 1997.

[6]Bondi, L. and Davidson, J. Troubling the place of gender. In K. Anderson, M. Domosh, S. Pile and N. Thrift (eds), Handbook of Cultural Geography. London: Sage, 2003.

[7]Butler, Judith. Gender Trouble: Feminism and the Subversion of Identity, New York: Routledge, 1990.

[8]Butler, Judith. "Sexual Ideology and Phenomenological Description: A Feminist Critique of Merleau-Ponty's Phenomenology of Perception." from The Thinking Muse: Feminism and Modern French Philosophy. Edt. Jeffner

Allen and Iris Marion Young. Bloomington: Indiana University Press, 1989.

[9]Caruth, Cathy. Unclaimed Experience: Trauma, Narrative, and History. Baltimore: Maryland University Press, 1996.

[10]Christian, Babara. "The Contemporary Fables of Toni Morrison", in Black Women Novelists: The Development of a Tradition, 1892-1976, Barbara Christian ed.

[11]Christian, Barbara. Mcdowell, Deborah & Mckay, Nellie Y. "A Conversation on Toni Morrison's Beloved", Beloved: A Casebook, ed. William L., Andrews& Nellie Mckay. New York & Oxford: Oxford University Press, 1999.

[12]Cixous, Hélène. "Extreme Fidelity," in Writing Difference: Readings from the Seminar of Hélène Cixous. ed. Susan Seller. Milton Keynes: Open University Press. 1988.

[13]Cixous, Hélène. "Sorties," in New French Feminism. eds. Elaine Marks. Isabelle de Courtivron. New York: Schocken Books, 1981.

[14]Cixous, Hélène. "The Laugh of the Medusa," in New French Feminism: An Anthology, by Isabelle de Courtivon, Elaine Marks. Schoken Books, 1986.

[15]Connor, Kimberly Rae. Conversions and Visions: in the writing of African-American Women. Knoxville, The University of Tennessee Press, 1994.

[16]Connor, Marc C. The Aesthetics of Toni Morrison: Speaking the Unspeakable, University Press of Mississippi, 2000

[17]Daly, Mary. "After the Death of God the Father," Womanspirit Rising: A Feminist Reader in Religion. Edited by Carol P. Christ and Judith Plaskow. San Francisco: Harper & Row, 1979.

[18]Davis, Cynthia A. "Self, Society and Myth in Toni Morrison's Fiction," in Toni Morrison, Linden Peach, ed. New York: St. Martin's Press, 1998.

[19]Doreatha, Mbalia D, Morrison's Developing Consciousness. London: Associated University Press, 1991.

[20]Foucault, Michel. Language, Counter-Memory, Practice, edt. Bouchard, 1981.

[21] Fricker, Miranda and Hornsby, Jennifer edt., The Cambridge Companion to Feminism in Philosophy, Cambridge University Press, 2000.

[22] Frye, Marilyn, "In and Out of Harm's Way: Arrogance and Love," in The Politics of Reality: Essays in Feminist Theory, Trumansburg, NY: Crossing Press, 1983.

[23] Fuston-White, Jeanna. "The Construction of Subjectivity in Toni Morrison's Beloved", African American Review, Vol.36, Num. 3. Saint Louis University, 2002.

[24] Giddens, Anthony Modernity and Self-identity, Cambridge: Polity Press, 1991.

[25] Gilroy, Paul. The Black Atlantic. Modernity and Double Consciousness. London: Verso, 1993. King, Lovalerie. "Introduction: Baldwin and Morrison in Dialogue", from James Baldwin and Toni Morrison: Comparative Critical and Theoretical Essays edited by Lovalerie King and Lynn Orilla Scott, New York: Palgrave Macmillan, 2006.

[26] Guthrie-Taylor. Danielle. Conversations with Toni Morrison, Jackson: University of Mississippi Press, edt, 1994.

[27] Harvey, David. "Between Spaces and Time: Reflection on the Geographical Imagination", Annals of the Association of American Geography, 80 (3). 1990.

[28] Heidegger, Martin, Nietzsche, Volumes 3and 4, Harper, San Francisco, 1991.

[29] Henderson, Carol E. "Refiguring the Flesh: the World, the Body, and the Rituals of Being in Beloved and Go Tell It on the Mountain", selected from James Baldwin and Toni Morrison: Comparative Critical and Theoretical Essays edited by Lovalerie King and Lynn Orilla Scott, New York: Palgrave Macmillan, 2006.

[30] Hirsch. "Maternal Narratives: Cruel Enough to Stop the Blood", Toni Morrison: Critical Perspectives Past and Present, Gates Jr. and Appiah, eds. 1993.

[31] Hooks, Bell. Feminist Theory: From Margin to Center. Boston: South End Press, 1984.

[32] Hurston, Zora Neale. "Charateristics of Negro Expression", from The Sanctified Church. Berkley: Turtle Island Press, 1981.

[33] Irigary, Luce. "The Universal as Mediation", in Sexes and Genealogies. Gillian C. Gill. New York: Columbia University Press, 1993.

[34] Irigary, Luce. This Sex Which Is Not One, translated by Catherine Porter and Carolyn Burk trans. Ithaca: Cornell University Press, 1985.

[35] Jaye Michael C. and Ann C. Watts eds, Literature and the American Urban Experience: Essays on the City and Literature (Manchester: Manchester University Press, 1981.

[36] Jennifer Fitzgerald. "Selfhood and Community: Psychoanalysis and Discourse in Beloved" from Toni Morrison, Linden Peach, ed. New York: St. Martin's Press, 1998.

[37] Koenen, Anne. "The One Out of Sequence: An Interview with Toni Morrison", from History and Tradition in Afro-American Culture. Gunter H. Lenz. Ed. Frankfurt, Germany: Campus, 1984.

[38] Lanser, Susan. Fictions of Authority: Women Writers and Narrative Voice. (Ithaca and London: Cornell University Press, 1992.

[39] Lefebvre, Henry. The Production of Space, Trans. Donald Nicholson-Smith. Cambridge: Blackwell, 1991.

[40] Lefebvre, Henry. Everyday Life in the Modern World, Trans, Sacha Rabinovitch, New Brunswick: Transaction, 1994.

[41] Lepow, Lauren. "Paradise Lost and Found: Dualism and Edenic Myth in Toni Morrison's Tar Baby", from Toni Morrison's Fiction—Contemporary Criticism, edited by David L. Middleton), New York: Garland Publishing Inc. 2000.

[42] Lerner Gerda. The Creation of Patriarchy, Oxford University Press, 1984.

[43] Lester Rosemarie K. "An Interview with Toni Morrison", from Critical Essays

on Toni Morrison, ed. Nellie Mckay (Boston: G.K. Hall, 1988.

[44]Lidinsky, April. "Prophesying bodies: Calling for a Politics of Collectivity in Toni Morrison's Beloved" in Carl Plass and Betty J. Ring, eds. The Discourse of Slavery: Aphra Behn to Toni Morrison, New York: Routledge, 1994.

[45]Lister, Rachel. Reading Toni Morrison. Greenwood Publishing Group. 2009.

[46]Lovalerie, King. "Introduction: Baldwin and Morrison in Dialogue", selected from James Baldwin and Toni Morrison: Comparative Critical and Theoretical Essays edited by Lovalerie King and Lynn Orilla Scott, New York: Palgrave Macmillan, 2006.

[47]Lyotard Jean-Francois. Discours Figure. Paris Editions Klincksieck, 1971.

[48]MacKinnon, Catharine A. Feminism Unmodified: Discourses on Life and Law, Harvard University Press, 1987.

[49]Merleau-Ponty, Maurice. The Structure of Behavior, Boston: Beacon Press, 1963.

[50]Merleau-Ponty, Maurice. Phenomenology of Perception. New York: Humanities Press, 1962.

[51]Millett, Kate. Sexual Politics, New York: Doubleday, 1970.

[52]Mori, Aoi. Toni Morrison and Womanist Discourse, Atlanta: P. Lang Publishing, 2000.

[53]Morrison, Toni. "The Future of Time, Literature and Diminished Expectations", reprinted in Toni Morrison, What Moves at the Margin: Selected Nonfiction Univ. Press of Mississippi, 2008.

[54]Naama Banyiwa-Horne. "The Scary Face of the Self: an Analysis of the Character Sula in Toni Morrison's Sula," Sage 2 (1985): 28. Quoted in Hudson-Weems and Samuels, Toni Morrison, 1990.

[55]Nelson, Lise & Seager, Joni. edt. A Companion to Feminist Geography, Malden, MA: Blackwell Pub., 2005.

[56]Oksala, Johanna. "Female Liberty: Can the Lived Body Be Emancipated?" by (p209-28), selected from Olkowski, Dorothea and Weiss, Gall edt, Feminist

Interpretations of Maurice Merleau-Ponty, The Pennsylvania University Press, 2006.

[57] Olkowski, Dorothea and Weiss, Gall edt. Feminist Interpretations of Maurice Merleau-Ponty, The Pennsylvania University Press, 2006.

[58] Peach, Linden. Toni Morrison, London: Macmillan Press Ltd, 2000.

[59] Peter R. Kearly. "Toni Morrison's Paradise and the politics of community", selected from Journal of American & Comparative Cultures, Summer 2000.

[60] Probyn, Elspeth. "The spatial imperative of subjectivity", in Kay Anderson, Mona Domosh, Steve Pile and Nigel Thrift (eds), Handbook of Cultural Geography. London: Sage. 2003.

[61] Ruether, Rosemary Radford. "Motherearth And the Megamachine", Womanspirit Rising: A Feminist Reader in Religion. Edited by Carol P. Christ and Judith Plaskow. San Francisco: Harper & Row, 1979.

[62] Scheler, Marx. The Position of Man in the Universe, (Die Stellung des Menschen im Kosmo), Darmstadt, 1928.

[64] Schreiber, Evelyn Jaffe. Race, Trauma, and Home in the Novels of Toni Morrison, Louisiana State University Press, 2010.

[65] Smedley, Audrey. Race in North America: Origin and Evolution of a Worldview. Oxford: Westview Press, 1993.

[66] Soja, Edward William. Postmodern Geographies: The Reassertion of Space in Critical Social Theory. London: Verso Press, 1989.

[67] Warren, Mervyn A.; Taylor, Gardner C. King Came Preaching: The Pulpit Power of Dr. Martin Luther King Jr. InterVarsity Press. 2008.

[68] Weeker, Jacqueline de. "The Inverted World of Toni Morrison's The Bluest Eye and Sula," CLA Journal 22, 1979.

[69] Wolff, Cynathia. "Margaret Garner: A Cincinnati Story", Massachusetts Review, Vol. 32, No. 2. Massachusetts, 1991.60. Birch, Eva Lennox Black American Writings: a Quilt of Many Colors, Harvester Wheatsheaf, 1994.

[70] 列维纳斯. 从存在到存在者[M]. 吴蕙仪译, 南京: 江苏教育出版社, 2006.

[71]鲍晓兰. 西方女性主义研究评介[M]. 北京: 三联书店, 1995.

[72]包亚明. 现代性与空间的生产[M]. 上海: 上海教育出版社, 2003.

[73]程志民. 绝对主体的构建: 费希特的哲学[M]. 长沙: 湖南教育出版社, 1990.

[74]卡西尔. 人论[M]. 甘阳, 译. 上海: 上海译文出版社, 1985.

[75]冯友兰. 中国哲学简史[M]. 赵复三, 译. 天津: 天津社会科学院出版社, 2007.

[76]多尔迈. 主体性的黄昏[M]. 万俊人, 朱国钧, 吴海针, 译. 上海: 上海人民出版社, 1989.

[77]海德格尔. 存在与时间(修订版)[M]. 陈嘉映, 王庆节, 译. 3版. 北京: 生活-读书-新知三联书店, 2006.

[78]黄华. 权力, 身体与自我: 福柯与女性主义文学批评[M]. 北京: 北京大学出版社, 2005.

[79]章汝雯. "天堂"的困惑和思考[J]. 四川外语学院学报, 2004(1): 69-73; 106.

[80]康正果. 女性主义与文学[M]. 北京: 中国社会科学出版社, 1994.

[81]舒斯特曼. 实用主义美学[M]. 彭锋, 译. 北京: 商务印书馆, 2002.

[82]李楠明. 价值主体性: 主体性研究的新视域[M]. 北京: 社会科学文献出版社, 2005.

[83]刘绪贻, 杨生茂主编. 美国通史(第6卷)[M]. 北京: 人民出版社, 2002.

[84]马克思, 恩格斯. 马克思恩格斯全集(第四卷)[M]. 北京: 人民出版社, 1972.

[85]兰德曼. 哲学人类学[M]. 上海: 上海译文出版社, 1988.

[86]辛格. 实践伦理学[M]. 刘莘, 译. 北京: 东方出版社, 2005.

[87]约翰逊. 海德格尔[M]. 张祥龙, 林丹, 朱刚, 译. 北京: 中华书局, 2002.

[88]麦克林. 传统与超越[M]. 北京: 华夏出版社, 2000.

[89]肖尔茨. 波伏瓦[M]. 龚晓京, 译. 北京: 中华书局, 2002.

[90]孙正聿. 哲学通论[M]. 上海: 复旦大学出版社, 2005.

[91]曾梅. 跋涉于泥泞中的"爱"[J]. 山东外语教学, 2004(5): 79-83.

[92]唐红梅. 种族、性别与身份认同: 美国黑人女作家艾丽丝·沃克、托尼·莫里森小说创作研究[M]. 北京: 民族出版社, 2006.

[93]童明. 空间哲学[M]. 北京: 北京大学出版社, 2011.

[94]王德峰. 哲学导论[M]. 上海: 上海人民出版社, 2000.

[95]汪民安. 尼采与身体[M]. 北京: 北京大学出版社, 2008.

[96]王玉括. 莫里森研究[M]. 北京: 人民文学出版社, 2005.

[97]王守仁, 吴新云. 性别·种族·文化: 托妮·莫里森的小说创作[M]. 北京: 北京大学出版社, 2004.

[98]谢维营. 哲学的魅力[M]. 上海: 上海人民出版社, 2006.

[99]杨国荣. 理性与价值[M]. 上海: 上海三联书店, 1998.

[100]俞宣孟. 本体论研究[M]. 上海: 上海人民出版社, 2005.

[101]多诺万. 女权主义的知识分子传统[M]. 赵育春, 译. 南京: 江苏人民出版社, 2003.

[102]普鲁姆德. 女性主义对自然的主宰[M]. 马天杰, 李丽丽, 译. 重庆: 重庆出版社, 2007.

[103]张抗抗. 女性身体写作及其他[M]. 上海: 文汇出版社, 2002.

[104]张曙光. 生存哲学: 走向本真的存在[M]. 昆明: 云南人民出版社, 2001.

[105]章汝雯. 托妮·莫里森研究[M]. 北京: 外语教学与研究出版社, 2006.

[106]张庆熊. 自我、主体际性与文化交流[M]. 上海: 上海人民出版社, 1999.

[107]张文喜. 自我的建构与解构[M]. 上海: 上海人民出版社, 2002.

[108]朱立元. 当代西方文艺理论[M]. 上海: 华东师大出版社, 2005.

[109]朱立元. 美学[M]. 北京: 高等教育出版社, 2006.

[110]杜志卿. 爱与死的悖谬——试析《爵士乐》中乔—特雷斯的悲剧及其心理意义[J]. 四川外语学院学报, 2002(1): 48-50; 53.

[111]何成洲. 性别研究的未来—与托莉·莫伊的访谈[J]. 当代外国文学, 2009, 30(2): 155-161.

[112]焦晓婷. 《爵士乐》的后现代现实主义叙述阐释[J]. 四川外语学院学报, 2005(1): 25-28.

[113]焦晓婷. 话语权力之突围—托妮·莫里森《爵士乐》中的语言偏离现象阐释[J]. 天津外国语学院学报, 2006(6): 65-70.

[114]彭富春. 身体与身体美学[J]. 哲学研究, 2004(4): 59-66.

[115]宋建福. 反拨"两权"女性神话的《新夏娃激情》[J]. 英美文学研究论丛, 2008（2）: 149-159.

[116]王钢. 福克纳小说的基督教时间观[J]. 外国文学评论, 2012（2）: 106-118.

[117]汪民安, 陈永国. 身体转向[J]. 外国文学, 2004（1）: 36-44.

[118]王玉括. 身体政治与《宠儿》再现[J]. 四川外语学院学报, 2006（4）: 53-56.

[119]王守仁, 吴新云. 超越种族: 莫里森新作《慈悲》中的"奴役"解析[J]. 当代外国文学, 2009, 30（2）: 35-44.

[120]徐蕾. 当代西方文学研究中的身体视角: 回顾与反思[J]. 外国文学评论, 2012（1）: 224-237.

[121]徐颖. 托妮·莫里森作品中的"替罪羊"原型研究——译论与实践的关系简论[J]. 天津外国语学院学报, 2007（2）: 62-68.

[122]胡强. 近年来身体美学研究述论[J]. 阴山学刊, 2007（6）: 5-9.

[123]许总. 中国古代身体观念的文化内涵与现代意义[J]. 江淮论坛, 2012（3）: 5-14; 1.

[124]严启刚, 杨海燕. 解读《宠儿》中蕴含的两种文本[J]. 四川外语学院学报, 2004（2）: 16-20.

[125]杨春时, 张海涛. 生存美学: 超越意识美学与身体美学[J]. 贵州社会科学, 2010（4）: 30-35.